REDEEMED

KATTY'S STORY

BONNIE LACY

FROSTING ON THE CAKE PRODUCTIONS

To God and all the Beings of Heaven.

You know Who You are.

"It is because of the Lord's loving kindnesses that we are not consumed, Because His [tender] compassions never fail. They are new every morning; Great and beyond measure is Your faithfulness." Lamentations 3: 22, 23. Amplified Version.

CONTENTS

Chapter 1 — 1
Chapter 2 — 17
Chapter 3 — 23
Chapter 4 — 27
Chapter 5 — 31
Chapter 6 — 37
Chapter 7 — 43
Chapter 8 — 49
Chapter 9 — 53
Chapter 10 — 59
Chapter 11 — 67
Chapter 12 — 73
Chapter 13 — 77
Chapter 14 — 81
Chapter 15 — 89
Chapter 16 — 99
Chapter 17 — 105
Chapter 18 — 111
Chapter 19 — 119
Chapter 20 — 123
Chapter 21 — 131
Chapter 22 — 141
Chapter 23 — 153
Chapter 24 — 161
Chapter 25 — 167
Chapter 26 — 171
Chapter 27 — 179
Chapter 28 — 183
Chapter 29 — 191
Chapter 30 — 199
Chapter 31 — 209
Chapter 32 — 213
Chapter 33 — 221
Chapter 34 — 227

Chapter 35   233
Chapter 36   237
Chapter 37   243
Chapter 38   251
Chapter 39   257
Chapter 40   265
Chapter 41   273
Chapter 42   281
Chapter 43   289
Chapter 44   295
Chapter 45   301
Chapter 46   309
Chapter 47   319
Chapter 48   323
Chapter 49   327
Chapter 50   331

Afterword   337
Author Notes and Acknowledgements   339
Thank You, Reader!   343
Also by Bonnie Lacy   345

ONE

Katty Randolph blinked her eyes. She blinked again. Eyes barely focused, crusty dry. She wiped them. Fingertips black. Make-up still on.

Well.

She sat near the kitchen, right where she figured she deserved to sit—on the floor with all the rest of the trash—the crumbs, candy wrappers, crushed Fruit Loops. The only thing worth picking up was a colored pencil.

Her head throbbed like a thousand frogs had jumped up and down in it all night long. They were still there. Bouncing. Leaping. Pounding.

She hated frogs.

She lifted her head, but only so far. Twisting it back and forth helped, but pain stopped her. She flexed her shoulders up, then down. Same thing. They hurt. Leaning forward released a groan. Back hurt, too. Her whole body felt like she'd been beaten—just like old times.

Katty cleared her throat and stretched her legs out in front of her.

Nightmares had definitely been wild … or had they been … real? Blinks of glowing yellow eyes, low growls, throbbing music shook her, even now.

She shivered. She knew she was in her trailer house—her crappy trailer house—right now. But those visuals seemed just as real as the dirty floor.

She leaned against the paneled wall. The brittle vinyl floor under her creaked as she moved and stretched.

Million dollar question—-why was she sitting on the floor, against the wall? Had she slept here all night? That might make a body sore.

She faced the kitchen. A chair lay on its side and … Bea was nowhere to be seen.

"B-Bea?" She struggled to get up. Woah. The room started to spin, so she slid back down to the floor. If there was anything still in her stomach, it threatened a reappearance. She blew out a breath. Blew out another. Slowly her stomach settled and she could get to her knees.

She crawled to the overturned chair, crunched on a piece of cereal, and pushed up to her feet, still leaning over. Not a good position. Her stomach was waking up too—only it was crabby from what Katty constantly poured into it.

Burp.

No. "Stay down." Katty willed her stomach to settle. "Not gonna come up." She tried to right the chair, but it fought her and she dropped it back down.

Bang!

"Bea? Where are you?" Hide and seek. "Where are you hiding?"

Sugar, sugar, sugar.

Belched again.

Each step was a struggle, like climbing up a mountain side, against a strong wind, in a snowstorm. Each one was measured and tested. Slowly. Then the next step. And the one after. At the wall, she turned and leaned her back against it.

She had quit drinking once. Why did she ever think it was okay to start again? Clarence had helped her get free and clean. Why had she started again?

Where was Bea?

Stumbling down the hall to Bea's room, she slid her hand along the old wood paneling to steady herself. "Ouch!" She shook her hand. Splinter. "Damn wall."

"Bea? You awake. Sweetie?"

What time was it? Was it day? She looked out the window in Bea's room. Day. Maybe.

No Bea.

Maybe Bea was in the car.

Purse. Where'd she put her purse? Back to the kitchen. Right where she'd left it—on the kitchen counter. Only most of its contents had fallen out. She pushed it all back in, but her keys were missing.

She grabbed the purse anyway. For some reason, Katty glanced up. The painted wall. Why had she painted on that old paneling? The tree, flowers and babies. She inched to it and traced the brush marks with her fingers. No. The babies always lined up and accused her. They all faced her and pointed. She heard their voices. "You're the one."

No.

One looked like Bea—her dark eyelashes closed against her pale cheeks—sleeping on the sofa. But then the babies all lined up next to each other and Katty couldn't tell the difference—whether one was Bea, or not.

Belched again. Her hand flew to her mouth. Her stomach needed more. Away from the painted wall. It only caused her pain. When she got home, she'd wash it all off. Get rid of the pain and the babies. Paint over it.

She stumbled out to the car … only Bea wasn't in the car.

Where were her keys?

Not in the console. Not in the visor. Under the seat?

Whoops. A shooter bottle slid to the floor on the passenger side. Didn't take her a minute to stretch to pick up the bottle and twist the cap off. A couple drops left. The deep golden color of that liquid.

Ahh.

It seduced her. Hypnotized her. Sunlight caught the drops just right. They glistened. "Beautiful."

A car drove past and out of the trailer park. Katty waved, without caring to see who it was.

She licked the mouth of the bottle and let the booze linger on her tongue. The anticipated burn never satisfied anymore. One more drop in the bottom. Tipping it into her mouth, her tongue caressed the opening. A deep moan vibrated in her chest. "Mmm.." She twisted her tongue to try and reach that last drop, but the mouth of the bottle was too small.

The little bit she got tasted delicious. She licked her lips. More. She needed more.

She threw the tiny bottle onto the floor of the passenger side and watched it bounce off the floor mat.

Where were those keys to the car? Nowhere. She threw her purse onto the passenger seat. Something rattled, jiggled inside. But … she dug in it again.

Damn! There they were. Odd. Someone must have put them there. She had looked before, in the trailer.

The car started right up.

The bottle rolled on the floor, taunting her, calling to her. *More! You need more of me.* Yeah. That was the next thing on her … to-do list.

Get more shooters.

Katty checked her purse again. Just enough money to buy twenty bottles. Wait. Weren't there some in the house still?

Yeah, but the weekend was coming and she'd need more. Maybe friends would stop.

Party on.

At the convenience store, Katty slammed the car door and stomped into the building.

She shouldn't be here. She ran back to the women's bathroom, passing people sitting at tables, eating. The store was busy. Eyes watched her. Busy mouths whispered words, heads together, fingers pointed. Old men didn't whisper as much. They were louder—probably because they couldn't hear each other and were too stubborn to get their hearing tested. Either that, or they wanted her to hear them.

"Did you hear ...?"

"Did you see what she was doin?"

"She needs to get—"

The bathroom. Why hadn't God made a bigger place in her body for the pee so she didn't have to stop so often. She snickered. If she didn't pour in so much, she wouldn't have to pee so much.

Two women waited in line for a free stall, but that didn't stop Katty from laughing out loud at her own joke. The ladies didn't seem to catch the joke.

Of course.

Katty hadn't told them the joke. If you didn't drink, you didn't pee so much. She almost choked at the extra meaning ... if you didn't drink ... which was exactly what she was doing.

She leaned against the wall and sighed, but accidentally slid too close to one woman. The woman jumped and stepped away like Katty had some sort of disease.

Stupid idiot.

Katty snickered again.

The lady probably didn't have a sense of humor like Katty did. Everything was funny right now.

The stall door opened. "Hi Katty!"

Oh-oh.

Who was this? Looked familiar. Katty rubbed her eyes. Nursing home nurse? Katty chuckled. That was funny. Nursing home nurse!

"Uh, hi." Glad she'd put some lipstick on. Not. "Lisha. Hi."

"What are you up to today? And where is that beautiful daughter of yours?" Lisha punched the soap dispenser for a dollop of soap and rubbed her hands together forever, then finally rinsed under the faucet.

"She's … she's … out in the car." There was no answer that would please this little gathering of bitches—Lisha included. If Katty said Bea was home, they'd think she left her home by herself … which is maybe what she'd done. If Katty said Bea was looking at candy out in the store, they'd tell her that someone could kidnap Bea—like it wasn't happening already with Bea's dad, Phil Daynton. If Katty said Bea was in the car— same thing—someone could kidnap her.

The real answer?

Katty didn't have a clue where Bea was.

"Well, I hope you have a great day together." Lisha grabbed Katty in a crushing hug before she could refuse.

Where were her breath mints?

Katty watched Lisha open the door and drift into the store.

Another woman finished, washed her hands, and pushed the door open. Only she didn't hug Katty, nor did she smile. As she turned to shut the door, she glared at Katty. Her eyes spoke of a knowing.

Experienced.

Dumb broad. Whatever that bitch was thinking was wrong. Katty might have had a few shooters, but she was a long way from drunk. "Take a picture. It lasts longer." Katty hiccuped and laughed.

Another funny joke. She was hilarious today. Might have to

go on the road. "I might have to go on the road, if you don't hurry up." She pushed against the other stall door and it opened to reveal a brown mess on the toilet seat and a toilet bowl full of paper and brown.

Katty belched. Oh-oh. Gasp. She rushed to the sink, pushed the lady away and puked.

"Oh God. You are disgusting!" The woman rushed out of the bathroom, yelling. "Mess in the women's bathroom. Some drunk is throwing up in the sink and it's gonna need a—"

The door slammed on her words, but the judgement and shame stayed in the bathroom with Katty.

One look at the sink and she hurled again, but a hand reached in and supported her forehead with a damp paper towel.

At the same time, morphed over that hand, was another one. But this hand was raised, ready to slap, rather than comfort.

Katty peeked at the mirror in front of her. The nursing home nurse. Er, Lisha. Only she wasn't smiling this time. Tears dripped into the sink, disappeared into the mess.

Breathe.

Kind voice. "It's gonna be okay, Katty."

Katty wanted to believe.

Why had she gone back to this?

Why was she drinking?

Again.

Something in her flipped and she shoved the hand away and stomped out, only the door caught on her cast. She shoved the door back open, slamming it against the inner wall, and pulled at the cast. Tried to rip it off, until she caught a man standing by the pop dispenser staring at her.

A line formed at the cashier. She slowed down, pulled out her money and her ID. The bitch who had reported the mess was paying—still harping on the mess in the bathroom. Get over it, lady. She wasn't the one who was … sick.

Right in front of Katty stood an elderly couple, who were both barely taller than Bea. The man wore a typical plaid shirt and jeans, and sported a terrible comb-over, mostly revealing what it was meant to conceal. The woman had long white hair, tied back with a bow and wore a long, patchwork skirt, blue blouse, and matching sweater. Her colors blended with the colors in the man's shirt.

They held hands.

Aww.

When had Katty held hands with a man without him wanting favors? Without him expecting a return on his investment?

When the couple stepped to the cashier to pay, they still held hands. "I'm buying my sweetheart here, brownies."

His sweetheart giggled.

"Well, is she going to share any with you, sir?" The cashier smiled and slid the tray of brownies into a plastic shopping bag and shoved it to the woman. He pulled the brownies back out of the bag and counted. "There's five for you … and one for him, right?"

The woman giggled again. "He gets some, too. He deserves them." She leaned over and kissed his cheek.

Katty blinked. Never in her life had she—

"How long have you two lovebirds been married, now? Two years?" The cashier knew Katty was in a hurry. He always did this, played on her needing a drink. Drag it out.

The couple turned to leave, still holding hands, only now Katty could see their faces. The gentleman had a kind look in his eyes, a sweet smile. He nodded at Katty as they stepped out of line. He held his arm out for his sweetheart to grab. She fumbled with the plastic bag, then found his arm. She turned directly toward Katty—face-to-face.

Katty blinked again.

Totally blind. The woman's eyes were white. Cataracts?

Katty couldn't breathe. She stepped back. The woman even smiled as she passed Katty.

"Sorry to make you wait for us old people, dear." The woman spoke like she could see Katty. There was no way she could see. The lady couldn't see the freckles on her own face.

The man gently grasped his sweetheart's hand on his arm and patted it, his eyes never leaving Katty's face.

"It-it's okay. Ma'am." Katty swallowed and blinked tears away. "I-I'm not in a hurry." *Liar. You want your booze. Bea is at home alone.* Holy cow. That man could leave his sweetheart forever and she'd never know it. Well, she'd know he was gone, but she couldn't do anything about it. She'd be all alone and helpless. But he stayed. Why? Why did a sweet man like he seemed to be, stay with a woman like that? Why did he stay?

The man seemed to read Katty's mind. "We've been together for sixty-seven years. Through the good times," he looked at Sweetheart, "and there have been some good ones, right Nelly?"

She nodded vigorously.

"And there have been really rough times, too." His eyes welled up. He checked Nelly's face—her eyes. Seemed to want to make sure she was okay with what he shared openly.

Nelly slowly nodded, blinking herself. The old woman didn't need eyes with sight, for tears to well up. Nodded again, turned her head toward him. "Fires." She breathed. "Babies dying."

Katty gasped. She wiped a tear running down her own cheek.

Nelly's face remained still, sweet—even though her own cheeks were wet, now. The man's were wet, too. They breathed almost in unison. She seemed to know he was looking at her and raised her hand to find his cheek. She held it there. "Such a good man." She tilted her head toward Katty. "He never left. He's a faithful man." She searched the air with her other hand, until she found Katty's and grabbed it. "Find yourself a faithful man—faithful and true." The woman's touch zinged Katty's skin. Nelly wouldn't let go, in fact her grip became almost painful. "You'll know, dear—you'll know when you've found him. He sees you like a queen, when you know you're still a scullery maid." She shook her head, her face toward his. "A queen."

He nodded. "A queen." He smiled at Katty as they walked to the door.

No one in the store said a word. Only four or five people had heard or even seen what Katty had—close up—but each visual became a snapshot in Katty's brain. Like her photo app on her phone held progressive shots—blink, blink, blink of a scene when Bea licked her first ice cream cone. Lick—click. Expression on Bea's face when she tasted—actually tasted the treat—click. Another lick—click.

Katty's brain had a whole movie sequence of screen shots with the old man and blind old woman in her head.

Breathe.

The casier tapped the counter.

Katty stretched to watch them leave the building. Slowly the man helped Nelly into their car. His eyes never left his wife as he made his way slowly around the car to the driver's side and got in.

"Ahem. You gonna take pictures?"

"Uh, what?"

She'd never have that kind of love. Like Clarence and Mrs. T. Their kind of love. They probably didn't even have sex anymore—it's all kindness and love. A deeper kind of love that Katty has never experienced—or never will. If that bastard, Phil, had not been at the convenience store that night. But then she wouldn't have Bea.

Bea! She had to get home!

Katty turned away from the couple and back into the store. She was living inside a dream or a movie. She twisted to watch them drive away. A big truck blocked her view, but when the truck pulled away, their car was nowhere to be seen. Katty stood on tiptoes and searched the parking lot. They just disappeared. Gone. Vanished.

Slowly she regained her bearings of standing inside the store, people making noises, a cash register ringing up items. Back to reality. Back to … shit!

Katty stumbled up to the cashier. He was ringing up a young woman, lugging a little girl. The woman glanced at her. "Hey, don't butt in line." She tilted her head behind her. A whole line of people waited their turn.

"Uh, sorry." Katty glanced at the cashier. Dork was smiling to himself. Damn him. He won. She glanced back outside as she took her place last in line. They were gone. The line moved forward and she followed. Gone. She studied the freckles on the guy's shoulders standing in front of her. He carried a twelve-pack of beer. She studied the colors on the cardboard box. Blues. Back outside. She shook her head. Her stomach rumbled. Belch. She covered her mouth with her hand.

Where had the couple gone?

Her foot tapped the floor—almost on its own. Bea. Shooters. *Breathe.*

"Can I help you?" Same cashier that had sold her the shooters before—he had ripped her off. She held up ten fingers. Twice.

He reached into the case and pulled out shooters of whiskey, tapped on the cash register, and dropped the tiny bottles into a bag, just out of her reach.

Bastard.

She threw the money at him, along with her ID, climbed up the shelves of candy in front of her and grabbed the sack out of his hand. Bea would never have gotten away with kicking all those rows of gum and candy bars around. She gave them another kick, scattering some onto the floor.

She made her way to the door, but as she pushed it open, she glanced behind her.

The cashier waved her ID. "Need this?"

She took one swipe at his hand and nailed it. "Dork." Slid it into her back pocket and rotated again.

The store spun.

No.

Help. Help. It had been so sweet and pure just a minute ago and now, the world, *her* world, crashed down around her again. A sob threatened to surface, but she choked it down. She left the building and once more, searched the parking lot. She hadn't even seen what kind of car they drove off in. White something. Nowhere. Gone.

Just like Bea always said, *Bad Mommy was back.* "You are so stupid." She opened her car door and slid into the car, glaring at herself in the rear view mirror. "Never happened. They weren't real. You are the crazy person. Love like that doesn't exist! *They* don't exist!"

Slammed the door shut. Hard.

Bea would have been spanked by now for kicking all that candy off the shelf inside.

She unscrewed the cap on one bottle and slugged it down. Someone sitting at a lunch table inside pointed at her. Yeah. She just openly took a drink.

She started her car.

They still pointed.

She flipped them off. Tears stung her eyes.

One person's hand flew to their mouth. Another grabbed a cell phone.

"Bitch."

Katty backed out, muttering. "Damn them. What's it to them? None of their business." She shifted into drive. "What should they care if I drink and drive?"

A car passed beside Katty's on the way to park at the gas pumps.

Noell.

Katty swallowed and tried to calm down. Slow down.

Noell waved. She was so beautiful—all that blond hair. She couldn't be Katty's cousin. Oh no. She was rolling her window down. *Breathe.* "Hi, Katty!" She was so excited. "How are you?" she stretched to see the back seat. "How's Bea?"

Katty chuckled. Play along. Pretend. "We're fine." She nodded toward the back seat. "Bea's at my neighbor's right now. Mrs. Nosy? She babysits sometimes."

Noell smiled. "That's great."

"Yeah. It's pretty convenient , too, so … and Bea likes her." Bea didn't have a clue. Lies.

"Well, anytime you need someone else, or if Mrs. Nosy can't babysit, I'd love to play with Bea." Noell shut off her car and opened the car door.

Oh no. Not gonna happen. No long cousin visit today. "Well, I should get back and relieve Mrs. Nosy." She started to leave. "But thanks for the offer. Maybe that'll work out. It'd work out great."

Noell nodded and waved.

Katty pulled away.

Not on your life, Noell.

Not going to have Noell babysit. Not today. Not ever. She already suspects something. She'd seen Katty drunk probably. Not ever going to have her babysit.

Bea would tell it all anyway.

She stomped on the gas and barely missed a truck. "What do they care? I'm gonna drink until I'm so sick, I'll never drink again. Or I die." She yanked on the steering wheel and swerved out of the parking lot onto the highway. A car took to the shoulder to avoid hitting her and an oncoming truck screeched their tires.

She gunned it, as she swerved around a slow moving camper. "Out of my way!" Swerved back in her lane just in time to avoid an oncoming semi.

The driver laid on the horn, as the truck passed.

"Damn you!" She flipped him off and kept on driving.

Katty patted her pocket. Where were those bottles? She'd bought extra. Just in case. She'd heard somewhere that it made a person stronger if they could quit drinking with booze still in the house. She was gonna try that. Make sure she had some, but not drink it. She patted the seat next to her—there. In the plastic shopping bags.

Her insides jiggled. She could do this.

A mile passed.

Who was she kidding? She pulled over on a side road and ripped open the cap. She loved that sound. It even said, "Rip." Rip rip rip. She was gonna drink them all. Or at least one right here along the side of the road.

Bea might be watching TV at home, so she was okay. She even knew how to get her own supper. Cereal bowl, spoon, cereal box, and milk. They might be out of milk, but Bea had munched on dry cereal before. Many times. She was okay. Pretty strong for a four-year-old.

Katty downed the shooter bottle and started the car again. Checked her mirrors. Nothing coming. At least she could see behind her, toward the convenience store. There had been a time, not too long ago, when she'd checked her mirrors on the way home and cop car lights flashed right behind her. Not this time.

The sun was bright this time of day. Sunglasses. Where was her purse? She dug for her purse, but only found bottles. She twisted open another one and downed it. Nothing coming. Easy to make sure nothing was coming up behind her from the direction of the convenience store.

But from the west, toward home, it was impossible to see. She shielded her eyes. Dang. She carefully edged onto the road.

Back on the highway, she sped up. Gotta get home to Bea. She reached for another bottle and braced the steering wheel with her knees. There. Perfect driving. Rip. She lifted the bottle to her lips, looked ahead on the highway and the sun completely blinded her. She blinked and dropped the bottle without taking a drink.

Blam!

Katty gulped and threw up.

And blacked out.

TWO

"Mommy?" Bea Randolph wandered into the kitchen, rubbing her eyes. "What was that noise?"

A chair lying on its side on the floor completely distracted her. She didn't usually take an afternoon nap, but had fallen asleep reading Daryl & Dumpty books on the sofa. Seeing the chair on the floor stopped her and she tipped it upright. She climbed onto a different chair—her chair—and folded her hands. "This is the church." She looked around. "Mommy?" Two fingers up. "This is the steeple."

She rubbed her eyes again, yawned, and tapped the paper she'd been coloring earlier. The grocery store had given out pictures of a lady and three kids pushing a cart—the lady almost looked like Mommy. They handed the pictures out for a coloring contest. Bea's was gonna be the best. Forgetting all about Mommy, she colored a section of the drawing, first red, then she changed her mind and picked up blue. "Oooo. Purple." She picked up the red crayon again and colored the rest of the shape, then picked up the blue one and the yellow crayon. Dozens more crayons scattered across the table.

Tiny, sparkly lights appeared on the table, scattered in between the crayons—just like the little Christmas lights they strung on the tree. Bea blinked. Crayons moved. The purple crayon rolled off the table. She held out her hand and a light landed on it, tickling her. She wanted to laugh, but what if she scared it away?

It tickled.

"Mommy." Bea whispered. She didn't want to scare them. "Mommy, the lights are back." She slowly raised her hand and the light flickered off. "Oh. It's gone. It shut off it's light." Then back on. Bea giggled.

Off. On. Off.

Other lights gathered around her hand, her arm, her face. In front of her eyes, making her go cross-eyed. Lights like when Mommy and Bea were in the car. They had stopped Bad Mommy from being … bad.

Deep sigh.

"Pretty lights. Does Mrs. T know?" She sucked in a breath. "Are you really angels?" They flitted on top of a crayon, lined up on a green one. "You don't look like Michael when he gets dressed up in his costume." She thought a minute. "He has wings. Do you have wings?"

She waited, watching.

They blinked off, one-by-one. The last one flew right past her eyes. Bea had seen gnats—really little flies. She squinted—it was a really little, little, angel?

One last crayon—a pink one—rolled just to the edge of the table and no farther and that angel blinked off, too.

Bea watched for a little longer. "Please come back. Please?" She picked up the pink crayon, hoping the lights would turn back on. She waited.

Nothing. Bea held her breath. If she was real quiet and very good … but no lights. They didn't come back.

Back to coloring.

If Bea colored with kids at story hour at the library, she

stayed between the lines and colored the leaves on the trees green, the sky blue and the sun yellow.

But when she was by herself at home or at Clarence's house, she let her every whim come out and rule. She tried to make the sky all the colors, like when the sun came up on those mornings when Mommy had been gone all night and didn't come home until Bea had used up a whole jar of peanut butter and every cracker in the house. There was never any bread that wasn't green. Mommy always said not to eat that green bread—it might make her sick.

She had once.

Didn't taste very good. Had a funny taste and smell—like when Mommy had to buy pills from that icky man and she dragged Bea into his house. He had kept wanting to hold Bea, but she never came out from under Mommy's arm. His house smelled like that green bread.

She leaned forward in her chair now, her feet hanging free, swinging back and forth. Her toes weren't in socks, so they could stretch and move.

Growl.

"Mommy?"

That lady's hair in the coloring book page would look fun in rainbow stripes.

Bea picked up the red, green, blue and purple crayons and started coloring. One red stripe first. Then green. Her head popped up. Pink. She scattered the crayons till she found it. Pink next to green was really pretty—just like in her room. She finished the lady's hair with one red stripe and filled in with green and pink, green and pink.

She stretched back and checked what she'd done.

Pretty.

Growl.

"Mommy?" She rolled onto her back, hanging on the chair,

her head down on one side and feet dangling from the other. Then sat up. "Where are you, Mommy?"

She pushed her crayons together in a pile so she wouldn't knock them off the table and break them. She really liked when they stayed new, even if they got shorter, the more she used them.

Mommy wasn't in the kitchen or in the living room.

Potty. She must have had to go.

The bathroom was a mess … just like when Mommy used to dress up and put on make-up … to go out.

"Mommy?"

Nobody in the shower. Nobody on the potty or in the little closet for towels. Bea checked to see if she still fit in the bottom where Mommy kept the vacuum.

Yup. But she must have gotten bigger though, because her head hit the shelf above when she sat beside the big vacuum. That thing didn't seem so big anymore.

The lipstick was still open. Bea loved how smooth it felt on her own lips, but she didn't stop to play this time. The counter was covered with little flakes from Mommy's blush. That was still open, and the perfume bottle cap was off beside the bottle. Mommy always used to say that a girl needed to smell nice for the men. She hadn't used it in awhile.

But had she now?

The little towel was on the floor. Bea stooped to pick it up and uncovered a tiny bottle. Empty. The little cap was under the sink. She reached down, picked it up, and sniffed the bottle.

Ugh. That smell.

Pictures swirled around her—pictures of Mommy tipping the bottle to her lips, then smiling in an odd way, like it tasted good but more. Kind of like when Mommy licked an ice cream cone at Clarence's house. She'd always smile and say it tasted good.

That smile when Mommy took a drink from one of those bottles was different. Her eyes looked different.

Bea sniffed it again. Put it to her lips and licked it. The stuff tasted icky. Terrible. Tasted like medicine. Even though it tasted terrible, a little flutter tickled her tummy. An excitement, like when she got a new Daryl & Dumpty book.

"Don't drink that stuff!"

She dropped the bottle and it bounced off the tile floor. "What?" She spun in a circle. Who said that?

Nobody.

She tried to push the taste out of her mouth with her tongue. A drink of water would help only the plastic cup that was knocked over on its side smelled the same way.

She ran back into the kitchen and found her cup from earlier, filled it with water and drank, spit into the sink, then drank and swallowed.

Better.

"Don't drink that stuff."

Bea dropped the cup and turned. "Boy?" She squealed. "Boy!" She jumped and hugged him. "I missed you!"

He hugged her back.

Bea let him go and patted him on the shoulder. "You're my brother, right?"

"Yep." He nodded.

As they walked back through the hallway on the way to her bedroom arm-in-arm, something caught the backdoor and blew it wide open—screaking as it swung back and forth. She shivered and peeked outside—stood there beside Boy. The only thing out there was the fence they'd had fixed when the front deck had been replaced.

"Mommy?"

The door swung back and forth, like someone was pushing it. The sun was going down. It was getting dark out. The doorknob was too far away to reach. Her hand only went partway there, her fingers grasping what she couldn't reach. If she was bigger—to have her head touch the bottom of the shelf in the vacuum closet

—then she guessed she would be able to touch that doorknob soon.

She tried again. Stretched, completely sure her body would either become like Elastic woman or break like a rubber band that had been stretched too thin.

"I can't reach it." She tried batting at it to make it swing shut, but she couldn't hit it hard enough.

Boy reappeared with books.

They both sat down on the floor, their legs swung free out the open door. Her thumb slipped into her mouth. Boy opened a book and began to read to her.

THREE

"On my way." Mark Scott raced to his squad car, started it and radioed in almost at the same time.

"Guy here." He followed Mark out, into his own car.

Sheriff Dennison and another deputy, Deputy Tyler, jumped into the pickup.

All ready to hit the road. They had a protocol when all three vehicles were called out. No matter who needed to go, the vehicle closest to the corner took off first, then the one next to it, then on down the line. Today it would be three cop vehicles.

Mark followed Sheriff. Guy followed Mark. Lights flashed. Sirens blared. They took the usual route out of town. At one intersection, a lady stopped just in time to let them pass. Her hand flew to her mouth as Mark's car followed the sheriff's. Wonder what she did when Guy passed her.

Mark's stomach growled. He had been ready to take a bite of leftover chili that Chantelle had shared when the call came. Just took it out of the microwave and was literally lifting the spoon to his mouth. It would wait. If he knew Chantelle, she'd cover it and put it in the fridge for him.

Turning onto the highway east, traffic stopped, giving them

all three the right of way. Bad accidents happened when people didn't stop to let emergency units or fire trucks pass. People needed to focus when they were in their cars. Always too busy checking their phones, texting, or just listening to music. All distracted.

Mark gauged his speed behind Sheriff to keep up. This time of year people needed to watch out especially. This time of day was bad. Mark checked his rear-view-mirror. Yep. The sun was glaring behind him.

His phone vibrated. Not now. He wasn't gong to even check the screen.

They slowed as they drew close to the scene of the accident. One big grain truck parked on the highway, its blinker still flashing—like it was preparing to turn—even now.

The call was probably Mom. God, please have her pray. Have her call all the Bible study ladies she knows. The scene looked very serious—*very* serious.

The truck driver had exited his vehicle and was crouched beside the driver's door, his head in his hand. Might be okay. Mark pulled off the highway directly across from him, on the other side, avoiding debris and car parts scattered. Not good.

An ambulance was there already. Fast response. They had a gurney out. Not good. An older man—so far. Their car had been sandwiched between the truck and … oh no.

Dear Lord God in Heaven. Please don't let that be Katty's car.

He opened his car door and got out.

The EMTs had the older man.

Mark jogged across the highway to the truck driver and leaned down to his level. "Hey man."

The guy jerked his head up. His eyes were already red and face wet. He sobbed. "I was turning. I think I had my blinker on." He swallowed and sobbed again. "That's when I felt them—

heard the car hit. Blam!" He clapped his hands together, hard. "Like that." He glanced over at the emergency unit again.

"Are you hurt?" Mark stood. "We need to get you to the hospital."

The man stood. "No. I'm okay." He patted his truck behind him. "She never fails me." He tipped his head toward the old man. "It's them. God help them." He covered his face.

Mark led him to his cruiser. "Take a seat here and when the EMTs have a minute, I want you checked over. Okay?" Mark hated this part. "Do you have your drivers license on you?" Sometimes farmers didn't.

The man nodded and dug into his back pocket. Handed it to Mark, his eyes never leaving the gurney.

Mark called it in and he handed the license back. "Checks out, Tom. Take a seat here and I'll send them over to you. He opened the back door and covered Tom's head as he eased onto the backseat.

Mark glanced where the ambulance was parked, trying to remain calm and professional. Super impossible to do. Sheriff was taking the old man's information. Mark alerted the deputy that he had Tom in his cruiser.

To Katty's car.

FOUR

"Hello?" A man's voice. "You okay?" Someone touched Katty's shoulder.

"No. No. Leave me alone." Wha-where was she? She'd just been home ... or at the store. Where was she? "Bea?" She wiped her mouth. "Bea, you okay?"

No answer.

Movement in the backseat. She tried to see. "Bea? You okay?"

"Ma'am? Did you have a child with you? There's nobody here. Are you sure you had someone with you?"

She blinked and rubbed her eyes. Nothing made sense. Maybe she'd hit her head, but on ... what? The steering wheel? She rubbed her eyes again, and tried to peer through the windshield. Only it wasn't there. No glass. Shattered glass covered her lap, the seat beside her, the floor—all around her.

She reached out to touch the windshield—no glass—really strange sensation. Expected glass and there was none. Nothing.

Her car had just become longer in front. What? An unfamiliar back seat was *in front* of her. A backseat was her front seat? Wait. Where was her engine?

She opened her car door.

"Ma'am, wait."

"Katty, careful." A hand gently pressed down on her shoulder. "Slow."

Familiar voice. She tilted her head to see. "Mark?" She pushed her leg out, but stepped on a tire rim and faltered. Car parts scattered all over the highway. Strong hands steadied her. Finding her footing, she stood.

"Katty, it's Mark. Stop." He tried to stop her, resting his hand on her shoulder, again. He picked glass from her hair "Katty. Are you all right?" He stepped in front of her. "Looks like you hit your head."

The brain fog seemed to clear as she stood beside her car and the realization hit—punched her hard. This wasn't just her drinking or imagination. This had really happened. For real. "Let me … I want to see." She pushed around to the front of her car, or to what had been the hood and engine compartment, and stumbled. "Look, my engine is in their trunk."

No one laughed. Cops were busy. The sheriff was even there. EMTs and firemen worked on the people from the car ahead of hers.

Everything had been so funny earlier in the women's bathroom at the convenience store, but now, her funny joke fell flat. Not funny. Not here. Not now.

The EMTs lifted a body onto the gurney and covered it.

Katty blinked, her hand flew to her mouth. "There was someone in this car?" She pointed. "The one I ran into?"

Mark nodded and radioed in. "Chantelle, alert the hospital. We are bringing in two." He glanced at Katty. "Three people. Maybe for confirmation. Maybe for observation."

The EMTs wheeled the gurney toward the ambulance, but an old man followed and stopped them. "No!" He shook his head. "No, my love." He sobbed and leaned over the body on the gurney. "No."

Katty froze and pointed. "That car. Those old people at the convenience store were driving it." She strained to see around all the vehicles. Where were the people from the store? Not along the road. Not with the cops. Not in the tow truck. She pointed. "Where are the people who were driving this car?"

Mark stared at Katty. He nodded at the man who was crying over the gurney. Back at Katty.

Realization slammed Katty in the gut. She couldn't breathe. She'd pulled back onto the highway, twisted the lid off a bottle and slammed into their car. The sun. Blinding.

"*I* hit them. *I* caused this." She hiccuped. "I couldn't see." She pointed at the sky. "The sun." She sank onto the pavement. "I killed them. I did this. I didn't want to hurt anybody."

Katty had an immediate flashback to that very morning when she had hit Bea. Hard. She sobbed. "Oh God, help. I didn't want to hurt her."

Mark shook her shoulders and helped her stand. "Katty, come out of it. You didn't hurt anyone. They were blinded by the sun, like you were. We're assessing and taking statements. They slammed into the truck that was turning." He pointed ahead. "They couldn't see his blinker and slammed into him. You didn't hurt anybody. They are probably going to be okay, we are just sending them to the ER for observation." He nodded toward her. "You, too."

Katty stared into his green eyes. Those eyelashes.

He shook her again. "Are you okay? You didn't hurt anybody." He checked her car. "Is Bea at home?"

Katty saw him glance in her car. Little shooter bottles littered the front passenger seat and cup holders.

"Uh, I gotta get home." She slid away from him toward the open car door. "I'm okay. I'll just go now."

She sat down hard in her car and stared out the glassless windshield.

FIVE

Mark watched the ambulance pull away. He knew Katty was okay, except for hitting her head. He knew she'd be dismissed— not even admitted. He knew she'd been drinking.

Mom, pray. Gather your ladies in to pray. God tell the whole world to pray for Katty. And Bea. God, help.

The ambulance brake lights flashed as it steered around debris and a line of vehicles he had detained along one lane. Sheriff Dennison was helping the truck driver fill out forms. Katty would fill out hers at the hospital. Whether it was he himself or Guy or one of the other deputies, she had already given a report about what happened tonight and that was the most important thing.

He glanced at the sky. The sunset was stunning. Right now. He had no doubt that the old man and Katty had been blinded by the light. There was a song …

Sheriff motioned for the other deputy to help. Tow truck had arrived and there was a lot to do yet. Mark guessed about twenty cars waited in line until the road surface was cleared. Accidents were very messy. Cleanup in every way. Car parts. Oil on the road and ditches. Fires started. He glanced behind him at the two cars as they were being pulled apart. A miracle that they hadn't ignited. A true miracle.

His heart broke for the old man. The woman had been unresponsive but still breathing. They were from the area—frequented the ice cream shop, cafes—even the coffee shops. He just didn't know their names. He'd never talked to them more than saying hello. Didn't know their true age, or marriage status, their address. He guessed he would now.

Back to the line of cars waiting to be released. One young upstart gunned his engine. Mark pushed his hand at him. It would not go well for the kid to break out of line and drive over sharp car parts. Or if he disobeyed the law at the scene of an accident. That would be bad. He knew it was tough to wait. People had places to go—work, home, kids to pick up, or in the kid's case, maybe a party to go to.

A loud twisting of metal distracted even the kid, as the road department crew attempted to pull apart the two cars. Steve Ivertson and his crew did an amazing job. Mark turned to watch. Steve shook his head. The two cars seemed forever joined. They were actually pulling the first car out from under the grain truck by pulling on Katty's car. Two at a time.

Steve shook his head again, his jaw jutting out. Determination could only carry a man so far when faced with the realities of human and earthly life. He glanced up at Mark and shook his head, again.

Guy and Tyler had swept the south lane clear.

Steve motioned for the tow truck and trailer to proceed. Gonna take them both at once. The kid gunned his engine and Mark stepped closer to the car, made eye contact with the kid, and laid down the law. As Mark stared directly at him, the kid backed down. Being the second vehicle made it harder to jump line, but knowing kids these days, he'd find a way. Mark felt old. Even thinking the words, "Kids these days" made it clear that he himself wasn't one of them. He'd lived too much life, even at twenty-eight years of age. With his past and now this job. Life was short.

The woman in the first car kept moving her lips, like she was … praying.

Mark swallowed. Even for the old man and his wife—as old as they might be—tonight, life probably seemed too short.

Mom pray.

As if on cue, his phone buzzed. Not checking it, but he'd have to call her later, when he had a break. He knew it was her.

Watching the two cars being loaded would give the people waiting in line entertainment, if you could call it that. The noise was deafening. Even the truck driver stepped to where he could watch.

Mark nodded at him. "You okay, Tom?"

Tom stepped closer to Mark and they both watched the tow truck. "Powerful winch. That's crazy. I could use one at the farm." He nodded at Mark. "And I'm better. I saw her eyes move. Flutter maybe. She's in there." He wiped his eyes. "God help her. And him."

Katty's car and the old couple's car were slowly being winched onto the huge trailer.

Tom crossed his arms across his chest. "I've seen that man and his wife around before."

Mark checked his line. The kid was distracted by the tow truck doing its job. "Yeah, me too."

"Sweet couple. My wife says that she wants us to be like them when we're that age." Tom swallowed. "I pray we are as kind and loving still, as they seem to be. We can never see into their past or their problems. If I remember right, the wife is blind."

"Really." Mark blinked. "I didn't know that. You can't tell."

"No. They are like a dance together." Tom nodded. "I hope we can be like them right now. Yes as we get old, but now." He blinked and wiped his face again.

Would Mark ... and Katty ever get that chance? He knew it was crazy to even think that. But there was something between them that could blossom if given a chance. If his mom really knew he had those thoughts, what would she do or think? He was pretty sure Katty wasn't Mom's first choice for him.

They stepped to the side of the highway as the tow truck pulled past them. The engine roared as it worked hard with that load.

Mark checked behind him. Checked with Tyler, Guy, and Sheriff for the release signal. Sheriff nodded and waved toward the East. Mark stepped in front of the first car and checked the line. What? Fifty cars now?

"Tom, you okay?" Mark knew he didn't have to, but he held his arm in front of Tom like he was a child and gave a gentle push back. They stepped off the highway together and Mark signaled for the first car to pass. He pushed his hands down to go slow. "Be careful." He knew they couldn't hear him.

The kid drove past and nodded. Maybe he did have some brains after all. Seeing an accident this close had to be sobering for a kid his age. It sobered Mark every time. Tom was affected significantly. Good man, Tom.

People waved as they drove on past. One woman held her hands like prayer hands. Mark nodded.

The last car drove away.

"Thanks Deputy." Tom shook his hand, then grabbed Mark in a man hug—not too long, not too close—but meaningful. "Thanks for helping me ... uh ..."

Mark patted him on the back and released him. "All in a day's ... glad I was here."

Sheriff sent Guy to the hospital to check on the people. Odd. The whole department was always sending Mark whenever Katty was involved. Not this time. Sheriff and Tyler drove off.

Guy was never one to show emotion, but as he stepped into his squad car, he saluted Mark and nodded. Most people wouldn't think a thing about his movements. There was nothing to think about. Just a simple salute. But Mark had worked with Guy long enough to know it was more than just a salute.

Mark saluted back. Good to have friends. Mark knew Guy would check on Katty. Guy knew Mark wanted to be the one going to the hospital.

All for the best.

He patted Tom on the arm. "Ready to go home?"

SIX

"Thanks, uh, Officer." Katty slid off the front passenger seat as Guy stepped around to escort her to the trailer.

"No problem, Katty." He glanced at the trailer. "Please call us if you need anything. This was a traumatic event and … well, we know."

Katty jumped. "You know?"

Guy shook his head, a kind smile on his lips. "We understand what it's like to go through hard things—like the accident."

"Oh. Uh, yes." Super huge man. Dark skin. Dark eyes. He was so big that he could be scary, except he was kind and gentle. His touch at her shoulder was gentle. Safe. That sigh came from a deep place. She hadn't realized she had been holding her breath off and on, all evening. At the convenience store, at the accident, later at the hospital. The doctor there had taken her cast off, too. From one accident to another. Felt good to release the cast. Felt good to release that breath. She was safe.

But one glance at the trailer as they walked closer and the terror exploded. She rubbed her arm. "I better go in." She shrugged out from under his grasp and reached for the wooden railing of the deck steps. At the top, she turned. "Thank you, Officer."

He nodded and saluted her. "No problem. And I meant it. Chantelle, our dispatcher, takes all the calls and she's a big help. Has a big heart, so don't hesitate to call if you need anything."

She reached the door, her hand on the knob. She knew she was putting off the inevitable. Terrified. Her hand trembled on the doorknob. Where was Bea? Was she okay? Would Katty need to call Chantelle already—now?

She made sure to turn and wave as he drove away. Even smiled. Best acting award ever.

She turned the knob and pushed the door open.

"Mommy!" Bea screamed and rushed Katty, her arms in the air. She leaped into Katty's arms and they both tumbled to the floor. "Mommy, where did you go?" Bea sobbed into Katty's chest. "Why did you leave me?"

"Bea. I am so sorry." One of these days, sorry wasn't gonna cut it. It might work today, but the time was coming when Bea might not buy her apology. Katty pulled Bea onto her lap, Bea's head on her shoulder. What other words were there? When would Bea not be bought with tears and apologies? With sugar, sugar? "I'm so sorry. There was an accident."

Bea knew that word—accident. Accident had lived in her young life from day one. "It was an accident, Bea. I'm sorry, it was my fault. It was an accident." When would Bea finally see the truth and throw the lies back in Katty's face?

God, when would this be over? When would she ever be free of her demons? When would she be able to tell Bea the truth? What if Katty had not drank a drop today or yesterday? That she had just run out to the mailbox—not to the convenience store— seven miles away. With an accident in between that probably was her own fault for killing two sweet old people?

Katty lifted her head to the heavens. *God, when? God, please. Help, God!*

Tears coursed down Katty's cheeks onto Bea's head. She shuddered at the thought. Mark, and then Guy, had assured her that she hadn't caused the accident—that she hadn't killed anyone. The old man and his blind wife were going to be okay—just some minor bruises. The little lady had blacked out when she hit her head, but was awake and going to be fine. They were fine.

But still Katty couldn't get free of the visual of the man leaning over his wife on the gurney, crying, "No. No!" That one would remain in her permanent bank of memories—along with the other brutal visuals.

Breathe. Breathe in fresh ... wait.

Katty sat up. "Bea, is there a window open?" She twisted to see the hallway. "Why is the side door open?"

Bea lifted her head and glanced that direction. "Th-the door? The wind blew it open. I couldn't reach it. Boy couldn't reach it either."

"Oh." Katty stood and walked to the door. "I'll get it." She turned after closing the door. "Boy?" Bea couldn't have reached it and the latch wasn't very secure. How to fix it? She needed to save money for a hammer ... no, a screwdriver and some screws. Maybe ... naw. She couldn't ask Mark.

Bea was already at the table, picking up a crayon.

"Bea, who is Boy?" Katty sat next to her and unconsciously picked up a colored pencil. When Bea didn't answer, Katty looked up at her. She was engrossed in her drawing. Katty shook her head. Imaginary friend?

Soon Katty was distracted by her own drawing. The visuals from the accident kept popping into her mind. Of the old man and woman. Their love for each other. Their devotion. The brownies. Of Clarence and Mrs. T. Same kind of love for each other. Pure love. Sweetness.

"What color do you want, Mommy?" Bea dumped more crayons onto the table.

Katty jumped. Wow, crayons were loud. Katty rolled them around until she found one, "Red. I want red." Yes she did. She wanted red—real revenge against Phil. Interesting how colors represented emotions.

Bea handed her a piece of paper.

At least paper was cheap. Nothing else was.

Katty drew circles on her paper. Lots of circles. If each circle was a person, how would they intersect?

"What are you drawing, Mommy?'

"I'm drawing … circles."

Bea laughed. "I know what circles look like. How come so many?" Bea stopped her own drawing and watched Katty.

"I don't know yet. Just playing, I guess." Circles appeared all over the paper. All red. Something stirred in Katty. So many circles. So many people. None of them interested—just kept to themselves. All far apart from each other. All just circles. It was when she drew one into another circle that the drawing became more interesting.

For some reason she thought of Clarence and Mrs. T, again. They had gotten married, both in their eighties and it was okay. Even at that age. Katty didn't even want to think about how they did it. Maybe it was all about love and not sex.

The more she thought about Clarence, the darker some circles grew. She laid down the crayon. Damn. She missed Clarence. She needed his wisdom. She needed his humor. She needed his love. He'd become like a grandfather or even like a father and she missed him.

When she worked at the Agency, he was always busy with clients. Many new residents who had moved in recently, needed a lawyer. She just took notes and filed the results. Took phone calls. Booked appointments.

She needed Clarence the way he used to be. But she wanted him to be the now Clarence with Mrs. T.

She wanted to cry. She wanted to let it out. But not with Bea. Bea wouldn't understand. Bea would ask—

"Mommy? Are you crying, Mommy?" Bea pushed her own drawing away and picked up the red crayon and started doodling on Katty's drawing, too.

Bea colored in some circles.

That made them appear angry and red. But then as Bea did that, the color red seemed healing and calming to Katty, somehow. That was crazy because red was supposed to represent anger. Red represented blood—bad blood. Maybe it was just watching Bea's movements of filling in each circle that soothed Katty.

Odd ... before, each circle had taken on the idea of each being a person. And now, as Bea colored each one in, they became drops of blood. Katty had seem more blood in her life than most doctors and now watching Bea color the circles in became almost too much.

Katty had to restrain herself from shoving the crayons off the table and sending the paper flying.

What was wrong with her? She knew she was drinking again but what was all this emotion about blood?

SEVEN

Deputy Mark jumped at the sound of the phone. He should be used to that sound by now, but with all that had been going on lately: the recent accident and changes within the department itself. He was on edge.

Sheriff Dennison was always trying to find more help, and not only just help, but qualified help. Being a deputy wasn't an easy job for anyone. Mark knew first hand from Guy, who was married and had a couple kids, that working as a deputy posed many problems. Time with family being the main one. Mark had been privy to many conversations—one-sided of course—with Guy's wife. Guy was always respectful, but Mark could tell by the sound of Guy's voice and even overhearing his wife through the phone that there were times of frustration. Mark tried to help out. He wasn't married. He had no kids. His only commitment was the occasional dinner with Mom, so he offered to work Guy's shift if he could.

Trade-off when Guy worked for Mark meant Mark had dinner with Mom. Guy loved to share the leftovers that Mom aways sent. Mark was sure she over-baked and cooked just so he would have leftovers for the department as well. Maybe she and Guy were in cahoots.

For the moment, after the phone rang, things were quiet. Chantelle—who had been there for a long time and in addition to answering the phone, filing, and other tasks—cleaned and scheduled meetings for them all. She ran a tight ship for all who worked there. She even scheduled the work hours. She needed a raise.

Mark stared at the reports in front of him and sighed.

Paperwork always did Mark in. He knew the importance. Many times he'd needed to go into a file and look up background information to a case or a person's backstory. If the officer covering the case had done their job right, the extra information helped either solve a case or helped the officer understand it better. He always tried to remember that when he dragged through paperwork himself. He tried to make sense.

"Mark, you should be a writer." Chantelle had let the ear pod dangle from one ear as she talked to him.

"What? Why?" He shook his head. He loved to read, but write? Not.

"You have a way with words." She shook her head. "No. Everybody says that. What I mean is, you make the scene come alive. I can picture what is happening by the way you describe it." She pointed at her computer. "Some officers get me so confused, I can't make any sense of whatever it is they are describing. That's important, because sometimes the information is needed in court."

That made Mark sit up. Dang. She was right. If the officer didn't make sure the report was accurate, a case might go the wrong way. He knew the reports should be done well, but Chantelle had just reinforced that for Mark.

Nobody liked paperwork. But it was important.

Today. The accident. How to make sense of that accident?

He stood and stretched. Reaching for his coffee cup, he

stepped to the coffee maker. It might be a long night. Coffee helped. But water did, too. Important to drink water more than coffee. Guy always challenged him on that. Uncle Ted had drilled him on that, driving it home with many stories from his experience in the military. Crazy stories.

Dang, he missed Uncle Ted.

Mark yawned and stretched. "Chantelle, how's your kid? Your parents?" He hadn't asked in a long time.

"They're all great."

Ring!

Mark checked the time. One o'clock in the morning. Some nights flew. This one dragged.

"Yes, Ma'am." Chantelle looked straight at Mark. "Yes, Mrs. —Agatha. I'll send a deputy right over." She scribbled something on her notepad. "He'll be right there."

Mark stood up, popped his ball hat on his head, and walked to her desk. Wasn't it like that? Dead for hours, then one phone call exploded the rest of the night into action.

Chantelle tore off the paper and handed it to Mark. "Mrs. Agatha?" She shook her head. "Hard to understand her. But she is mad. She said someone is breaking into her trailer. You could hear pounding over the phone."

Trailer?

"Uh, okay." Mark held out his phone to download the address file.

"Be careful. She sounded mad. Isn't she the lady who shot the rifle in the air—not too long ago, right?"

Mark rushed to the door, but turned and nodded. Thought about it and nodded again.

As he started his car, his mind whirled. Trailer court address. But, Agatha? Who was Agatha?

Due to the late hour, Mark tried to be quiet. If he got there and it was an animal, he'd be fine. If it was a human, things might get strange.

Sure enough, it was the trailer court, but not Katty's trailer. Whew. He pulled to the correct trailer address on his phone and his computer. This was the right one. Slowly, he parked. He could just barely see someone on the deck. He turned down the volume on his radio, barely clicked open his door, and got out, his hand on his camera. He flicked it on, just in case. Never hurt.

As he walked closer, he could hear banging and loud yelling. What the?

Someone was pounding and yelling. This was Mrs. Nosy's trailer. She had reported Katty several times for child abuse. He swallowed. The closer he got to the trailer he could hear a woman's voice. "Let me in! I live here." Pound, pound. "Why is the door locked? Bea, let me in!"

Bea?

Oh no! Not Katty. He glanced over at Katty's trailer. All dark.

Back to Mrs. Nosy's.

Pound, pound. Sobbing. "Let me in!"

He stepped up on the deck. Mrs. Nosy still had her gun. He'd checked in with her after the last incident. Katty was lucky Mrs. Nosy hadn't blown her head off, because she wasn't afraid to use it.

Katty had slumped to her knees. "Bea. Let me in." She sounded and appeared very drunk.

"Katty." Mark stepped to her side where she would be able to see him. "Katty."

She jerked her head up. She patted the trailer siding. When she looked up at him and recognized him, the expression on her face broke his heart. "No." She glanced at where her hand rested on the side of the trailer. She patted it again—must have taken awhile for it to sink in. "This isn't my trailer, is it." She let her head fall to her chest and sobbed. "I'm at the wrong trailer." She peeked up at him.

He nodded. "Katty. Here. Let me help you up," So hard not

to break protocol. There was always a chance Katty could draw a gun. Did she even have one? He knew Mrs. Nosy was just inside. She definitely had one.

Katty pushed him away. "This is so stupid. I'll go home and be quiet." She patted the trailer again. "This is Mrs. Nosy's trailer, isn't it."

She didn't appear to have a weapon. His flashlight revealed too much. She was a mess, her hair was partly up and partly down, make-up smeared across her cheeks, eyes red.

Another squad car pulled up beside Mark's. Guy. *Good job, Chantelle.* He must have gotten back from the investigation.

Mark stooped to grasp her arm and help her stand. She pushed him away again and lunged for the edge of the deck, almost falling over the side.. "No. No. I'll go home. I'll be good. I won't hurt anybody."

Mark caught her in time, just as Mrs. Nosy opened her door. No gun. No lipstick this time. "Go back inside, Mrs. .... Um, please go back in. I have help."

Guy stepped onto the deck. "Katty, we're gonna have to take you in." He gently grasped her arm on the other side. "It's late. Let's let this kind lady go back to bed."

Something must have snapped in Katty and she kicked at Guy's leg, almost falling over. "No! I can't go to jail. I have a job. I have a kid." She tried to point behind them to her trailer, but got the wrong direction, "I have a kid and I need to go home."

Mark swallowed. Bea. He gulped and swallowed again. Guy glanced at him and raised his eyebrows. Mark shook his head. *Swallow it down. Swallow again.*

Katty swatted at Mark, then at Guy. She swung wide, missed by a mile, but lost her balance and fell. Guy caught her hands behind her back and reached for his handcuffs. "Katty you can go in quietly and not wake up the neighborhood. Or not."

Click.

Katty continued to thrash. She cussed and screamed. Cried.

The lady edged out her door.

"Mrs. ..." He couldn't call her Mrs. Nosy. What was her name? "Not a good idea. We need you to go back inside."

As if in response, the lady spoke. "My name is Agatha. Just Agatha."

"Okay. Agatha." Guy's stature and girth must have impressed her enough so that she stepped inside.

"Katty, we're taking you to the department to sleep it off."

She collapsed on the deck.

Both men reached down and lifted her to a stand.

Mark swallowed hard. His stomach wanted to heave. The smell of booze choked him. Body odor from a woman. Surprising and offensive. He wanted to run behind the bushes and hurl. He knew she needed to quit. He knew she should go to some kind of help group, or rehab. She needed it so bad.

But he also knew that, for some reason, he'd die for her and her little girl.

EIGHT

"Ow." Katty's arms were pulled behind her back. "That hurts." Her shoulders felt like they were tearing apart. The metal handcuffs cut into her wrists. She wiggled against the two men. No use. Her mind, her thoughts were ragged, she couldn't keep them on any one thing. From the red circles Bea had colored in, to the smell of Bea's dirty head against her shoulder, to the visual of a row of tiny shooter bottles lined up behind the cans of vegetables. To the babies floating on clouds about her right now.

So mixed up. So crazy. That was it. She was crazy. Not going crazy. She *was* crazy. And she would never be any good to anyone, much less the cute cop or Bea.

Her stomach lurched. Swallow. Swallow. No. She cleared her throat. Belch.

Now here. Not with them.

Her whole body wanted to revolt. She needed to get off the stuff, but her body screamed for more booze. What a way to go. She wanted more to feel better, but needed to get off it to feel better. To live her life.

One step at a time. Her small shoes next to the men's huge boots on the ground.

As soon as her feet hit the gravel of Mrs. Nosy's driveway, it all came up.

Both men groaned. Mark turned away and threw up.

She couldn't wipe her mouth. She couldn't pull her hair out of the way with her hands cuffed behind her back. She couldn't wipe the mess off of her shoes or their boots.

Sobs began to build from a deep place within her as she bent over. She'd never stand upright and look into another human's eyes again. She tripped over their boots and landed hard on her knees. In the muck. In her own vomit.

Fitting.

That was the only thought that made any sense. That was all she deserved.

Sobs took over, in spite of big hands lifting her upright. The higher they lifted her, the lower she crawled.

The car door opened and she all but crept into the car. A hand gently pushed her head down so she wouldn't bash it against the car. What was the point? She wouldn't ever be worth anyone saving or keeping safe. Why should they start now?

Once on the backseat, she slid down, her hands still cuffed behind her. Tears silently rolled down her cheeks, off her nose.

This was it. She was dying.

The end.

What had she done?

Deputy Scott didn't say a word to her until he pulled into a parking place in front of the Sheriff's Department.

She didn't want to go in. It felt like the end of the line for her forever. Her clothes felt clammy against her skin. She was sweating and freezing at the same time.

"Katty." He looked at her in the rear view mirror.

She couldn't meet his gaze. Tried to sit up.

He turned around in his seat and looked directly into her eyes.

She couldn't look away. He was so cute. She had blown anything from happening with him, too. The tears flowed.

She nodded slowly, not trusting herself to try her voice. Clearing her throat didn't help. She was numb but at the same time felt every cell in her body screaming, "stop this," but "give us more."

All she could do was nod.

So ashamed.

All she could do was shake her head. She couldn't even wipe her tears away.

The big deputy had opened the door to the back where she sat and held out his hand to grasp her arm.

Deep breath.

This was the end.

She scooted to the edge of the seat. Looked through the Sheriff's Department door. Was that Clarence?

"No."

"Katty—we had to." He helped her out the rest of the way and steadied her. "Just stand here for a minute and get your bearings. Breath slowly—it might help."

She nodded slightly.

"You can do this, Katty. This isn't the end."

Then why did it feel like it?

NINE

Bea shoved the book back onto her book shelf. Not that one.

She had a certain one or two in mind and she couldn't find them.

"Daryl & Dumpty." She sang the lyrics, remembering the melody as she went. "Had a great fall. They climbed and they bumped and then built a great wall."

She knew this by heart after watching the program every day, sometimes several times a day. Sometimes all night when Mommy left her alone while she ran out and did whatever she did all night.

"They shoveled and hammered and soon it was tall. Daryl and Dumpty had a great wall." Whenever she sang the song that went along with the TV program, she pictured the scenes in her mind. The way the characters moved and the way they were dressed. She heard the voices and how funny they sounded. She loved what they built. Every week it was a different wall. A different place. A garden wall. A house wall. Walls for chickens. Mostly to help someone out, but always to have fun and make things pretty. To never give up.

But, always have fun.

There they were. Just on the bottom of the pile. Mommy must have picked them all up, not remembering that Bea liked Daryl & Dumpty books right on top, so she could find them fast. So she could reach them.

Fun.

Knock. Knock.

Bea froze.

That wasn't Mommy.

Who was there?

She wasn't about to go to the front door because it was probably those old creepy men—the ones who stunk like those pretty bottles Mommy had hidden in the cupboard in the kitchen.

No.

Bea covered her ears and tried to sing the song from the Daryl and Dumpty show. "Daryl & Dumpty had a—"

Knock. Knock.

Wait. She rotated to the hallway. Was that the door there? It had come open before. Had Mommy fixed it shut?

Someone shoved the door open.

Every cell in Bea stopped. She held her breath.

Tap. Tap.

Bea pulled the blanket over her head and tried to breathe quietly. She had practiced that for a long time. Through her mouth. And slowly. She knew she didn't make a sound. She almost couldn't hear herself breathe.

Prickles on her skin. Shivers like when she got out of the bathtub and didn't have a towel.

The door creaked. Was it the front door or that hallway door?

"Mommy?" Bea crawled out, her tent blanket trailing along with her. "Mommy? That you?"

She held her breath and listened.

Took a short step toward the living room, but stopped.

Listened again.

"Mommy?" Her voice squeaked. Tears threatened.

She wiped them away and swallowed. Hard to swallow. She sniffed, wiped her nose on the blanket, and turned back to the rocker but almost bumped into a little boy. At least he looked like a little boy. He was shorter than Boy and his clothes were funny—like he still wore his Halloween costume. His shirt had all kinds of fun characters on it—kittens, dogs, mice, ducks. Even Daryl & Dumpty. All kinds of colors, like on her bedspread. His sleeves looked like the frogs skin she'd found last summer.

Bea pointed at his shirt. "You like Daryl & Dumpty, too?"

He nodded and grinned. Funny teeth ... all crooked and some pointed. Mommy always said she should brush her teeth every night. Maybe his mommy forgot to tell him.

"Can you talk?"

He shook his head. He held out his hands to her, but they were different than hers. His fingernails were long—like the girl's at the fingernail place.

He blinked.

Bea jumped back. His eyes blinked like the cat that hung around Mrs. Nosy's house. Skin closed over his eyes two times. Then his eyes turned black, then yellow and black again.

"Ick! Who are you?" Bea backed away toward the hallway. She bumped into something and turned. "Boy!"

Boy stepped beside the other kid. Boys eyes were pretty and just like Michael's. Michael liked Boy.

Bea glanced from one boy to the other. Back and forth. She knew Boy. He was her brother. He was kind and Michael knew him—loved him. But this other one ...

"Is he—"

"Let's go read some books." Boy grabbed Bea's hand and led her into the living room.

Boy read to Bea ... three books. She leaned over next to him on the sofa. Boy stood to look at Mommy's painting. He knew all the babies by name. "That's one's Sally. That's

Billy." He pointed at each one. "And that one's name is Alice."

Bea clapped her hands. They all seemed real to him. And they were. When he pointed at one, the baby flew to them, as if to meet her. They never talked. Babies can't talk, but they giggled. Lots of giggles.

"What's *your* name?" Bea pointed at Boy. "We just call you Boy. Do you have a name?"

He shook his head. "Naw. The angels say my mommy has to name me. Michael just calls me Buddy."

Bea nodded. "He's nice." She faced him and held his cheeks in her hands. "You want me to call you Boy or Buddy?"

He shook his head. "I don't care. Either one. Both."

Bea tried it out. "Buddy Boy. Boy Buddy." She shrugged. "I like Boy Buddy." She shook her head. "Boy is good. I already know it." She pointed at the kid who had followed them from the bedroom. "Who is that little boy? He's scary but he's got a Daryl & Dumpty shirt on."

"He's a demon. He'll go away if you ask God to get rid of him."

Bea looked in that direction. "Okay. He's creepy." She folded her hands and closed her eyes. "God please make him go away!"

Boy pointed at the kid. "Go!"

The kid popped like a balloon and disappeared.

"Cool! How'd you do that?"

Boy shook his head. "You did it. You asked. And God answered." He turned a page. "So when does Mom get home?" He closed the books and shoved them beside him on the sofa.

Bea breathed out a sigh. "I never know. Sometimes after I fall asleep. Sometimes not until breakfast time."

"We could go for a walk, or something." He patted the books. "I like your books but I'm done reading." He stood up. "Let's go and see if we can find her."

Bea stood, but didn't move from where she was. "But ... I'm

supposed to stay here and wait for Mommy." She pinched at a couple lose threads on the sofa and pulled them out. "We could watch TV."

Boy smiled. "That's okay. I'll be okay." He tilted his head from side to side. Smiled again. "I'm an angel, so I can't get hurt." He stepped toward the front door. "Michael and the other angels take care of me." He opened the door and waved.

Bea watched him close the door, then ran to the window. "Where'd he go?" She ran to another one. Nobody on the driveway. Not on the street. Wait. Was he on the street already? Maybe she could just go out and check. She wouldn't go very far.

She patted her books on the sofa. "I won't be gone long. I'll be right back." She snagged her blue sweatshirt from one of the kitchen chairs and pulled it on as she opened the door. "Bye Daryl & Dumpty books. I'll be right back."

She stepped onto the deck and carefully closed the door behind her. Was that Boy, beside the big tree? She ran to meet him.

"Boy!" She waved. "Wait for me."

TEN

"But where was her kid?" Chantelle filed some papers in the four stack file cabinet and turned to face Mark and Guy. "Where is her little girl?"

Mark looked at Guy. Guy stared back at him. Both shook their heads. How stupid was that? They both knew she had a kid, Mark especially, but neither had checked to see where she was.

"I figured that since Katty was pounding on Mrs. Nos—er, Agatha's trailer to get in, that Bea was with her. That Agatha was babysitting for her."

Guy stood. "I'll check to see if Katty is still passed out."

Mark shook his head. "I shoulda looked. I should have asked." He avoided Chantelle's accusing eyes. "I didn't even think." He glanced at her. "Okay. I didn't think."

Buzz.

He checked his phone. Not now Mom. He was legitimately being thrashed by Chantelle, with good reason, and Mom calls.

Chantelle pushed her phone at him. "Answer it."

He turned away. "Hi Mom."

"Hello, Mark. Uh, if you're busy, I can call back tomorrow."

"It's okay. You're up late." He checked the wall clock. "1:30 a.m. Mom. You been out on a date or something? It's past your bedtime." Felt good. Getting called out by Chantelle and passing it on to his own mom.

She chuckled. "You know me better than that. I was getting ready for bed and praying. I had a thought. I know this is very unlike me, but … is that little girl okay?"

Mark sat down hard at his desk. "What little girl, Mom?"

Chantelle looked up—on full alert.

"You know. The little girl and that lady you—you know." She cleared her throat. "I think I saw her at the grocery store the other day with the little girl. I was shopping there with Lucille and we were planning the Bible study luncheon. We found--"

"Mom." Mark interrupted her. "You mean, Katty? *Her* little girl?" He couldn't stop shaking his head. His eyes locked with Chantelle's.

"I know this is really unusual for me to ask about her, but for some reason, I keep seeing her little girl … uh, what's her name … little—"

"Bea, Mom. Like the bumblebee."

"Yes. I keep seeing—you know how I am … I sometimes see things. Anyway, I saw her all dirty and crying. Like she fell and hurt herself." She stopped. "I know this is crazy, but I couldn't stop thinking about her, about that child. I couldn't sleep without knowing if she's okay."

Mom was trying. Trying to be gracious, even when she didn't approve.

"Did you see where she was? Like what street, or town?"

Chantelle picked up a pen, still watching him, still listening.

Guy walked in. "She's still out."

Both Chantelle and Mark shushed him.

"I'm sorry Son, if you're busy."

"No Mom. It's okay. We've had a busy night, but we are

always interested in your proph—uh, in any help you can give us." He paused. "Is there anything else?"

"No. Just that she was hurt and really upset." Mom hesitated. "She is sweet and so tiny, Mark."

"I know, Mom." He turned away and covered his face with his hand. "Thanks, Mom. We'll check into it. I'm sure she's alright." He turned back to Guy and Chantelle with wide eyes. "Sleep well."

"Thanks, Son. Be safe. I love you."

"I love you too, Mom." Mark clicked off and stood. "I don't know how you feel about that call or what it might mean. Or how you feel about Mom and her ... I don't know where I'm gonna look, but I'm starting at Katty's trailer and branching out from there. No. Agatha's trailer first."

"Wait." Guy followed him to the door. "What was that all about?"

Mark stepped back to check with Chantelle. "Am I crazy?"

Chantelle shook her head. "Not in my book." She tapped her pen to the paper. "Even if she's wrong, we follow up on leads. And in my book, that woman hears from God."

Mark blinked. "Like has she ever—"

Chantelle stood and pointed at the door. "Go find Bea."

Out in the parking lot, Guy slid in the passenger side as Mark started the squad car and checked in. "What is going on?"

"It's kinda hard to tell you. Mom called." He glanced over at Guy. He might be crazy, but he knew his mom. "She ... called about Bea."

"What about Bea?"

Mark shifted into drive. "I uh, I." He glanced over at Guy. "It's just a hunch."

"You mean a premonition or—"

"Something like that." Mark turned the corner.

"What'd your mom say, exactly?"

Mark blew out a breath. "She said she saw Bea."

"Saw Bea."

"Not for real, but—"

Guy shook his head. "Like a dream?"

"Kinda. Just listen." Mark shook his head. "She saw Bea dirty and crying, like she hurt herself." Mark flipped on the blinker and turned on the next street. "I know she doesn't like Katty or Bea. Or at least she doesn't want me to be involved with them." Dang. Let's get it all out of the bag and in the open.

Guy didn't make a comment. He didn't even smirk. "Go on."

"But she kept seeing Bea. That's it. Like she was hurt."

"Okay. Let's get after it. Where do you want to start?"

Mark turned into the trailer court. "I say start with Mrs. … Agatha."

"Why do you keep calling her that?' Guy did grin that time. "You're talking about Mrs. … Nosy, right?"

"Because she got mad at me and told me to call her Agatha." Mark pulled up in Agatha's driveway and got out. "Poor lady. We just left here. I hope she's not asleep yet."

Knock, knock.

There was rustling at the door and Agatha opened it. "What is it? Why are you back?"

"Sorry to bother you again … Agatha. We needed to check on the little girl. Little Bea. Have you seen her?" Mark pulled out his pen and pad. "Is she with you?"

Agatha shook her head. "Why would she be here?"

Mark checked Guy's face. "Okay. Have you seen her tonight?"

She shook her head. "No." She stepped out on her deck, pushing the men back. "She is a sweetheart, so you better find her." She pointed at Katty's trailer. "Did you check there?"

"No. That's next. I was just hoping Katty had asked you to babysit and that was why Katty was … pounding on *your* door earlier."

"Nope. Katty was drunk. Find her. Find that little girl."

Mark nodded and stepped down her steps. "Thanks, Mrs. Agatha."

"Agatha. Just Agatha."

Mark raced to Katty's trailer. Guy drove the car there.

He pounded on the door. Tried the doorknob. Unlocked. Guy right behind him. He opened it and pushed it in. "Bea?" Louder. "Bea, are you in here?" He flicked the lights on.

What a disaster.

Guy right behind him. "What's all that?" Guy pointed at the paintings on the wall.

"Katty is an artist." Mark checked under the table. "Bea?" He yelled now. Back down the hall.

Guy checked the living room, under cushions, behind the curtains.

A kid could hide anywhere. Bea's room. Under the bed, in her closet. Nowhere. The bathroom was easy. Shower and tub. Storage cupboard behind the door. Perfect hiding place. No Bea.

Katty's room. Damn. He pulled the blanket from the rocker, knowing the stories about Bea's hiding place. He pulled the comforter off Katty's bed and shooter bottles flipped into the air. Damn. Under the bed. More. In the closet. Madness.

No Bea.

He rushed into the hall and slammed into Guy.

"No Bea." Both at the same time.

Guy lifted his hands. "Where would a little girl go—?"

"To find her mommy?" Mark finished the question. He blinked. Where had he seen Bea and Katty before this? "I've seen them at the park a long time ago."

Guy shook his head. "That's too far." He swallowed. "Isn't it?"

"I don't know. You've got kids." Mark tapped on his radio. "Chantelle, you there?"

"Yes. Here."

"You sitting on your radio?" Mark shook his head. "Where would Woodrow hide?"

"She's not at the trailer?" Chantelle blew out a breath. "Wow. He hides, but dang. Kids hide in old refrigerators, in trees. You know I just finished reading … " Papers rustled. "Here. It just said that kids don't go far from home. Even when they run away, they truly want to be found, so they don't go very far. I don't know."

Mark and Guy walked into the kitchen when they heard a screech and both turned toward the sound.

"Did that? Did that come from back there?" Guy pointed to the hallway. He rushed back the way they'd just come and flicked the light switch on in the hallway.

The hall door swung open.

"I didn't know there was a door here." Mark pushed it wide open and peeked outside. Grabbed his flashlight and flicked it on.

Guy jumped out onto the ground, stepped to a fence and tripped on some mangled old pipes. He fell into a hole. Someone had been digging a basement. Another tiny house.

Mark followed him out, his flash light illuminated a child's book. He leaned to pick it up. "This is Bea's—I know it is. She loves these books." He wiped the dirt off onto his pants.

"Here. She left a good trail."

Thank God. "What'd you find?"

Guy held up a tiny bottle—empty.

Mark sucked in a breath. "Dang." He made it around to the driver's side, tossed the book in back, and got in. Guy radioed Chantelle.

They pulled out of the trailer court and turned onto the street.

Whatever was that in the middle of the street?

Some little dog must have gotten out. He checked the number for the dog pound, then glanced up as he put in the call.

"Hello, Dog Pound. Sandy speaking."

"Hi Sandy. Sorry so late. You are always so upbeat. It's just worth the call in to hear your happy voice." He grinned envisioning this woman who was grandmother to all—dogs and people alike. "Hey, it's Mark and I might have a … "

What on earth?

He slowly drove closer so as not to startle the animal, only it was no dog.

It was a child.

No.

He drove closer, braked, shifted to park and Guy jumped out.

"You still there Mark?" There was a lot of yapping on her end of the connection, but he could still hear the concern in her voice. "You okay?'

Mark leaned down to the child. "I'm okay." He lifted the child's hair off her face. "Bea!" He dropped his phone, then scooped her up.

Guy grabbed the phone, ran to the squad car, and opened the back door. "Hey Sandy. Sorry, gotta go."

Mark slid onto the car seat with her in his arms, shoving the papers, book, and lunch over, until they were all the way in. Just as she opened her eyes.

"Mr. Depdy, sir." Bea licked her dry lips. "My arm hurts. Can you take me to the doctor?" She sucked in a deep, ragged breath. "Please?"

"Bea. It's gonna be alright. We'll sure take you to the doc—er—hospital."

Guy shifted to drive and radioed in. "Hey Chantelle, our little dog turned out to be a child. It's Bea. Heading to the hospital."

"Dear God. Just like Mom saw." Mark choked.

Mark adjusted Bea in his arms. "Bea?" Nothing. No response. Her face was wet. She'd been crying. Mark gently held her close. He didn't bother to wipe his eyes. "Mom pray."

Louder. "God, get Mom to pray." He didn't bother to hide his face from Guy, who could see him in the rearview mirror—tears and all.

This little girl. And her mommy.

There had to be a way.

ELEVEN

Jasper breathed, his eyes closed. He slowly breathed Father in.

He felt the physical world on Earth. He stood in a jail cell. But the Breath of Heaven was breathing through him now. Breathing into him Peace, Love, Joy. He sensed and heard the worship going on in heaven, even as he stood on Earth.

Powerful.

Katty lay on the cot, out cold.

Jasper guarded her as part of Father's plan for her.

She rolled over and groaned.

He'd learned that some of the things humans used—like food or drink or other earthly things available—made them sick. That always puzzled Jasper. When they could have all kinds of foods the Lord had created for them to eat. When they could have Jesus. When they could actually have Jesus, the Way, inside of them.

Angels couldn't have it like that. They communed with Jesus, knew him, and could see him. Knew Him.

But not like the humans could.

Not like Jasper hoped for Katty. She breathed in a deep breath.

Belched.

Uh-oh.

She blinked several times and tried to open her eyes. Rubbed them with her fists. The look of confusion on her face when she saw the blank walls, the windows.

Closed her eyes again.

He knew she was still drunk. He'd been with Katty since she had come to Earth—experienced everything she'd been through —with her. Seen it all.

She belched again. He knew the signs. He never entertained critical thoughts toward her. Even though he loved her, the Father had made angels so they would be kind, faithful and loyal but never unkind or cruel. Never accusing. Angels that were still of the Kingdom of God didn't have any evil in their beings.

They were curious though. Somedays they'd go back to heaven and ask the elders questions. Like … what does that yellow liquid do to the human body, exactly? On the day Jasper had gotten up the nerve to ask, the elder just shook his head. "Be thankful you don't know."

So Jasper watched as Katty threw up the contents of her stomach onto the floor. It was a messy one. Smelly, too.

He began to flow the music of heaven in. Softly. He piped it into the room, into the jail cell. "Fasten me upon your heart as a seal of fire forevermore." He loved the depth of the choirs of heaven. "This living, consuming flame will seal you as my prisoner of love." At times when he heard the singing from heaven, the veil was thin, and a mist broke open. The angels and saints leaned down, their faces glorious as they sang and prayed.

Katty stirred again. This was going to be a long process.

But Jesus had eternity.

Jasper knew the prayers of Jesus for His church. He knew the words of Jesus on this earth—"Our Father …."

Satan had words too, but he was a liar.

The words of the Psalmist, King David, floated into Jasper's heart and he piped them into the cell. "The Lord is close … the Lord is close … to the brokenhearted. The Lord is close to the brokenhearted. He rescues those who are crushed. He rescues them. He rescues them. The Lord rescues those who are crushed."

Tears gathered at the corners of Katty's eyes. Even though she wasn't fully conscious, he knew she heard those words.

He piped the song in again. He knew Jesus was layering His words over Satan's lies, washing the lies away through Katty's tears.

"Oh, Father …."

<hr>

Katty leaned over the edge of the cot and threw up. "Oh, shit. Oh no." She'd have to check out one of those carpet cleaner things …

Wait. She really opened her eyes. No carpet. Just floor. Tiles. Wha? Covered in her vomit. She closed her eyes. *Breathe.*

Onto her back. Belch.

Out again.

Shadows moved. She opened her eyes. Closed again. No. Don't come up. No. Not again. *Breathe. Breathe.* She didn't even dare to wipe her eyes. She'd throw up again. *Breathe.* She willed herself to open her eyes. Slowly. The shadows again. Long windows up high. Dark sky. Tree shadows waved, taunting her.

Close eyes.

"I am here. I am here. Close to your broken heart."

No.

Breathe.

She heard it again. Music. Voices. The words. Those words. "I am close to your broken heart." Tears rolled down her cheeks, into her hair. "I am here." She swallowed. Then "Worthless." Tears. Worthless. Then, "I am here."

Stop the voices! She balled her fists at her eyes. Stop those voices.

She tried to roll over and open her eyes again.

Those windows up high. Black sky. Street lights. Waving shadows in the wind. Tree shadows waving. Making her dizzy. Even the trees hated her. Just like the tree she'd painted at home on the walls.

Everything up again. Everything she'd poured in yesterday and last night—up and out.

She couldn't even cuss.

Nothing.

Nothing left in her stomach and nothing left in her heart.

All empty.

All darkness.

She glanced out the windows again. Dark. Black. Was there even a human heart inside her body? She placed her hands on her chest. Barely shook her head. No heartbeat. Nothing there. No beating of a heart. Dry. Empty. Nothing.

She'd always felt overcome by something so deep and heavy, something so depressing, so painful. There must be spiritual blood somehow. Not physical … well, yes. Physical. She'd seen enough of that.

But, there had to be blood, blood of the heart. Blood of the wounded heart. Blood that poured out of the heart, out of the eyes. Out of a place so deep no x-ray could ever detect it, no surgeon could ever sew it back together.

But it was there. Churning. Painful. Spewing blood.

Katty blinked. Rubbed her eyes. This bed was terrible. It wasn't her bed. Her bed wasn't perfect, but it was … her bed. She slowly rolled to one side. A cot. She was on a cot?

Back to the windows. Two side by side, close to the ceiling. Still dark outside. Still windy—the shadows seemed to be like fingers pointing at her. Yes. No. Yes, you are in trouble. Yes, you are a murderer. Yes, you are in jail.

Her eyes popped open.

She sat up too fast and threw up again.

Shit.

Jail.

She *was* in jail. For real.

But this time she stayed sitting up. What on earth? It had been years—at least five—since she had spent a night in jail.

The cot. The windows. The floor tiles. Again.

All over again.

The smells. Pine-sol.

She blinked. This *was not* her house.

Her house.

Shit! Where was Bea? What had she done?

This was really the jail—she was not dreaming. Painted concrete block walls. The windows. The tiny sink. The toilet. The walls had funny texture all over them. White, like the paint, but speckled and each minute as she stared at the walls, they morphed into bubbles, into misty bubbles. Clouds. Little clouds like steam.

Giggles. Clouds … coming closer.

The babies.

No! Not here.

"Help." She stepped over the vomit. The door. The thick steel door. Closed. Locked. The only barrier to freedom.

Bea.

Where was Bea?

"Help me." Someone's ragged voice cried. Tears flowed faster, now. She glanced back at the walls. If only she could transform this cell into her living room at home. Paint herself back home. Bubbles of babies floated toward her. How had they found her? How had they gotten here from home?

Her hand on the door was cold. Oh, Lord, what had she done? What had she done with Bea?

She didn't even remember getting here. How had she gotten here?

The babies closed in. Their eyes appeared different. Each baby's eyes appeared blue, green, brown. Were they accusing? Were those giggles—that morphed into growls and evil laughter? Accusing eyes. Accusing laughter.

She slid down the door to the floor. Oh, Dear God. Flat on her face. Hands on the floor, her face on her hands. No tears, just sobs. What had she done?

She was the only barrier to freedom. It was her—all her. "Oh God. Help me." She sobbed. "The things I've done. The terrible …." She glanced up. "My babies. Forgive me."

Sobbed.

"Oh, God, what have I done?"

TWELVE

Mark gently scooped Bea up and held her against his chest as carefully as he could and still walk. He tried to not jar her but walked smoothly to the ER entrance.

Guy bumped the automatic door button and waited for Mark to walk inside.

Mark watched Bea as it opened. She was so pretty. Her dark eyelashes rested against her pale cheeks. Tears still pooled in the corners of her eyes.

He accidentally jostled her as he leaned against the inside automatic door button and her eyes opened. She looked up at him, blinked and then smiled.

"Hi Mr. Depdy, Sir."

Never was there a more profound moment for Mark than now. He smiled down at her as he walked through the now opened door. "Hi Bea."

She stared up at him for a long time before becoming aware of her surroundings. She must have seen the overhead lights along the ceiling as he walked her inside. Before she thought about it, she raised herself up and looked at the walls. She winced. "Hopistal?"

A bubble of joy tried to work its way up from his gut. He kept his cool but he so wanted to laugh out loud. "Yes. Hopistal."

"I tried to walk, but I got so tired. Boy left me and I tried to follow him." She looked down at her hurt arm. "And my arm hurt, so I had to sit down on the ground."

"Boy?"

"Yes. He's my brother."

She must have hit her head. This kid was so precious. "Well you're here now and you don't have to sit down on the ground."

The nurse opened the door to an emergency room and pulled the sheet back. "Here you go."

"You can have a bed instead—not the ground." Oh, this might hurt. He rested her bottom on the bed first, then her back and legs.

"Where is she hurt?" The nurse pushed a crash cart beside the gurney and felt Bea's forehead. "I'll take vitals."

Bea was still looking at Mark from under the nurse's hand on her forehead. "My arm is hurt."

He smiled down at her.

Guy signed her in and filled in a form.

The nurse began asking the intake questions. "What is your name little one?" She started to rush through to the next questions.

A doctor walked in and spoke his own questions and orders. He assessed Bea. "What's your name young lady?"

Bea glanced at the nurse, then back to the doctor. "My name is Bea Randolph." She watched the nurse tear open some packages. "And my mommy's name is Mommy." She kicked her feet a little, seemingly uncomfortable. "And I don't have a daddy." She looked up at Mark with such pain in her eyes.

He could have cried. He reached for her good hand and squeezed her fingers.

"And this is Depdy. My friend."

Dang. This was going to be hard. He didn't usually get this emotional on the job, but this kid got to him. Her big brown eyes were so pure and innocent. What was to become of her? He knew too much about her young life.

"Yes. And you are my friend, too."

THIRTEEN

Jasper watched Katty's features writhe with pain, her brow tightened, tears wet her pillow, her chin quivered as she tried to hold it in. Her arms hugged her body tightly. She leaned over from the cot and threw up again.

What did that make? Three times. There couldn't be anything left in her stomach. The dispatcher had come in to offer Katty some breakfast of coffee and a bagel, but Katty had refused it. The lady kindly helped her lie down again.

She'd had nothing—no booze—for twenty-four hours? Her stomach should be empty and she should be closer to sobriety than she'd ever been. By now, going on her past experience, she would have started drinking again upon waking.

It always seemed like pouring down more booze when Katty woke up, helped—that it somehow settled her stomach and kept her from vomiting.

Life with these humans, especially his assignment, was quite confusing.

Jasper shook his head. He had no authority to change things —to change the humans. Only the Lord did that—if the human was willing and wanted the change.

He'd heard Katty say many, many times that she wanted to change. Or that she wanted to not drink the stuff anymore. Or she wanted to be a better mommy to Bea.

Jasper didn't understand. Why didn't she just quit? He'd seen Jesus raised from the dead. What was so hard about stopping something that was making a human sick? He didn't have the position or authority to condemn them. Condemnation was Satan's job and humans had to learn the difference between condemnation and conviction that was brought by the Spirit. The Spirit pointed out the wrong in love. He didn't condemn to destroy.

Katty lifted her head and rolled onto the floor, her hair tangled into her face, dragging across her back.

Jasper guessed from the human standpoint that she needed a shower. She had a strong stench about her. If he didn't know better, he'd think there'd been demons around and because of the constant drinking, there had been. Jasper didn't get too worked up when the demons appeared. He knew who they were. They knew him.

But those demons knew they only had a short time with each human and each nation to interfere and influence before they were cast out by some believing follower of Jesus, the Christ. Then it was over and those demons had to find another place to inhabit and inflict their evil. They might be able to trigger the human after that but only if the human agreed.

Mrs. T prayed constantly with those words—God's words through her. Those were strange words to humans—different languages—but angels mostly understood them. Mrs. T prayed for everyone—Katty, Bea, her own husband—Clarence, the people at Hillcrest Nursing Home. She saw and knew Michael, the angel over Clarence. She held a high position in the Kingdom of God—even though she was a tiny, frail human. It didn't matter. They were all part of God's plan—whether they were angels, humans still on the earth, created creatures, or humans that had gone from the earth to their place in heaven. They all had a part in God's plan.

And in the end, God's plan won.

Katty rolled over on the floor, trying to sit up, unsuccessfully. Chunks of hair tangled into her puffy, red eyes and around her ears. "What have I done?" She sat up, startled. "Why didn't I think of this until now? Those babies I painted on the wall at home. They float. They are alive. They fly to me and call me Mommy."

Father's voice rumbled gently into Katty's spirit. "You *are* their mommy."

Katty's eyes popped when she heard His voice. She sat still for a long time. Quiet. "They are ...." She swallowed and pointed at her chest. "They are *my* babies?"

Why hadn't she figured that out until now? No condemnation again, but babies who gathered to their mothers, both in the human kingdom and the animal kingdom, were the babies of that mom.

Katty spoke out loud again. "God, You are here?" She swallowed and glanced around the cell. "You just spoke to me. You are here?"

Jasper pulled back, as a mist filled the space. A huge Presence dominated and filled the cell. The Presence of the Ever Living One, the Great Almighty God, Jehovah.

Jasper knelt on one knee, his right arm across his chest, head bowed.

Katty closed her eyes, gasped for breath.

As she breathed and struggled for air, Jasper heard Father download messages. They slammed into her, one after another, until she was sobbing on the floor again.

The Strength, the Truth, and the Power of Father flowed into Katty, in response to her cries. Jasper knew Father was reminding her of His love. Giving her Truth. As each message flowed into her, an angel accompanied it to protect it, to make sure it wasn't stolen by the enemy. One-by-one, the messages hit the mark, like a movie screen, one frame at a time. The angels made sure she heard the Voice that went with each screen.

The enemy accused her and right away an angel brought the Father's words, "You are my Beloved."

Demons brought nightmares of brutality.

Angels brought more Words from Father. "My Son died for you."

Demons pointed and accused Katty.

Father stretched out His arms and gently covered her with His blanket of love—ever-forgiving, ever-loving.

Sobs erupted from her.

Demons gathered in, but at the same time Jasper and his angels formed a tight circle around her, swords weaving a living, impenetrable mesh that kept the demons from getting through. One might stab her on the head and try to insert a thought or accusation, but it sputtered out like a match stuck into water.

Nothing getting through today.

FOURTEEN

Mark sat at his desk and pulled the top drawer open, then closed it. He clicked on his computer and watched it load up. The network at the department was fast, but Mark figured it needed to be. Click on. Find the background or record of a person they had just rescued or detained. They needed information quickly to make a better decision.

He clicked through a couple reports and new messages. Sheriff sent out several a day to keep the deputies updated. They were always good and kind, but necessary to keep his people on task and informed of any legal changes or new results of court cases that they needed to know about.

He checked his phone. No messages or calls he might have missed. Made sure it was not on silent. He'd done that before because of too many calls from Mom, while he attended a conference or training. She'd understood, though.

It was on. All okay there.

Coffee would help. He grabbed his mug. Yuck. Old and cold. He rinsed it out and poured hot, fresh coffee. Mmm. A full pot. He breathed it in and glanced up.

Chantelle grinned at him. "Made it fresh."

Mark nodded. *Get it together.* "Smells really good. Thanks for making fresh." Better yet. "Thanks for all you do around here. Makes it a better place to work."

She frowned. "Are you okay, Mark?"

"What? I can't thank you for all you do?" He sipped the hot coffee and sat down at his desk. Dang. What was wrong with him? Pretending. Trying not to think that in a cell just a few feet from his desk, Katty was incarcerated. Just to dry out and be released.

She was all he could think about.

Chantelle smiled and returned to her desk.

She knew. What of it? He could trust her with his life and at least, *some* secrets. She was a good friend, even. She was a good mom to her kid. Woodrow. She helped take care of her elderly parents. She had tons going on, but she could be trusted. She always offered part of her lunch—she brought some to share— whether it was roast beef, or green beans or strawberries from her garden. A generous woman.

She turned back to him.

Oh-oh.

"Have you … have you gone back there and tried to talk to her?" She tilted her head and shrugged her shoulders. "At least to see how she's doing? She was pretty drunk when you brought her in."

Drunk? She had passed out just from her trailer to the department. What? Two, three blocks? "Is Guy around? Maybe—"

"He left on a call. Something about a car inspection. They usually bring them here—well, you know—but for some reason they couldn't, and needed it inspected, so they could drive it." She shook her head.

Mark nodded. What would he say to her? Even if Katty was awake, what would they say to each other? How did he do this?

Buzz.

Always. Always, without fail. Mom called at the worst times. Better check to see how she was doing.

"Hi Mom."

"Hello, Mark. Did I catch you at a bad time, Dear? I mean, I can call back some other time." She cleared her throat. "Sorry, Son. Allergies."

"No problem, Mom. No this is a good time. I have a few minutes."

Chantelle shook her head.

Mark crossed his eyes at her and stuck out his tongue.

"Well, I was just wondering … you remember the last time we talked, right? About the little girl? I was just wondering if … well, if I was crazy." Tap, tap, tap. "I was just curious."

Chantelle turned to face Mark, her dark eyebrows raised.

Dang. What was protocol right now? It was his mom and she had seen evidence. He almost said he didn't know, but Chantelle floated him a look that could kill and shook her head. "What? Do I or don't I?"

"What? I didn't hear you, Mark."

"You need to tell her the truth." Chantelle turned back to her computer, then swung to face him again. "And thank her."

"Right." He stood and walked outside. Dang Chantelle. Get him in trouble. But she was right. "Yeah. About that Mom. Right after you called, Guy and I took off to see if we could find her. We went to the trailer house—"

"Oh, those trai—"

"It's been fixed up, Mom. Looks better on the inside than on the outside." Flashback—maybe better on the outside than the inside. "They've fixed some of it up." He was making excuses for Katty. Some. "Anyway, She wasn't there. Nobody home."

"Oh." Her voice sounded deflated. "I was wrong." She sucked in a deep breath. "It was such a powerful, strong vision. We can't get it right all of the time."

"But you did get it right." Mark ran his fingers through his hair. Where was his ball cap? "Mom, what you saw was exactly the way she looked. We found her. She must have hit her head, because she was saying funny things, but she was dirty and had been crying." Mark wiped his wet cheek. "You helped us find her, Mom."

A sob broke on the other end of the line. "Oh, thank You God."

"You okay, Mom?" Mark nodded. "She's okay because of you."

"She's okay, then? I saw her so many times. And I know I haven't been very nice about her mom with you. I'm so sorry. I don't mean to." Deep sigh. "She's okay."

"Mom, I know you just want what's best for me. You want me to be happy. I think I get that." Guy pulled up. Just in time. "Hey, I do have to go now. Breathe easy." He sucked in a deep breath, himself. "Breathe. And go back to bed." He checked the time. "Go to bed, Mom." He laughed. "Not very often I get to tell you what to do."

Guy walked past him, making kissing noises with his lips.

Mark flipped him off.

She laughed. "I need it sometime, though." She sniffled. "Thanks Mark, for telling me. I'm not sure about the legal thing. The privacy thing. But as long as she's okay."

"She is, Mom. Thanks to you." He hesitated. "And God, right?"

"Right. I'll get off the phone and go back to bed. I love you, Mark."

"Thanks Mom. I love you too." Mark looked up at the sky. Must be cloudy. Not very many stars. Windy, too. Stormy almost. The whole night felt stormy—people, too. And now, he turned and faced the building, sucked in a deep breath, and offered up a prayer. "God please help. I have no idea how ..."

He stood for another moment then took a step, then another. With each successive step, he became more sure and determined.

He opened the door, avoided looking at Chantelle, but felt her glance at him. She knew. He sensed it. She was deeper than he gave her credit for. He knew his mother was praying, too. Guy might laugh. Maybe. But Mark knew that this was one of those destiny moments. A pure moment in time, led by God, to change a life—maybe Katty's, maybe his, and possibly Bea's, too.

He opened the door and marched directly to the cell block, listening, thankful that Phil had been transported to another county jail. It had been inappropriate having him here and Katty, too.

All was quiet.

He stepped to Katty's cell door and almost unlocked it, but stopped.

Voices.

Katty's voice. Sobbing. "What have I done?" Sobbing. Crying. Gasping.

He almost inserted his key, but something stopped him again.

"My babies." She must have pounded on the floor? "Bea. What have I done?" Sobs. Painful, gut-wrenching sobs.

Mark knelt on one knee without thinking about it. He just found himself kneeling on the tile floor right outside Katty's cell door—listening, hearing her pain, her heart. Her words. Never had Mark connected with another human on this level. As he heard her words, something broke in his own heart—his own pain, his past, his wounds—all broke and stirred, mixed with Katty's. His own stuff was hard, but Katty's grief was deep and crushing

"Oh God, what have I done? Killing my babies." Katty sobbed and seemingly pounded the floor with her fist. "God forgive me!"

Mark found himself kneeling facedown on the floor outside her cell door, weeping. His tears joined hers with just a door between them.

"God take away the voices, these awful voices. Give me my babies back. Please, Lord." One last plea. "God help me. Don't give up on me."

Mark crouched almost in a fetal position, his face in the palms of his hands. Crying, weeping soundlessly. Touching her heart. He knew he was connecting with her heart. He stretched out his hands on the floor and touched something.

He jumped. What? He opened his eyes and there were boots on the floor in front of him.

He froze. Boots.

Oh no. Guy?

Instinct and training tried to kick in. Those boots hadn't been there before he'd knelt down. He wasn't alarmed or afraid. Just … startled. He'd been tapping them for a couple seconds before he realized that they shouldn't be there. The material was not leather like he'd ever seen before. He was afraid to look up. Cloth draped above the boots. Fabric? A robe?

Not Guy.

Visuals misted over the actual physical walls and door, the floor. He could still see them, still hear Katty inside her cell, his heart still connected to hers. But at the same time, these boots, the robe layered over the rest.

He felt that if he just peeked up, he'd die. This was something so powerful, so jarring, that he'd just lay down and die. Guy or Chantelle would walk into the short hallway to the cells and find him flat on the floor—dead, no longer breathing. Or disappeared somehow.

But, he had to. He had to look up. Al-l-l-l the way up.

Oh dear God in heaven.

A huge man hovered, stood over him, gently smiled down at him. White hair streamed around his face, some kind of armor covered his muscular body, robes flowed from under the armor. Dark blue eyes pierced Mark's own.

Deep breath. Tears wouldn't stop.

At the same moment that Mark noticed a sword, a knowing stabbed Mark's heart. This was Katty's angel. He was guarding her. Mark didn't understand how he knew, but he knew. He was more sure of that, than he was of his own being, of his own humanity. This was Katty's own personal angel assigned to protect her.

Terror invaded Mark as he realized who this was. He also realized he was still tapping the angel's boot. He peered all the way up to the angel's face, again.

The angel was smiling. Kind of. He was. Really smiling. But, at the same time, there seemed to be some kind of threat or reminder. Communication without words.

Again, Mark knew, just by looking up at the angel, that this angel would not allow Katty to be harmed, in any way. Yes, she harmed herself, but from this moment on, any threats from anyone else—including Mark—would not be tolerated.

The angel glanced at his sword.

Damn. Mark removed his hand to just beside the boot.

Katty had quieted, but seemed to be hiccupping. Still moaned. Grieving.

One quick glance up at her angel's face.

Terrified.

FIFTEEN

Bea burst out of the front door and screamed, "Mommy! You're here! Noell said you'd be here soon." She waved her hands out wide. "And here you are."

So now, Katty wasn't the most important one? Noell was?

Bea grabbed her Daryl & Dumpty blanket from Katty and half of her books. She skipped ahead and partway up the sidewalk to Noell's house, then dropped one. Then another. "Mommy. This way. Noell showed me around her house. There was a big storm last night." She looked at the house. "We cleaned up the branches that fell down at the park." She giggled. "Then we played on the swings."

Chatter, chatter, chatter. *Take a breath. Take another one.*

"Noell took me to the store and we got more coloring pages." She jumped up and down, dropped another book. "I'm gonna win the contest, Mommy."

Katty stooped to pick the books up, still dragging their rolling suitcase behind her. "Bea. Slow down. We have time to bring our stuff inside." She straightened and looked up at the house looming in front of her. Even halfway to the house from the street, it was huge. A white—a little chipped paint here and there—but mostly white, two-story house with a basement. And a yard. And evidently a garage out back. She even remembered a small creek running through, way behind the house, with a garden.

Gamma's garden. Paradise.

Belch. Please not here. Not in front of Noell. Or Bea. Bea had seen enough. *Breathe. Breathe.* She knew she was better— almost sober, maybe, maybe not—but she had a long way to go to forever sober. She closed her eyes and stood still.

"Mommy. Come on." Bea reached the front step.

"Bea. Wait. This isn't our house." Even though Gamma and Mom had been sisters, for a reason Katty had never known, Mom hated Gamma. And Gamma had always loved Mom … and Katty. She should find a time to ask Noell. Maybe Gamma told *her* what happened. And why did Katty even call Gamma, Gamma? She was her … aunt? She'd always been Gamma. Maybe because that was what Noell always called her and when they played together, what one did or said, the other one did. For awhile Noell had been jealous of Katty playing there. She'd always claimed Gamma as her own and didn't want Katty calling her that.

Katty smiled. She'd always been beaten and pushed around, but she always found a way. Gamma had sat them both down and told them—no, told Noell—that there was enough Gamma and Gamma love for both of them. Ha.

"Noell, said it is. I lived here last night." Bea pursed her lips and raised her eyebrows, jutted out her chin. That funny expression. "Noell said I can live here as long as I want. I can bring all my toys and pictures. I can draw and color and … I don't 'member what else. But she said."

Little smarty pants. She'd found an ally? She'd use it, too.

Katty had to smile, even though she felt like crap. Tears sprang to her eyes just thinking about jail time. Had she really said all that to God? Was He mad? She stood still and made herself breathe. Did He hate her for killing her babies?

She wiped her face before Bea could see. At the jail, she'd made the deputies bring her a mop to clean up her vomit. She would have given almost anything to sneak out the backdoor—straight from the cells to the back parking lot. But no. Walk out—drag out, rather—in front of the dispatcher lady, Mark, Guy, and Sheriff Dennison.

Worst one? Clarence Timmelsen stood in the hallway between the cell block and the office. He grabbed Katty in a hug —and she let him.

She had crumbled to the floor.

Shame, shame, shame.

Mom had been right. She was a scab on everyone's life.

And then outside—in front of the whole world—the post office, coffee shop. She'd felt their eyes on her—their fingers pointing, whether they were or not. Maybe it was God's finger pointing at her, accusing her.

She'd never anticipated living in Gamma's house, though. She couldn't remember what she used to call her. Aunt Gamma? She'd dreamt of it as a little girl—maybe Bea's age. Katty remembered running along the creek and playing dolls in the closet upstairs. It wasn't very often she could play at this house. Mom wouldn't let her come over.

Mom had hated this house and all who lived in it.

Maybe she wouldn't have to stay here very long and they could go back to the trailer house. That was home. This was—

The front door burst open and Noell ran out. "Bea!" She held out her arms to Bea. "Oh, wait. You were here already."

Bea giggled and hugged her anyway—books and blanket and all.

"Did I hurt your arm?" Noell held her away so she could look at her. "Are you okay?"

Bea giggled. "It's only a flesh wound."

Katty shook her head.

Noell laughed out loud. A true belly laugh. "Oh, you're gonna be fun." She stood and held out her arms to Katty. "C'mere cousin."

Oh. No. Katty and Noell barely knew one another. It apparently didn't make much difference to Bea, because she climbed the concrete steps up into the porch already—like it was her own. She'd probably made her nest, since she'd stayed with Noell while Katty was in jail. And today, they were going to live together. One big happy family. Katty was certainly the black sheep. She had proven it by being locked up in a jail cell.

Noell hadn't put her arms down—still holding them out to Katty.

Katty let go of her suitcase and the books and blindly walked into Noell's hug. So embarrassed, terribly shaken, still sick, but suddenly very thankful. Katty opened her arms around Noell's neck, as Noell embraced her. Gently at first, but both hugging as if lives would end if they parted. A sob broke loose in Katty. She couldn't help it. She tried to hold it in, but there was just something about being loved by … like … real family … that overwhelmed her. Noell hugged even tighter until Katty couldn't breathe anymore and they released.

Bea stepped back outside with an old doll and more books. "Can I play with these, too?"

Both young women turned to face her, arms around each other's waists.

"Bea. This isn't your house. You have to ask Noell what you can play with and what you have to leave alone. Ok?"

"I … did." Bea blinked. "I thought I just did. Ok." Deep sigh. Again. "Are these for me?"

Noell had the most delicate and melodic laughter. "Yes, those are for you, Bea." She patted Katty's shoulder. "Always and forever." She stepped toward the house, grabbed Katty's suitcase handle and pulled it up a couple steps. "Come in and I'll show you around and you can tell me where you might be the most comfortable. Bea, too." She lifted the suitcase, then stopped. Blew out a breath. "That man."

She whispered it so softly, that Katty figured she hadn't heard her.

"Here, I can take that." Katty shook her head. "And we can sleep on a sofa somewhere, or—"

"Mommy!" Bea back outside. "Mommy, there's a big bed with Daryl & Dumpty blankets on it." She dragged her own dirty blanket back outside and held it up. "This one's mine." She looked at it. "Well, the one on the bed is new. They're clean!"

"Noell, what did you do?"

Noell paused, closed her eyes, expelled a couple of deep breaths, and stepped inside. "I spent some of our inheritance money on a new bedspread and sheets for your bed." She chuckled. "Well, if it's okay for you to sleep on a Daryl & Dumpty bed … with Bea."

Inheritance money. Wha?

Noell pulled Katty inside, chattering almost as much as Bea. "I know. It's a mess. Gamma was a terrible hoarder. I have a deal going with Mrs. Bertrand."

"Mrs. Bertrand?" It *was* a mess. Not dirty like the trailer, but stacks of boxes lined every wall of the enclosed porch. Some stacks were two deep. But it was an organized mess. Some had writing on them in black marker and were neatly stacked, but a couple stacks seemed ready to topple. No writing. The room had a distinct smell—like old stuff. It probably smelled better than her trailer did right now.

"She owns the thrift store." Noell carefully placed the suitcase beside a doorway going into the kitchen.

"The what?" Katty sucked in a deep breath. Her stomach lurched. She swallowed. How was she going to do this? She needed a drink. Belch. The day had started out okay—not sick at least. Now? Sick. Distracted, they walked through what might be the living room. The only clue to what room it might be was an oversized red sofa along one wall, completely surrounded by boxes and totes and stuff.

Noell kept on chattering.

"The what?" Hard to focus on what Noell was saying, when there were so many distractions.

Then a room. A ... room full. No clue to it's function. Maybe a ... no.

"It's okay, Katty." Noell beckoned Katty into the kitchen and sat her at the kitchen table. "The thrift store. The consignment store." She picked up a glass and turned to face Katty. "Haven't you ever been in there?"

Katty barely shook her head, she was so distracted by the contents of the kitchen. Stacks of books lined each wall—floor to ceiling—insulation with cookbooks, maybe. Spices, cans, stacks of plates and cups covered the counters, leaving very little space for cooking. Cupboard doors hung open—one had been emptied out. Another held a stack of plates matching the ones already on the counter. The stove was clear—better than Katty's in the trailer. Something was off or missing though. There stood an enormous refrigerator. Probably the dishwasher was ... nope. There it was.

Noell placed the glass of water in front of Katty and poured one for herself and a little one for Bea. "I've ... I've been doing some reading on what if feels like."

"What it feels like?" What was Noell talking about? What it feels like to live like this? There was more stuff in this kitchen alone, than Katty's whole trailer house. Maybe.

"Well. When they called me last night to see if I'd take Bea, they just said that you had too much to drink." She sipped from her glass. "I wanted to know what that was like. So I did some reading ... on the computer."

She wasn't. If Noell thought she was going to be Katty's own personal therapist or her rehab, she was damn wrong. She wouldn't. How did she think she knew? Katty started to stand. "What ... *what* feels like?"

Noell sat still, evidently thinking. She glanced at Katty, pulled in a deep breath and opened her mouth.

Here it comes. Here comes the bribe, or the I'll do this for you, but you are locked in to do that for me. The I'll scratch your back, if you'll scratch mine sort of thing. The, I'll get you sober if you promise to go to church or have sex. She'd been in those situations before. It was a kind of barter, only probably more of a locked in model. I'll do this for you, but you'll owe me your first-born. Katty looked at Bea, sipping from her cup.

She needed a drink—badly.

"I don't quite know how to say this, but—"

"It's okay, Noell. We don't have to stay. It's nice of you to invite us, you kept Bea last night, and I know we're cousins and all—Clarence's adoptees and all, but—"

"Katty. Stop. I'm not asking you to leave or don't drink. I'm not telling you there are any rules." She glanced around the house. "Are you kidding me? This place is crazy messy, and I have cleared out a lot. I've taken trailer loads to the dump." She leaned forward on her chair, her eyes intent on Katty's face. "I can feel things." She blew out a breath and glanced out the window. "I don't know why I'm telling you this." She swallowed. "When I touch people. Or touch ... uh, door handles or mail." She picked up an envelope lying on the table.

Katty stood.

"Hear me out, Katty." Noell sipped from her glass. "It's not something I asked for. It's something that ... when I was struggling about Mom ... well, I still struggle."

Katty slowly slumped onto her chair. "About your mom?"

Noell nodded and rubbed her upper arm. She sucked in a deep breath and plunged in. "Mom drowned when I was little."

Katty's eyes popped. Her body jerked back.

"I was with her. When she drowned." She stared out the

window a long time before talking again. "After that, I lived with Grandpa and Gamma … until Grandpa died. I don't remember when they started, but I started to have nightmares about Mom."

Why had Katty never been told all this? She'd thought Noell's mom had for some reason just moved away. In Katty's world, that's what people did. They left—abandoned. She remembered Noell being small and quiet, but Katty had always thought she was just shy. Noell seemed to have everything—a house, a Gamma. "Nightmares?"

"Yeah. I still do. I see Mom and me in water." Noell stopped and hesitated. "In fact sometimes the nightmares turn real. Like I see water on the floor. Like right now."

Katty lifted her feet without thinking, shook her head, and peeked at the floor. Old wooden floor boards with no paint or varnish. Just smooth, beautiful wood. She pointed. "R-Right now?" No water, so she put her feet back down.

Noell nodded. "I hear it, too. I also saw something about you and Bea when I took your suitcase."

Katty's hand fluttered to her chest. "About me and Bea?" If this was going to get weird, she was packing out of here, no matter how bad she felt. Her stomach clenched and sweat trickled down her back under her shirt and jacket. "What. What did you see?"

Noell swallowed. "When I touch something, I hear people say things. I see things they've been through. It's weird."

Katty stood up. "Yeah. That is weird. I don't need anybody—especially you, my cousin, Noell—seeing my stuff." Visions of the babies floated through her mind, the tree waved at her, clouds, blood. Oh she wanted a drink. Visuals of her crappy trailer also hit her. There were still little bottles in her cupboard, right behind the row of canned vegetables. But. She had nowhere else to go. She sat back down hard. Now that Clarence and Mrs. T were married, Katty and Bea couldn't go there. The sheriff's department had released her to Noell's, but they'd never know if she left.

The only person she really belonged with—Phil Daynton—was a criminal, a cruel, evil man. He had a place right now and it was somewhere in jail—exactly where she had come from today. Exactly where she still deserved to be. Phil was the only person she deserved.

Katty slumped back in the chair. Weird or not, Noell's place —Gamma's old house—was the only place she had to go.

SIXTEEN

Bea stood just outside the kitchen door and let her eyes roam over the rooms there. Deputy Mark had brought her to Noell's last night, after dark. Nighttime. Bedtime. She'd been scared, even though she knew Noell. But she'd barely spent any time at her house, so at that time of night, it was scary.

Though she'd been scared, it had taken no time to fall asleep. Sleeping in Noell's bed right beside Noell. Snuggled her. Bea had hardly been snuggled through her whole life. She'd probably needed it many, many times before now. She'd wanted to ask more questions and she'd asked Noell and Deputy Mark many before she finally fell asleep. The warmth of another human being close beside her, in the same bed, comforted her into a deep sleep until she felt Noell get up in the morning.

Bea rubbed her arm, as she stood by the kitchen door. It was better today, but it was starting to look like she had colored it purple. She had a crayon that color. Noell called it a bruise. All Bea knew was that it still hurt.

Mommy and Noell talked in the kitchen. Noell had told her that she could go anywhere she wanted to in the whole house. The big red sofa called to her. She stood in front of a wooden door that she knew led upstairs—that's where Noell's room lived. The room she was in must be the box room. All boxes. Boxes lined up in rows, like at the grocery store.

Deep sigh.

She decided to go to the room where she knew the bed had Daryl & Dumpty on it. She stood at the door. This room still had lots of stuff in it—big boxes all along the walls—but no trash. Pictures hung on the walls. Lots of photos in frames lined up on a dresser—some little and some big. All side by side.

Bea found Noell in several photos, as she stepped closer to the dresser. There. Little girl with long braids. There. And another picture with an old lady and a young lady. The baby with them was for sure Noell.

One. Two. Three. There was another one with two little girls —arms around each other's shoulders. One. Two. Wait. One little girl was Noell—the shorter one. And one looked like … Mommy?

Bea scanned all of the other photos. Some were on top of a chest of drawers. She couldn't see all of the ones on top, but one in front stood out—Noell and Mommy? Another one on the wall had a man, the old lady and young lady and Noell. Noell had been cute as a little girl.

Bea snooped in the rest of the room. A small bathroom opened off the bedroom with a tub, potty and sink. A closet opened there with flowered sheets and soaps, shampoos. Girl stuff. She breathed in the smells—smelled like flowers. She sneezed.

Wandering into the bedroom again, she picked up one photo with a little girl who was for sure Noell and another girl that might be Mommy. Three ladies were sitting on chairs behind the little girls.

"Mommy?" Bea stumbled into the kitchen, dragging her Daryl & Dumpty blanket, holding the photo in her other hand. "Mommy? Is this you?"

But Mommy didn't answer. Noell didn't either.

Bea glanced from one to the other. Were they fighting?

Why weren't they talking?

Bea sat down on the floor, her blanket cushioning her bottom. She looked at the photo in her hand. The three ladies in back drew her attention. One might be Noell too. But the little girl was Noell. Who were they?

Mommy sat back down. "I don't need that, Noell." She shook her head. "I've had enough people analyzing me, telling me what to do. I already know I'm the black sheep of this family."

"Mommy?" Bea, still on the floor, slid to Mommy and tapped her leg.

"Not now, Bea." Mommy shoved her hand at Bea.

"Katty, I didn't mean to make you feel like that." Noell, covered her face with both hands, then raised her head. "I just wanted to tell you, that I know what you've been through. I saw it. No not exactly everything, but … my life hasn't been easy, either." Noell stared at Mommy.

Bea slid over to Noell, under the table and hugged her leg, the photo in her lap.

Noell patted her head, but still stared at Mommy. Sitting under the table reminded Bea of her rocking chair at home. She pulled the blanket closer, dropped the photo onto the floor and stuck her thumb in her mouth.

Noell still stared at Mommy and picked up the photo. She glanced at it, and then really looked hard. Her eyes got big. She looked down at Bea.

Bea squirmed away, or tried to, but Noell caught her and dragged her up onto her lap. "Was this what you were trying to show Mommy?" She almost shook it in Bea's face.

Bea nodded and squirmed to get away. "I'm sorry. I won't—"

Noell grabbed her tight against her chest, on her lap. Tight.

Bea squeezed her eyes shut as tears rolled down her cheeks.

She cringed and held her breath. She was in trouble and she couldn't get away. Noell held her tight. Just like right before Bad Mommy hit her. Bea braced herself for the slap.

But none came. She opened her eyes and saw Noell pass the photo across the table to Mommy.

Oh-oh.

Mommy took it and put it down on the table. Didn't even look. Still stared at Noell. "I didn't know. Nobody told me your mom drowned." Mommy shook her head. She picked up the photo and put it back down. Then picked it up again. Her eyes got big. She leaned her face closer to see better. She looked up at Noell. Then at the picture again.

Oh-oh.

Noell had relaxed her grip on Bea. Bea tried to slide off her lap, but Noell grabbed her again. "Not going anywhere, little Bea. You need to know this stuff. This is your family, too." She nodded to Mommy. "You know who all those females are, right?"

Mommy nodded her head. Her chin pouted, eyes wanted to cry. Mommy wanted to cry.

Bea wanted to cry, too, but Noell wouldn't let her go. Mommy blurred as Bea stared. Noell brushed her hair from her face and started to rock her. Like, baby rock her.

"I do." Mommy nodded. "That's you." She held it up to show them and pointed. "And that's me." She blinked. She didn't say anything for a long time and shook her head. "That's Gamma?"

Noell nodded, still rocking Bea on her lap, back and forth.

Mommy slowly slid off her chair onto the floor, her head low over the picture. She scooted over to Noell's chair and pointed. "And that's my mom." Her voice sounded funny—like she had a cold.

Noell held onto Bea and slid off her chair—all on the floor.

Mommy pointed. "Is that your mom?"

Noell nodded slowly, letting tears drip down on Bea's head.

Bea snuggled into her chest. Noell reached out to Mommy.

Mommy scooted right next to them and hugged Noell. She drew back and looked at the photo again. "She looks just like you." She shook her head and spoke again. "No. You look just like her." She took a breath. "I'm sorry. I didn't know, Noell. I'm so sorry I acted like that." She visibly swallowed. "Both of us have had a rough time."

She seemed to remember Bea in between them. "No. All of us—all three of us—have had a rough time." She nodded at Bea. "Right?"

Bea let out a wail, climbed onto Mommy's lap, and snuggled. Felt just like sitting in Clarence's lap. He always put his head on top of her head and made her feel safe.

Bea swallowed and turned to Noell. "I'm sorry I touched your pictures."

Noell reached for Bea's hand and kissed it. She shook her head. "You don't have to be sorry, Bea. You can look at and pick up any pictures—anything that you want to look at." Noell looked at Mommy.

Then down at Bea. "You helped your mommy and me be friends … again."

SEVENTEEN

Noell had seen some very bad things in her life because of her gift. Even calling it a gift was crazy—it wasn't a gift—it was probably a curse, except … sometimes it seemed to save her or protect her. Every time she touched a door knob or handle—every time someone tried to hug her—she saw everything and heard everything. She saw whole life events played out like scenes in a movie, heard words spewed out—bad and good. Mr. Grimes was an awful, creepy example of learning about her gift. That's the day she had come to think of her gift as a curse.

He still lived down the street—just two houses away, in fact. Noell thanked God for putting at least one house in between his and hers. She still caught him gawking at her out his windows. The day he had lured her into his house still gave her the creeps. As a young girl, she had suspected that he was faking his need for a walker. He forgot it in his car once at the post office and hurried back to get it. But when he asked if she could come into his house and help him, she figured he was legit. He needed her help.

Maybe she had trust issues since her mom had drowned, but there was something evil about that man. And not maybe. She knew. What Noell saw that day at his house was nothing but a demon. She had barely escaped. Gamma had been terrified and so mad at her for even stepping inside.

Noell could still hear Gamma's voice, "I told you! Never go near him!"

If only Gamma was still alive. Noell would pester her with questions about the creep. What had happened to Gamma because of him? Gamma knew things.

Oh no. What might have happened to Mom?

The day Noell had hidden and waited for him to leave the public power office was uppermost in her memory. He had faked injury with that cane or walker. She had hidden around outside the building, so he wouldn't see her, but also because she was always very leery and fearful of other people. She kept to the outside of the building until she knew who was working or who was inside paying a bill. He played his little scene with the walker, pretending to need a discount or help for his bill. That's what Gamma always said. Never trust Mr. Grimes.

When he finally drove off from the public power building, she took her chance to go inside. She was always careful to keep a sleeve of her jacket covering her hands or arms so she didn't touch any metal or anything. But for some reason that day, the sleeve had slipped and she'd seen and heard everything that Mr. Grimes had thought, said, or done.

The day he lured Noell into his house, he had no need for a walker. He was perfectly able to walk and tried to kidnap her without a walker or a cane!

Creeped her out for … even now.

She glanced at his house as she stirred the macaroni. Dirty old man. Demonic, dirty old man. As the pasta cooked, she guessed she'd be eating lots of macaroni and cheese from now on. For however long Katty and Bea lived with her.

There was a sweet contentment with Katty and Bea staying with Noell. It might be hard. No, it had already been difficult.

But Noell knew in her heart that God wanted this. That He wanted them together. He had some kind of plan and she maybe got to be a part of it.

She couldn't help thinking of what Gamma would think about Katty and Bea sharing her home. Gamma had a plan too, only now she was in heaven.

Already with snoopy, little Bea finding that photo, Katty and Noell realized that terrible things had happened to them—to them all. And somehow they both now knew more about their family together, than they ever had before.

Thanks to little, beautiful, sweet, snoopy Bea.

Noell poured off the water and stirred in the butter and milk and cheese, until it was all melted and mixed.

Even her inheritance. Noell knew that somehow it was for all three of them to live on. It was way more than she'd ever need in her lifetime alone. Amazing Gamma. And Gramps. So thankful. So very thankful.

She wiped her eyes, and turned to call for Katty and Bea to eat, but paused, scanned the house. It was awful. So much stuff. Noell sighed deeply. Too much to do. But she also realized and embraced the fact that this house had so much to tell them all—to teach them—her, Katty, *and* Bea. Even before now, there had been crazy answers as Noell dug through boxes or drawers.

More than a month ago, Noell had found her way into a room she had never been in or even known existed. Grampa's room. He had been such a man of honor and faith. Gamma had been, too, but his was different as he had served in the military. That would be a sweet day of celebration when she showed that room to Katty and Bea. He was their relative, too. What? Their uncle. So strange. She guessed she and Katty were about the same age. Katty maybe older by a few years. But Katty's mom and Noell's Gamma were sisters. Interesting.

Where were Katty and Bea? Too quiet. She tapped the spoon against the pan and tossed a hot pad onto the table.

"Hey guys. Supper's ready." She glanced at the table. It might not be enough. Well, she had more boxes. That side of hoarding was a plus, a bonus. She always had enough to eat. Fresh food, like bread and produce needed to be bought again, but cans and boxes of food seemed plentiful. She still struggled on how to organize such a huge amount. Having cousins here for awhile would help clear it out.

Applesauce. Maybe Bea liked applesauce. She had plenty of that.

Nobody came. She dropped the lid onto the pot.

Where were they?

Interesting to have them here in her house. She didn't always have to be careful about what she touched here, unless she was unpacking a box from a long time ago. Then she pulled on gloves or a sweater to protect herself. That usually took care of creepy visuals or sounds.

She didn't even think about protecting herself when she grabbed Katty's suitcase to help her come inside. It didn't happen right away, either. It took a couple seconds before the horror started to pop into her brain.

Oh Lord, dear Lord.

What awful things Katty had been through. Just gripping the handle. The blood. The cries. Pain and bruises. Dead … oh she couldn't go there.

Phil was Bea's father and he had broken into this very house. Noell had experienced *his* DNA, his memories afterward when she found her baby bracelet—the one thing that had been so precious from her mom—broken. He had broken her baby bracelet, scattered the tiny beads all over the floor. She remembered his visuals. She knew about him. The things he had done. It had taken days to put those visions somewhere so they didn't haunt her. She had enough of her own torment.

And now his own living daughter was here in Noell's house.

She realized she'd been holding her breath.

Study. Study. Study.

She had *his* memories from the beads and she now had *Katty's* memories of the same man—him—abusing *her* and killing … how does that happen? His molecules from both downloads—his direct DNA, but his through Katty. The same DNA through different sources. He had a direct part in Katty's abortions.

She blinked. The blood made her gasp. Help, God. This was crazy and she needed Gamma here to talk her through it. She needed—

"We're here!" Well, Bea was here.

"Are you hungry, Miss Bea?" Noell lifted her up and hugged her. Ahh. Maybe she needed Bea to help her, too.

"I am hungry." Bea climbed down, checked the table, and picked up the lid to the pan. "Macaroni and cheese! My favorite!"

Noell laughed. "I thought your favorite was peanut butter."

Bea nodded. "It is. It's my favorite, too."

EIGHTEEN

Katty shoved her underwear into a drawer. Noell had emptied it, claiming it helped her clear stuff out. "Look at all the rest I have to do." She had swung her arm around the room. Bet the room was bigger than it seemed. She and Bea got to stay downstairs in Gamma's room. Stuff, boxes and totes insulated every wall. Each stack had to be two feet wide. That made four feet of room space lost in all directions. She wasn't a mathematician but that was lots of space.

She stood. At least the windows weren't covered. Even though she lived in a trailer house, she loved light, so she always had the windows clear. No curtains … well, there were crappy blinds, mostly broken. But, no heavy curtains or drapes. No furniture blocked the crappy view, but none blocked the sunlight, either.

The neighborhood at Gamma's, er Noell's, was pretty. Nothing like where she lived either. Trees. Gardens. Nice view down to the creek—not even hidden by the old garage or shop or whatever it was in back. Old camper trailer to the side. That was cool. Did Gamma and Gramps have a camper? She couldn't remember one, but then again, she wasn't allowed to visit hardly at all.

Noell had called. Supper must be ready.

Katty's stomach had settled some. Then without warning, everything came up. Barely made it to the tiny bathroom. Even if there wasn't much in her stomach. Oh God, please help.

Breathe.

She wiped her face with a wad of toilet paper.

The curtains in the bedroom were lacy. Pretty. She backed away from the window. The curtains fell all the way to the floor. She followed the pattern. Followed the woven threads with her fingers. Tears pooled. She couldn't fall apart right now. Noell would come in to find her for supper. They were having macaroni and cheese. Yippee.

She appreciated Noell taking them in. She did.

But, it was humiliating. Shame, shame, shame.

Clump, clump.

Katty wiped her eyes. Noell must be coming.

Knock, knock. Noell pushed the door open. "You want mac and cheese?"

Katty started to answer, but choked on the words. She swallowed and tried again. Nothing. Katty didn't have to turn and look. Noell stood right beside her—not touching her, but close. She didn't say anything. Didn't open her mouth to try to say anything. Just stood.

Hadn't this ... hadn't Noell? She tried to remember. In the hospital when Bea was hurt? Months ago? It was all a blur. Someday if she stayed sober, would she remember?

That didn't help Katty at all. Tears flowed even more freely. She was such a failure. Couldn't take care of her own kid. Couldn't live by herself—at least for now.

Noell touched the lace curtains. "Pretty aren't they." She chuckled. "There are more—in fact twenty more in a box in the dining room."

Katty blinked and wiped her face. "What?"

"Gamma must have liked them. Maybe planned to hang them at every window, because there are probably twenty or more windows in this house."

Katty smiled in spite of her tears. "Thasalotta windows." She wiped her eyes. "I heard you call." More tears. "I'm just not sure what my stomach will do." She turned and searched Noell's eyes. "I'm never sure. Sometimes food sounds good, but it doesn't go well. Or … *always* a drink sounds good. And sometimes that doesn't go well, either." She turned back to lift the curtains away to see the rest of the back yard. "It's so pretty here, Noell."

Noell stood closer, her arm gently around Katty's waist. "It's beautiful. Lots to keep up, but I have a guy." She chuckled.

Katty interrupted her. "You have a guy? Like in a boyfriend? Or a gardener?"

Noell shook her head. "No. Yes. He is like a boyfriend. Kinda. We're good friends. But he comes over sometimes and helps me mow or fix something." She paused. "His name is Fletcher."

Katty smiled. "You like him, don't you."

Noell tilted her head, and pursed her lips to the side. "Well … yeah. I like him. A lot."

Bang.

Katty jumped. "That came from the kitchen."

Noell nodded. "I believe it did, but just sounded like the lid from the pan." She faced Katty. "If you don't feel like you can eat tonight—"

"I'll come in and help. I'll try. I've got to start sometime. It might take a while."

Noell nodded. "One day at a time." She glanced around the room. "Maybe after we're done, we can come in and create more space for you and Bea. Dig into some boxes and get more stuff ready to give to Mrs. Bertrand. I have a load ready to go again."

She shook her head. "And take you guys—or you, Bea's seen some of it—on a personal tour of the house. I haven't even seen some of it."

"What? You live here." Katty caught herself. "Oh. Some places must be hard to go into."

Noell nodded. "Yeah. Rooms should be meaningless without the human to inhabit them."

"That sounds like a line from a book … or a movie." Katty wove her arm around Noell's waist. "I'll go try. Maybe *your* mac and cheese will be better than mine at home."

They walked through the living room and dining room into the kitchen—arm-in-arm.

Bea scrambled the minute they entered the kitchen. The lid was perfectly centered on the pan. The pan was in the middle of the table, right where Noell had left it. Maybe. Each plate had a serving of yellow mac and cheese with a side of green grapes. Bea squirmed on her chair and twisted fingers of one hand with the other. "I found some grapes in your … your frigger-frigerater."

Noell clapped her hands. "Beautiful, Bea. Thank you!" A couple rolled on the floor under the table. "I forgot about those."

Katty sat beside Bea and hugged her. "This is so nice Bea. Sorry it took me so long to get in here."

"Let's pray." Noell peeked up at Katty. "Okay with you?"

Katty nodded.

Bea folded her hands. "Now I lay me … oops!" She tapped her mouth with her hand. "Wrong prayer. It's okay. Mrs. T says it doesn't matter what we pray, just as long as it's to Jesus." She resumed her prayer stance—hands folded, eyes closed, deep breath. "Jesus thanks for this mac and cheese and grapes. Thanks for Noell letting us stay with her in her Gamma's house. Please keep us healthy because I dropped all the grapes on the floor. Thanks, Jesus. Amen." She clapped her hands. "Let's eat!"

Katty closed her eyes and chuckled, shaking her head. She wanted to burst with joy for this little girl in her life. What if—

"We have our own Bible study leader." Noell picked up her fork. "Thanks Bea. Who taught you how to pray?"

Bea chewed and thought a minute. "Well, Mommy tried."

Oh no. Katty concentrated on her food. Or tried to. Don't come up. Don't come up.

Bea popped a grape into her mouth and her cheek bulged out. She popped it from cheek to cheek, then answered. "Probly Mrs. T, though. She's a good prayer. Michael listens to her." She nodded and dove into her mac and cheese.

Noell's eyebrows were raised. She stirred her macaroni. "Who's Michael?"

Dang it, Bea. Way to go and raise the weird questions. "He's a fr—"

"He's Clarence's angel." Bea chewed and swallowed quickly, her eyes big. "He has an angel costume with wings and every-thing." She stretched her arms wide, her fork still in one hand. "But he only dresses up in it when it's a big occa-occa. What's that word Mommy?"

Katty blinked. Laugh or cry. Laugh or cry.

"Occasion?" Noell jumped in. She visibly checked her grape before popping it into her mouth. "So … he has an outfit that he wears just for those important times?" She chewed and paused. "Wha-what does his angel costume look like?"

Good one, Noell. Way to lead Bea on. She comes up with enough crap on her own without giving her ideas. Katty stabbed one piece of macaroni and inspected it. She hesitated and took stock of her stomach. She wanted to literally ask it, "Can you take this one little piece without making it burst out again?" *Breathe. Breathe.* Nope. Nope. She hadn't even taken the bite and … run!

Katty backed away from the table, held her mouth with her

hand and ran for the bathroom in Gamma's room. God help. God help!

As she left the room Bea was talking. "She does that some-times. Throws up."

Katty envisioned Bea nodding so matter-of-factly as she ate. Little Smarty-Pants. Know-it-all.

Back at the trailer it might not have made any difference. She would have gotten to the bathroom just in time. And she did here, too. But it wasn't so easy in a strange house. Leaning over the strange toilet and puking in it made her system even more upset.

Oh when? When?

She was not going back into the kitchen with those two. And for some reason, she felt Noell would not expect her to. Katty shook her head as she leaned against the wall next to the toilet. If she wasn't so sick, she'd enjoy this little room. Well, she kinda did right now.

Creative floor plan in an old house. It was pretty big for a bathroom, because they had stolen space from under the stairway going upstairs, maybe. The shower bathtub was against the outside wall and under the top steps, she guessed, and a sink was below a little mirror. A tall narrow window was squeezed between the shower and the mirror. Sweet, white sheer curtains fluttered. The window must be just cracked open—enough to move the curtains. The toilet was under the lower steps—perfect when you sat down, and perfect when you stood up so you didn't bump your head. Bathroom planning was a great distraction.

For some reason, the more Katty let herself ponder the little room, her stomach settled itself. Must be Gamma's presence or her influence. Interesting to find herself and especially Bea, living here for now. She'd wanted so badly to stay even one night at Gamma's when she was little. Mom probably didn't trust Gamma. Katty might have come back realizing that Mom was evil, which she was. Or even, Katty might *never* have come back to Mom—which would have been great. Gamma would have let her stay—maybe wanted her to stay.

That photo Bea had found. Katty shook her head. Of all of them. Why couldn't it have been the way the photo looked—all together—one big happy family? Gamma, Mom, Berniece, ... her and Noell?

Katty pushed up from the floor and slowly stood, assessing her body, her stomach. Each breath became intentional and planned. Cleansing, hopefully. In and out. In and out.

She wiped the toilet down and washed her hands. The hand towel seemed to pretty to dry her wet hands on, but there was nothing else. She held it to her nose. Oh my. Sweetness of laundry soap? Gamma's presence?

Don't look up. Don't look up.

Katty blinked. A scared, young woman with a messy brown bun on the top of her head stared from the mirror, back at her. Look away. Don't look. But she couldn't take her eyes off the young woman in the mirror. Red-rimmed brown eyes full of pain. Tears tracked down the young woman's cheeks. Katty didn't wipe them away. Those brown eyes carried painful and bloody memories, so carefully hidden, deeply buried. The images and visuals floated between the woman in the mirror and Katty looking in.

She normally didn't let herself look. Even when she put on make-up to go out. Don't look too deep. Those images were always there, buried way down deep. Inaccessible to anyone— much less herself.

But today, there they were. Between the woman in the mirror and the one staring back. Little Katty stared back at her after being beaten by Mom—no tears—she'd been screamed at to never cry. But the face of that little girl, so resembling Bea, crumpled before her.

Whew.

She patted her pockets. Jacket and jeans.

Breathe.

Katty could only stand to examine those memories honestly for a short time. She opened the mirror to a small medicine cabinet.

She flinched. Maybe she shouldn't have. But someone might have cleaned it all out. No medicine. No drugs. Just makeup. Makeup and bath products. Noell had stocked it with store-bought bath products. She opened one and sniffed. Very light which was what she needed right now. Anything heavy or floral might have sent her over the toilet, again.

Towels had been hung—Bea's were obvious—Daryl & Dumpty. Next to those were a set of very light pink towels, with white trim. Guess she'd never mop the floor up with those. She held them against her cheek. So soft. Tears. She hadn't realized she'd been crying until she felt the towel against her cheek.

Slowly Katty stepped into the bedroom, the towel still against her cheek.

The stacks of boxes and totes had been organized more here than other rooms, or at least pushed against each wall—probably for her and Bea. Noell had worked hard if the whole house looked like the living room and what might be the dining room.

But it wasn't really what Katty saw in Gamma's room. It was what she felt. There was kindness here. Love was here.

Healing was here.

Gamma was here.

NINETEEN

Those words he had heard, as Mark lay prostrate outside Katty's cell door that night still haunted him. *"God forgive me. My babies. What have I done?"* He still heard the pain in her voice, sensed the tears and the choking. He could almost visualize her as she lay just inside the cell door. Him on the outside and her just on the inside. Only a metal cell door between them. Separating them.

He wiped his eyes and pounded the steering wheel.

"What, God?" Mark sucked in a ragged breath. "It's not cool to cry on duty. Not cool to be so attached, er attracted to … a woman … who spent time in jail." He shook his head and turned a corner. What was he thinking? He'd been in trouble. He must be driving in circles. No route. No plan. No calls over the radio. Just endless, no-plan circles. Unconscious driving. That'd be a good one in court. "No Judge. I was just driving around in circles." He paused and started again. "Driving in circles thinking about a woman." A woman who'd spent time in jail, who'd been so abused by a man that she'd lived through many abortions, and escaped with a baby intact.

A woman who, when she really, but rarely smiled at him, had

beautiful brown eyes that sang a sweet tune. Or maybe something in her eyes, made his own heart sing. There was something very tender inside of her that she buried deeply. For self-protection. For self-preservation.

He sucked in a deep breath and realized he was on a different street than his usual. He wasn't at the sheriff's office or at the trailer court—which was where he usually found himself—driving in circles around the trailer court, convincing himself that it was part of the route. His job entailed covering the town of Osceola, Nebraska, but all of Polk County. Every road. Every street. Just because he made repeated visits to one trailer court, past one unique trailer house, didn't make it wrong. He was, as a deputy, covering his area, his route, his beat. Like he was trained to.

But today. This time, he found himself driving a different street … right past Noell's house. Where he knew Katty and Bea were staying.

It wasn't the trailer court.

It was Katty. Those brown eyes were at Noell's. That beautiful, wavy, thick, brown hair was at Noell's.

He pounded the steering wheel again. "God, what is it? Why do I love her?" He stumbled over the word love. Had never spoken or thought that word in relation to Katty.

Bea, yes. He knew he loved Bea. Without a doubt.

He drove to where Katty was. Automatically. He couldn't help it. She was like a magnet, drawing him to wherever she happened to be.

And her broken words cried out last night. *"God what have I done?"*

Crushing. If Mark really let himself think about it, talk about it, he'd be just as crushed as she seemed. Not seemed. She *was* crushed. She would see her life and the choices she'd made through clearer eyes now that she was getting sober. No numbing out now. She'd see the truth and that was the problem. The truth was horribly scary.

Without thinking about it, he found himself parked and walking up the sidewalk to Noell's house. He didn't even remember parking—even *deciding* to pull in. Who had unbuckled his seatbelt, for Pete's sake? Getting out of the car and finding himself at the steps to the enclosed porch … impossible.

He needed to leave.

He turned to do just that, when the front door opened and he heard a squeal.

"Depdy Mark!" Bea leaped off the inside porch and landed in his arms. If he'd turned just a moment sooner, he'd have missed her. But no chance of that. He was supposed to catch this kid—in midair. No matter what.

"I almost didn't catch you. You're so fast." He hugged her to his chest. If he could only hide his expression on his face from Noell, who stood in the now wide open doorway. He was sure his face said everything his heart burst with at the moment. "Hi, Noell." He adjusted Bea to his hip and smiled. "How's it going? Is Bea running you ragged?"

Noell grinned.

She knew. She read his heart.

Dang.

"No. She fed us supper just now. Helped me clean up and wash dishes."

He made a pretend face of shock. "Wash dishes. You mean you put them in the dishwasher, right?"

Bea giggled. "Nope. I washed them in a sink with all sudsy water. With a dish-clo—"

Noell laughed. "Dishcloth." She stepped to where Mark stood and held Bea's cheeks in each hand. "Dish."

Bea repeated. "Dish." Followed it with a giggle.

Noell didn't give up. "Cloth."

"Cloth." Bea jumped from Mark to Noell's arms. "Dish.

Cloth. I can say it." Back to Mark's arms. "And Noell dried them and put them away. Wanna see?"

Oh-oh. Exactly what he wanted was to go inside and see … Katty. "I'm working tonight Bea. Gotta get back in my cruiser and go take care of bad guys."

"Do you kill bad guys?" She fiddled with the radio on his shoulder, next his badge, and then his name tag. Then her brown eyes met his. "My daddy is a bad, bad, bad guy. Is he 'rested?"

Mark swallowed. "Uh. He is." He glanced at Noell. What to do? Honesty.

"Hey Bea. Isn't it about time for the Daryl & Dumpty show?" Noell raised her eyebrows. "Maybe?" She held her hands out to Bea. "I think?"

Bea shimmied down Mark's leg and landed next to him. "I think so. Yeah." She ran up the steps to just inside the porch. "Do you have a TV, Noell?" Bea rubbed her hands together and licked her lips. "B'cause we need a TV to watch it." She glanced at Mark. "Right?"

Mark nodded his head and laughed. "Right, Bea." He shrugged at Noell. "So do you?"

Noell laughed, her head tilted back. "We have a TV. I know it is crazy that we do." She patted Bea's behind. "Go find it and I'll be right in."

Bea nodded. "Oh. You're going to talk 'dult talk, aren't you." She turned. "Don't forget about me Mr. Depdy, Sir."

He shook his head. "Now how could I ever do that? Never!"

Noell stepped inside to watch where Bea went. "She's a clever one."

Mark nodded. He glanced up at Noell, then down at the steps. Back at Noell. "How is she?"

"I'm pretty sure you don't mean Bea, right now." She glanced behind her. "You mean Katty."

He blew out a deep breath and nodded. Squinted up at Noell. "Yes. How is Katty?"

TWENTY

Knock, knock.

Katty jumped. No one ever knocked at her bedroom door in her trailer house. "Noell." She swallowed. So awkward. "You don't need to knock. This is your house. Your Gamma's room."

Noell peeked in and shook her head. "No. It's yours and Bea's room now. My room is upstairs."

Bea jumped in. "And it's awesome. Wa-a-a-ay up the steps. It's so clean and all put away."

Noell laughed and shrugged. "I'm kind of a neat freak. Well … I'm probably what people would call a germaphobe."

Katty blinked and glanced around Gamma's room.

Noell laughed again. "I know. Gamma was a hoarder and I'm a germaphobe. Quite a contrast. Quite an interesting way to live."

This young woman, her new cousin was a lot deeper than Katty ever realized. Her mom and the nightmares. Being a germaphobe. What else was there? "So … do you … what? Wash your hands after every time you blink? Or after every time —" She checked behind her at the bathroom.

"Yeah. All of that. Probably more." That melodic laugh, again.

"What's a germa-germa-what?" Bea bounced on the bed.

"Bea! That isn't your bed. Don't jump on it." Katty caught her in mid jump and thought better of it. *Breathe.*

Noell sat down on the bed and Bea scrambled out of Katty's arms to sit beside her. Noell pulled Bea onto her lap and thought a second. "A germaphobe is … a person who … likes everything clean. No germs. No dirt." She looked at the walls and boxes. "No boxes or mess anywhere. But almost like I get scared if it's dirty." She hugged Bea. "Make sense?"

Bea nodded.

Katty hugged her own sides. *Don't say it. Please don't say what our house looks like. Please don't say—*

"Well, our house is messy b'cause Mommy and me are artists and we leave our papers and colors all over the place. They even fall on the floor and sometimes we don't pick them up until we need them."

What? Katty realized she'd been holding her breath. She blew it out and tried to relax.

Noell nodded. "I get it. There are things I like to do and I make a mess, too. I don't think that it's a good thing to be as obsess … as crazy as I am about it. I'm learning to get better." She stood and opened a box against the wall near her. "Somewhere between what Gamma was and what I am would be good." She pulled out a smaller box and opened it. "What?" She looked up at Katty and Bea. "Gamma must have known you two would stay in her room." She slowly pulled out a bundle of very long necklaces.

"Ooo!" Bea scrambled to stand on the bed and held out her hands. "For me? Pretty!"

Katty jumped. "Bea, those might be special to Noell. You might break them."

Noell shook her head, mouthed no, and grinned. She held them to her chest and posed. "You think I'd wear these? No."

After they had explored the box, Noell sat down and scanned the room. "Fletcher helped me get this room ready for you guys."

"Fletcher?" Katty looped a necklace around Bea's neck. "Oh yeah. He's the boyfriend."

"Uh. Yeah. He lives just over there." Noell pointed, blushing. "He's helped me clean up a lot around here. Inside and outside."

"Oh yeah. I remember. He's just a friend?" Katty grinned. So good to not be focused on her own struggles. "You're blushing."

Bea jerked around to check Noell. "Let me see." She shook her head. "What's blushing?"

Katty leaned into her and pointed. "Blushing is what Noell is doing right now. See her pretty pink cheeks?"

Noell hid her face with her hands.

Bea nodded. "Yup. Her face is red." She gently touched Noell's forehead. "Do you have a fever? Are you hot, Noell?"

Noell laughed. "Stop you two!" To Katty. "I'll get you back." And to Bea. "I'm just hot. No fever."

Katty chuckled. "She's just hot, Bea. That's it." Katty shook her head. Thankful. Deep breath. What if *she* had a friend. Yes, legally and according to bloodline, she had a cousin. But what if she had a friend?

Noell seemed to be thinking the same thing. Her eyes were kind as she looked into Katty's eyes, deeper into Katty's heart. But only as deep as Katty's fears would allow. There. Soul mates? Katty had read about such things but had never had one. Phil was, or so she'd thought, at the beginning of their relationship. Never again.

"What is behind that big stack of boxes?" Noell had been staring behind Katty at a wall between the window and the bathroom door. "The window is odd right there. I don't remember it angled that way."

Katty stood up and looked where Noell pointed. "Where? You don't know?"

Noell pointed and shook her head. "There. That window wasn't built into a flat wall, it's built into the corner." She stepped to it and made a corner with her hands. "Look. It's just an angle, not a full corner." She stepped to the stack of totes between the window and the bathroom door, then backed up. "Looks like a door behind those totes. I guess Gamma would need a closet. She didn't have a dresser—at least not when I lived here. Maybe when Grampa was still alive, I think they shared this bedroom." She started to pull the totes away. "Help me pull this out of the way."

Katty pulled one tote off the top. She was stuck. "Put it in the living room?"

Noell looked up. "Yeah. Just anywhere." She pulled the next one down and followed Katty into the living room. "There's fine." She laughed. "It *is* better in this house, Katty. Believe me. There was just a pathway from the entrance—the porch door—to the kitchen. Then there were break-off pathways to the other rooms."

They started a stack then went back for more.

"Last one." Noell brushed her hands together. "I'll have to give Fletcher a bad time about covering up a closet door." She slowly opened the door and peeked. "Wow." She opened the door wide and shook her head, gasping. "I can't believe this. I don't remember ever seeing this closet." She checked the window, then the bathroom door. "It's almost like they built a secret closet here. Or maybe she did. Someone did." She clapped her hands. "Come and see!"

This wasn't really her stuff, so Katty held back. Still very curious. She'd always dreamt about finding a magic closet or a secret castle. This might be as close as she would ever get.

She stepped next to Noel and sucked in a breath. "Oh my—"

"I know." Noell slowly crumpled to the floor. "There's bookshelves of notebooks?" She crawled inside and pulled one out. "No." She flipped through the pages. "Maybe her journals? It's her handwriting." She held it to her chest. "Oh Gamma."

Tears visibly filled Noell's eyes.

What wouldn't Katty give to have a Gamma like her. To leave a legacy like this. She knelt and put her arm around Noell's shoulders. "This is beautiful." The closet had literally been lined with paintings, bookshelves lined with journals. "Can I …." She reached out to feel the wall nearest her.

Noell slowly nodded. "Of course." She blew out a breath. "I feel this is just as much for you, as me."

Bea crawled between their legs. "Me too?" She started to pull a book down.

"Bea. No. Let Noell." This wasn't theirs. It was amazing, but—

Bea plopped onto the floor and cried. Bedtime.

Noell leaned down and picked her up, still holding the book against her. "Bea. It's okay when Mommy says. But we just need to be careful and make sure we don't break anything. It's what Gamma left to us. Just be careful."

"What's a Gamma?" Bea hiccupped.

Noell checked Katty. "Uh."

Katty had never thought of that before. Bea didn't really have a grandma. Not here anyway. She had Clarence as a grandpa and he was a good one. Katty's own mom could have been. Katty trembled at that thought. No. Phil had never talked about parents. Bea didn't know what one was. She reached for Bea. "A Gamma or grandma is … would be like my mom to you, if she was here." So hard. Katty had never thought of that. She'd never had one—from her mom's side or her dad's. Every kid had a grandma—at least one. And a grampa. She sucked in a breath. "Like Clarence is our grampa, but a Gamma is a girl."

Bea scrunched her face. "Gamma is a girl grampa?"

Katty shook her head, but stopped, and switched to nodding. "Kinda."

Katty glanced at Noell as she touched the wall near her. Most of the closet was lined with shelves, stuffed with journals, books, and art? But someone—Gamma maybe—had wallpapered or painted the walls. They were beautiful as they peeked through and between the books.

Not wallpaper. She touched other places and it was painted. Wallpaper would have some kind of texture and it always felt like it wasn't completely bonded to the plaster wall—like in an old house. Like this one.

She became aware that Noell was still holding Bea, patting her back, but not digging into the seeming treasures in the closet. "Noell, aren't you going to explore all this? It's almost like Gamma has left a legacy or wisdom for you. Like ... here you go. Here's your life wisdom."

Noell wiped her face. "I'm scared."

Bea's head popped up and she gently touched Noell's cheek.

Katty looked at the closet then back at Noell. "Scared? O-of what?" Everybody had secrets, but Gamma? Naw. Katty vaguely remembered several fights between her mom and Gamma, but the one doing the yelling was always Mom. Gamma just tried to be nice, as Katty remembered. After that Katty was never allowed in Gamma's house, again.

She glanced around the room. And now, here she and Bea had been invited to sleep on Gamma's own bed. On Daryl & Dumpty sheets, even. Well, Katty needed a safe place to dry out. Oh God, please let this be it. But Noell. What on earth was wrong with discovering treasures left by her own grandma?

"Would you ... Would you help me go through this?" Noell stuttered her question.

"Sure I will. They are yours, but I'll help stack them and clean them. I do it all the time at Clarence's office. I dig through the boxes from when he was in prison, categorize everything, file everything, find important papers that change people's lives—get it?" She started to tap her cousins's shoulder but stopped. "Noell. What … what gives?" Katty gently turned Noell to face her, as Bea still played with the necklaces dangling onto her chest, but obviously listening.

Noell appeared to be terrified.

"Noell."

Noell wasn't in there. She was somewhere else and Katty didn't know how to get her back. Katty gripped both shoulders and gave her a little shake.

Noell blinked. "Oh, Katty."

"Where did you go?" Katty had never seen her like this.

"I-I went …" She shook her head and hesitated. "To my mom. I went to the nightmares, the actual night she died." She slumped onto the floor.

Bea snuggled in, fiddled with the beads, almost unaware of the difficulty Noell seemed to be having. "Nightmares? I have nightmares." Nope. Bea was aware.

Katty drifted down beside them both, her arm around Noell's shoulders. "I had no idea Noell. I'm so sorry. All I think about is me and what I'm going through while you are living in hell."

"Mommy. Bad word."

"Only one, Bea. And it is the only word I could use for what Noell is going through."

Noell pulled another book out. "If I know Gamma, or if I can guess what she'd do, every book here will have something about Mom's death. Something. She always said she was doing well. That's what she'd say when you asked her. 'I'm well.' But if I'm right, every book here will spew out her pain of losing her only daughter. Then loosing Grampa."

"And that is your pain, too, then. Because you have the actual visuals of her drowning. You were … there." Katty quickly glanced at Noell. "I shouldn't have said that. I'm sorry. I said too much."

"No, it's okay Katty." Noell wiped her nose on her sleeve.

Bea jumped up and ran to the bathroom, returning with a handful of tissues.

"Oh, thank you, Bea." Noell pulled her down onto her lap and blew her nose. "I meant what I said before. Please, would you help me with these? And what I meant was, would you read them with me? Beside me? To me? Would you help me read about my mom's death and Gamma's pain? Because I know that's what is in every one of these books."

Katty and Noell tipped their heads to follow the shelves of books from the floor clear up to the ceiling of the closet.

"Wow." Katty slowly nodded her head, her chest bursting for some unknown reason. "Yes. Absolutely, I'll help you." She grabbed Noell's hand in hers. Hadn't they, as little girls, before the stupid between her mom and Gamma, made a pact to be friends forever? Even if they hadn't really gotten to do that, it felt like they were doing that exact thing right now.

Becoming family.

TWENTY-ONE

"And just because you feel that way, doesn't mean you'll stay that way." Bea sighed and whispered the words to her favorite song. She rolled over and sank back into dreamland. She sang along with her dream.

"Bea. Stop singing and go back to sleep." Mommy patted her behind.

Awake again, Bea pointed at Daryl on the comforter. Then Dumpty. From character to character, she pointed at each one and whispered their name. "One, two, three. Daryl and Dumpty." Back again. So pretty. All new—all clean. "Four, five, six. Up in a tree." She rolled over. That didn't sound right—the words to the song were different. She needed Mommy's phone. She slowly lifted her head to peek.

No chance. It was way over on the other side of the bed beside Mommy. Mommy even had her hand on it—kinda.

Bea blew out a breath and kept on counting the characters. "One, two, three." She raised her head again. She should count all of them—the whole comforter. One look at Mommy changed her mind.

The characters sparkled against the clean, white background.

She pulled her own blanket out from under the covers. She loved it, but it was dirty next to the new one on Gamma's bed. Gamma's bed. Hers and Mommy's bed.

They'd never shared a bed before—well, they kinda had—but not as a plan. It had always happened if Bea was sick or Mommy was sick or Bea got scared in a dream, or Mommy got scared.

Bea smiled and rolled toward Mommy. She could barely see Mommy's dark hair above the comforter. She snuggled in deep.

Deep sigh. "One, two, three." Deep breath. "Four, five, six, seven." She tapped each character as she counted along. "One, two, three."

"Shh, Bea." Mommy shushed her. "Go back to sleep. It's early still."

Bea zipped her mouth. She'd been on the other side of Bad Mommy before. And even though they were at Noell's house now, she never knew when Bad Mommy would strike.

A bird chirped outside the window.

Mommy groaned and pulled the comforter over her head.

The bird sat just outside—Bea could see it through the fancy, lace curtains. It bounced from one branch to another. The sunlight outlined certain branches, making them brighter so Bea could see them better. Bea held her arm up and outlined the branches with her finger in the air, following each bend and curve of the branch.

The bird opened its mouth and sang a song.

Oh-oh.

Bea checked Mommy. She couldn't even see her head, she was under the comforter so deep. Bea slowly slipped out of bed and parted the curtain, but the bird must have seen the movement and flown off. "Oh, no. Come back little birdie."

Mommy sat up. "Bea!" She tried to whisper, but Bea knew she wanted to yell. If they had been at their trailer house,

Mommy would have yelled. "Get back to bed and go back to sleep!"

Bea jumped up onto the bed and ducked under the covers. Mommy laid back down again and started to breathe slowly.

Deep sigh. She peeked out at the window again. The bird was back. "Pretty, pretty, pretty bird." She knew Mommy hadn't heard that. She had barely moved her lips. "Pretty bird." The bird moved its mouth with its song. "Tweet, tweet, tweet."

Bea yawned and snuggled in, keeping her eyes just above the covers so she could keep watch on the bird. She closed her eyes and yawned again.

What would they do today at Noell's? A picture of the closet full of books and treasures blinked into Bea's imagination. A long time ago, Noell had invited them over and showed Bea a closet upstairs with her old toys in it. They could clean that out. A picture of the big red sofa popped into her mind. It was so soft and smooth. She'd never seen a red sofa before. Gamma must have liked red.

She tapped her foot against the mattress and peeked over at Mommy. She made her ears listen carefully to see if Mommy was asleep again. Even the bird outside was quiet.

Bea carefully slipped out of her side of the bed, and tiptoed to the door. One last look at Mommy and she gently opened it and stepped into the living room. She closed the door carefully but just when it was almost closed, it squeaked long and loud.

Bea stopped and listened, holding her head against the door. Nothing. No sound. Mommy hadn't yelled.

Okay. The door was closed.

And Bea was free.

The totes and boxes. The pretty red sofa. Free to explore.

The windows in Gamma's old house were big—bigger than the trailer house windows—and morning light streamed in, making sun lines on the floor. Bea couldn't resist. Stepping onto the sunlight on the wooden floor, she paused. It was warm to her feet, like when Mommy used to pull a towel out of the dryer and wrap her in it. Bea hugged herself. Where was Noell's dryer?

She tiptoed and followed the sunlight across each floor board. Step. Step. Stop to feel the warmth and breathe. Her eyes were drawn to the sunlight streaming in. She stepped closer and closer to the window. The light from the sun was almost a hug. The time at Clarence's house popped into her mind. The bird. The bird feeder. But that minute with Clarence when she thought the sunlight was like love.

She felt it now. The warmth. The comfort. Her comforter at home on her bed.

No matter where she was, the sunlight made her feel better.

Mrs. T always made her feel better, too.

Mrs. T.

Bea breathed in again, remembering what she'd ben taught.

"Jesus. My friend. Jesus. You love me."

A warmth—just like the sun shining on her body, her face, her arms—grew from within her. The sunlight was warm on her skin and hair as she touched it. Jesus made her warm inside as she held her hand to her chest.

She patted her chest. "My friend. Jesus." She swallowed. "Help Jesus. Help Mommy and me. And Noell. And Mrs. T and Clarence. And Depdy Mark Scott." She glanced at the room behind her. Still alone. Mommy could sometimes sleep all day, only right now, she was Good Mommy. Noell helped. "Jesus, please help Mommy be Good Mommy."

A big breath pushed out.

"Thank you, Jesus."

Big stacks of boxes and totes filled the other room—what Noell called the dining room—what was a dining room? But this room, right next to Gamma's bedroom, where she had slept, held a chair and that great big red sofa. And all the boxes.

Bea tiptoed to the sofa and stopped just before she touched it.

She glanced behind her at the door to Gamma's bedroom. Didn't move a muscle. Just listened.

Just the bird. It stood in a tree just outside the living room windows.

Bea slowly took a step closer to that window. "Did you follow me, birdie?"

The bird opened its mouth and sang its song. Twitter. Tweet. Up and down.

Bea held her breath. The bird sang its song just to her, she was sure of it. She stood still. From the warm sunshine to a birdie singing a song to her.

Deep sigh.

There weren't any curtains at these windows and she could see the bird, straight through the glass. She sang softly along. The bird's beak opened along with the sound. Bea opened her mouth along with the bird and pretended the sound came from her, instead of the bird.

Every time the bird opened its mouth, Bea opened hers. "Tweet, tweet, tweet, tweet." She mouthed the words with no sound. The bird seemed to know when Bea moved her mouth because it sang just at the right time when she opened her mouth.

Bea tried not to giggle.

She stepped on each long line of light along the wooden floor, following the long wooden boards. She pushed at the light in the air and blew with her lips, making the streams of sunlight lift and move—almost dance. Mommy called it dust, but Bea wasn't so sure.

Wow. Sun didn't do that at the trailer. Back and forth, up and down, she danced and the sunlight moved with her. She was careful to be quiet.

She sat on the floor and watched the sunlight creep closer. It didn't touch the wall by Gamma's bedroom door anymore. It stopped just before her toes. She wiggled her toes until they touched the sunlight. It moved away again. She moved her toes into the sunlight again and wiggled them.

She touched the red sofa, warm from the sun already. Mommy called it leather. Bea had never heard that word. What was leather? But it was red. Her new favorite color. Mommy colored lots with red crayons at home. She rubbed her hand against the leather. Soft. Smooth. A couple other chairs stood in the room surrounded by boxes, but they weren't as pretty as the red sofa.

Oh-oh. She better be quiet or there'd be trouble. She didn't want to wake Noell up either.

She sat.

Creak.

She stood quickly. Was that her? When she sat down on the sofa, there was a squeak. She turned. Had she made that noise?

Creak.

Bea sucked in a breath. What was that? Oh-no. She was in trouble. Mommy was coming. It wasn't too bad in their trailer house when Mommy woke up, but here in Noell's house, she didn't know what would happen. She didn't know the house or the rules.

Another creak. A foot stepped onto the floor as the stairway door opened a little.

Bea rushed to the opposite end of the sofa and watched. Hide.

Another foot.

"Peek!"

Bea breathed out. Not Mommy. Not a ghost. Not scary men. "Noell." Bea started to run to Noell, but Noell stopped her just in time and whispered.

"Shh. You'll wake your Mommy. She needs her sleep."

Bea covered her mouth and nodded. She crouched down on the floor beside the end of the sofa. Noell sat down on it and reached for Bea. She snuggled her on her lap and whispered in her ear. "You want breakfast?"

"Yes!"

"Shh." Noell picked Bea up and carried her into the kitchen. "What do you want to eat?" She sat on her chair. "I have toast with peanut butter. I have bagels with cream creese or either one with just butter." She looked to see if Bea liked anything.

Bea shrugged and patted Noell's shoulder. "What do you like to eat for breakfast?"

Noell hugged her. "Well, I like coffee."

Bea wrinkled up her nose and shook her head. "I don't like coffee."

"Okay." Noell put her down on her chair and opened the refrigerator door. "We have orange juice. Apple juice."

"Orange juice is my favorite."

Noell pulled it out and set it on the table. "Okay. Toast? Cereal?"

Bea stood up on the chair. "You have cereal?"

Noell jumped. "Don't fall. That would not be good to explain to your mommy why you fell off the chair." Noell sat her down then opened a cupboard door. "Let's see. What do we have?" Noell pointed at a box. "Os?" She turned to see Bea's face. "Cheerios? No?" Back to the cupboard. "Fruit Loops?'

Bea jumped up again and clapped her hands. "Fruit Loops!"

"Shh!" Noell grabbed the box and a bowl and put them in front of Bea. She opened the box—it was new—and poured cereal into the bowl. "Is that enough?"

Bea's eyes were big. "Wow. That's lots." She patted it level, then picked one up and popped it in her mouth. "Yum. I like Foot Loops."

Noell giggled softly. "I do too. They're my favorite." She found another bowl and two spoons. From the refrigerator, she pulled out the milk and sat down. "Oh. Glasses. I should get some for your mom when she comes out."

"What about your coffee?"

"Oh, Bea. I'm so glad you reminded me." Noell got up, opened the coffee and let Bea sniff.

Bea wrinkled her face. "I don't like it." She covered her nose and shook her head.

Noell smiled, made the coffee and tapped the start button. "Mmm. Smells so good." She poured milk on their cereal and dipped her spoon in and slurped a bite.

Bea giggled and did the same thing. "Mmm. I love Foot Loops." She chewed and crunched. "So good." She stirred the cereal. "Look at all the colors. Green. Blue. Yellow. Red. Mommy likes red." She scooped up another spoonful. "Red Foot Loops. Red sofa."

"What color do you like, Bea?" Noell stood and filled a cup with coffee. She smelled it as she sat back down. "Mmm. You sure you don't want any?'

Bea giggled. "Coffee is for a-dults."

Noell leaned closer and watched Bea's lips. "A-dults? Oh. Adults? Probably." She sipped from her cup. "Did you sleep well in Gamma's big bed?" She gazed out the window. "I used to love that bed. Gamma would let me sleep with her if I … if I couldn't sleep."

Bea nodded. "Like when you had a nightmare?"

Noell blinked. "Yeah. Like when I had a nightmare. She used to hold the covers up so I could climb in beside her and she'd hold me and sing to me. She'd be all warm." Noell nodded, hugged herself, and breathed a deep breath. "I miss her so much."

Mommy walked into the kitchen with a book in her hand. Her cheeks were wet. She held the book open. "I'm sorry. I shouldn't have opened one without you."

Noell shook her head. "It's all right. What has you crying? What happened?"

Mommy sat down beside Bea and kissed her on the forehead. She wiped her eyes. "You have Fruit Loops?"

Bea crunched another bite. "Noell gave them to me. I like Foot Loops." She reached for her glass." She gave me orange juice, too."

"I hope that was okay, Katty." Noell stood and poured another cup of coffee. She put it in front of Mommy and sat down.

Mommy started to read out loud. "Today, little Katty and her mom came over. I had kind of promised them a batch of cookies that I knew they both liked. Kind of lured them over because I missed my sister and her little Katty. I have no idea why Louise has become so mad and angry at the world. And at me. We used to be friends. Sisters. Now, she doesn't want to be a part of my life. I ask God and I ask God again, if there is anything I did to make her that way."

Mommy looked up at Noell. Then at Bea. "Mom was mean." Mommy almost said something else, but she wiped her cheek with the back of one hand and read. "Louise walked in the front door and spewed her filthy language from there to everywhere she walked. I caught her getting ready to slap little Katty for just spilling her milk. Kids spill milk." She glanced at Bea and blew out a breath. "I couldn't let her slap Katty. But if she does it here, in front of me, what does she do at home? I want so badly to adopt little Katty."

Mommy leaned over the journal and sobbed. She lifted her head. "Gamma knew." She held up the journal and shook it in the air. "She knew! Mom always told me that Gamma didn't care. That she wouldn't want me either."

Bea hopped off her chair and hugged Mommy's legs, then looked up. "Who's Louise?"

Mommy jumped.

Noell hugged Mommy from the other side and patted Bea's hand. "Louise is your Mommy's Mommy. Okay?" Noell looked at Mommy's face. "Gamma loved you and would have given anything to take you away from all that."

Mommy nodded and hugged Bea. "It must have been some-time after that, Mom told me she'd never take me to see Gamma again." She wiped her nose.

Bea ran for the tissues. "Mommy's mommy was meaner than *my* mommy." She whispered on the way to Gamma's bathroom. "Mommy's mommy was bad." She wiped her eyes. "Mommy's mommy is just like Bad Mommy." She let out a wail and ran back to the kitchen, the tissues fluttering in her hand. "Mommy, don't be like your mommy anymore." She wiped her nose with the tissues then gave them to Mommy.

Mommy pulled her onto her lap, hugged Bea tight, and held the journal against her chest. "Oh God help me be a good mommy to Bea. Help me be more like Gamma. Help me, God!"

She swallowed. "Somebody wanted me." She wiped her eyes. "Gamma wanted me."

TWENTY-TWO

Katty unbuckled Bea from her car seat. "Bea, you are so funny. You have a great imagination."

"It was real, Mommy." Bea pushed away from the seat and cupped Katty's face in her little hands. "The bird sang just to me. You weren't there. You were still in bed and didn't see."

So grown up. Katty tapped Bea's nose. "Don't grow up too fast, Baby Bea."

"But it's true, Mommy." Bea dropped her head to her chest. "You don't believe me."

Katty picked her up and hugged her, then set her on the concrete. "I believe you, Bea. I just … I just haven't ever done that before, that's all." She stood and read the sign on the store window. "The Used Cupboard. Huh." She pushed Bea in the direction of the sidewalk, and checked the store windows. "Pretty cool, Noell. I like the name."

Noell smiled and scanned the store window as she carefully shut the car door. "I love this store."

"Oh, wait." Katty fumbled in her purse, found the keys, and hit the lock button. She dropped the keys into her purse … did she really appreciate all that Clarence did? Another car?

Thoughts swirled through her mind as she followed Noell and Bea. This time, she hadn't caused the accident—she'd been drinking, but. This time, she didn't get arrested—just taken to the hospital. She glanced at the car behind her. Did she even deserve it? Did she deserve what Clarence did for her? Did she even deserve him?

Noell snatched Bea from running ahead. "I love Mrs. Bertrand. She'll try to get you to call her Gelda."

"I love that name, Gelda. So old-fashioned, but what?"

"Cute." Bea offered. "It's cute."

Noell laughed. "Yes. I agree. Cute." She tapped Bea's head. "You're cute." She walked Bea to the entrance and waited for Katty, who was shopping the front window.

"Is any of this stuff yours … stuff you brought in? Is that weird to see it for sale in here?"

Noell stepped beside her. "Yep. That was Gamma's. The green matching bead necklace, bracelet and earrings, there." She pointed again. "That set of cookbooks. Oh, the cookbooks she had."

Katty chuckled. "And still has." She faced Noell. "There is … uh, still lots in the house." Careful, Katty. The trailer house was awful, right now. "How do you go through something like that?"

"Cook." Bea nodded. "Bake cookies. Make spaghetti." She pointed. "Let's get that one. The one with little kids on the front."

Noell turned and looked at Katty. Her chin quivered. Her eyes teared up. But she wasn't crying. She bit her lips between her teeth.

"Was that one yours?" Katty raised her eyebrows and chuckled.

Noell nodded, finally laughing. "Yes. And we will buy it back for Bea."

Katty shook her head, grinning. Something about today,

about being here. About being here with Bea and Noell. Something within her wanted to bubble out in laughter—just like Noell now. Had she ever felt this before, anytime, anywhere? Had she ever laughed so freely?

Noell opened the door and held it for Bea and Katty. A tinkly bell announced their entrance. The smell of coffee welcomed them. Sparkly strings of tiny white lights outlined everywhere possible to hang them. Every top shelf, every doorway, every window.

"Wow." Katty stopped right inside the door, still holding the door open, but three ladies arrived behind her, wanting in.

One chuckled. "Popular place." She slipped past Katty to walk inside and the other two scooted around her, too.

Katty still hadn't moved much. "Magical." It was like two stores made into one. A partial wall had been opened up to make one big space. The coffee shop part was in the back of one, with a counter and tables and chairs to sit at. The twinkly lights followed everywhere. A coffee machine whirred and voices chattered happily.

Bea dragged Noell over to a child's play area and immediately befriended two little kids playing there.

Noell turned and shrugged.

Katty nodded. "Okay."

"Wanna grab a coffee and walk around?" Noell smiled. "Don't you love this?

Katty was still awestruck, but nodded. Deep sigh. "I don't know the last time I felt like this Noell." She shook her head and sighed again. "I can't stop having those deep breaths. It's like you feel first thing in the morning—if you go outside and the air is so fresh." She frowned. "It's not the air, though. I don't know what it is, but I'm glad we came. I really needed this."

Noell nodded, pulled her purse handle over her head and across her body, and sucked in a deep breath herself. "I know.

But you haven't met Mrs. B yet. She is a big reason why we feel this. Yeah. Coffee first."

Katty called to Bea. "Do you want something to drink, Bea?"

Bea hardly looked up. Busy, busy. They were playing blocks. Making stuff. Bea hadn't asked to color or draw yet at Noell's. Surprising, kinda. Finally, she hopped up and joined them. "Can I have hot chocolate, Mommy?"

"You don't want a smoothie or lemonade?"

"No. I want hot chocolate." Bea patted her tummy. "That sounds good." She turned to face the entrance and pointed at some little porcelain dolls. "So cute." She spun around in a circle —her arms outstretched. "And I love how the angels decorate the walls. So cute."

Katty paused and glanced at Noell. "Did she just say—"

Noell finished her sentence. "Angels?" She stepped close to Katty.

Katty shook her head. People in the store stopped moving and talking. The noise faded. Just her, Noell, and Bea existed in this moment, this space. This moment.

Angels?

Bea skipped to the play area like nothing had happened. The mist lifted. People shopped. The coffee machine whirred.

Back to what it had been?

Noell hugged Katty. "Did that just happen?" She stepped to a shelf and laughed. "We need to go through everything before I bring more down here. We might find stuff Bea wants."

Katty picked one up. "Was this yours?"

Noell nodded and laughed. "I haven't brought a lot down here, yeah the cookbooks and some dishes. Some things I want others to check out, see if it has any meaning. Like you. I'm so glad you're there now, because some things might be for you and Bea. I want to clear out, but I want stuff to go to the right places."

Katty hadn't been back to the trailer for a couple days, since before jail, but she guessed that there wasn't anything of hers anyone would want to take. It was all junk. A visual of the painted wall dropped into her memory. But that. That. Crazy stuff. Trees and babies and clouds that came alive and moved. Crazy.

The door bell dinged again.

"Mr. Depdy Mark Scott!" Bea pointed at the entrance door and ran to him.

"Hi Bea." He was carrying a big cardboard box.

Bea hugged his knees and almost made him fall—box and all.

"Bea. Wait." Katty rushed to his rescue before he dropped the box.

He moved it to one side, as Katty grabbed it on the other side, with Bea underneath. His green eyes were so close. Those eyes. Those eyelashes. He grinned. "I'm stuck."

Katty let go and pulled Bea away. "I'm so sorry." She didn't move away.

Bea didn't either.

Mark didn't either. "It's good to see you."

The last time he'd seen …. Whew.

Bea jumped up and down, up and down. "Good to see you Mr. Depdy Mark Scott."

Someone entered just behind Mark and the entrance area got crowded.

Katty backed away. "I'm sorry. We're in the way." She swooped Bea back to the counter and coffee area where Noell had claimed a table and placed their drinks. Katty turned so she could see him as she sat on her chair. He was still smiling as he walked to the back with the box. A woman followed him to the back of the store, carrying another, smaller box.

The woman tilted her head toward them. "Who was that, Mark? That little girl." Her voice was loud in the lull between coffee machine grinds and hisses. The woman seemed to smile.

"She knows you." She watched to see where Bea and Katty, and Noell sat. The minute her eyes landed on Katty, her expression changed. From happy and enjoying Bea's comment, to almost a scowl.

What?

Was this Mark's mom?

Katty held Bea's hot chocolate for her, the straw between her fingers, as she sipped from her own cup. Her eyes followed what she could see of Mark and the lady. Awkward.

"No I can do it, Mommy." Bea tried to brush Katty's hand away, but Katty held firm.

"Hey, Noell. How much for our drinks?" Katty moved to open her purse. "Bea stop. You're going to spill it."

"No. Nothing." Noell kept her bag close on her lap, her arms wrapped around it.

"Are you cold?" Katty imitated Noell's posture, shrugging her shoulders. Then it dawned on Katty what Noell was doing. She leaned closer. "Can you feel … stuff, or … hear … people in here … from this … junk?" Katty glanced around her. She held her breath. There had to be millions of kitchen goods, books, clothing, even furniture in the store. From every household in Polk County.

Noell slowly nodded.

"Oh my gosh. Is that hard? We don't have to stay. We should leave." She reached for her purse.

Noell slowly nodded, but then jumped up. She reached for a cookbook off a shelf and hugged it. "I know this one. I can feel her, smell her, hear her when I hug this one." She swayed side to side. "Gamma was so sweet." She held it out and read the front. "I should buy it back."

"Uh, hi." Mark stepped up to the table. "I didn't want to leave without saying hello. Or, good-bye." He tapped Bea on the head. "How's your arm, Bea?"

Bea blew bubbles into her hot chocolate through the straw,

then jumped off her chair and hugged Mark's knees again. "It's good." She lifted her sleeve. "It's purple."

He laughed and picked her up. He checked his space around him and threw her into the air.

She squealed, then drooled hot chocolate all over his shirt.

Katty jumped up and grabbed her napkin. "Oh no. She got you."

He shook his head and laughed. "It's alright. It's old. Needs to be washed." He held Bea. "It's my fault. I should have checked her mouth. Could be dangerous." He tickled Bea in her tummy. "Oops! Should have checked your mouth again!" He directed a question to Noell. "How are you doing? House guests and all."

"I love it. That big house is … big." She smiled. "So good to have the time to get to know my family better."

"Family?" He looked at Katty and Bea, then smiled. "Oh. I forgot."

The woman joined them. "Hi Mark. Why don't you introduce me to these ladies?" She *had* to be his mom—she reached up and tickled Bea in the same spot he had. "Who are you little lady?"

Bea giggled.

Katty wiped Bea's mouth before anything could spew out onto Mark's mom.

Mark shook his head. "Mom, this is Bea." He tickled her again, and turned to Noell, first. "This is Noell … Carpenter, right? Did I get your last name right?"

Noell stood and nodded. "Perfect." She held out her hand to Mark's mom. "Uh, Mom."

Mark laughed and shook his head. "Sorry. This is Phyllis, my mom."

"Hello, Phyllis. Good to meet you." She shook hands with Phyllis and sat.

"Mom, this is Katty, Bea's mom." He was blushing. He had

to be blushing … or very hot. Maybe wrestling Bea had made him heat up.

Katty stepped to Phyllis and held out her hand. "Good to meet you, Phyllis." Good to have Noell be her model so she could imitate her and offer her hand in greeting. Work on her please and thank you.

Phyllis didn't offer her hand. "Nice to meet you, Katty."

Awkward. Guess she didn't like her already. Hand down. Katty sat. Was she invisible? She'd been invisible before. Why not now at one of the most awkward moments of her life.

"C-can you join us for a drink?" Noell and her good manners.

"Uh, sure. Mom? We can pull a couple chairs over." Mark hadn't put Bea down yet and when he sat on his chair, he let her sit on his lap.

Phyllis stood for a couple seconds before pulling a chair up beside him. "I don't think I want anything."

"You sure?" Mark glanced at her. "You are in organizing mode, aren't you, Mom." He shrugged. "We don't have to stay if you have more you want help with."

She stood up. "I do. Thanks." She stepped away and waved. "Nice to meet you girls. And you Bea."

Was Bea not a girl? Katty wasn't impressed. She waved and picked Bea up from Mark. Their eyes met again, inches apart. She smiled a sheepish smile. The last time she'd seen him was at the Sheriff's Department. Yeah. What a contrast with here.

"Bye Bea." He bowed. "Have a good day."

Bea giggled and curtsied.

"What?" Katty laughed, thankful for the comic relief. "Where'd you learn to do that? No wait. Daryl & Dumpty, right?"

Bea nodded, very sure of herself and the attention she was getting at the moment. Little stinker. "Bye Mr. Depdy Mark. Sir."

Phyllis laughed. "She has all that down, doesn't she?" She turned to go. "Smart little girl, Mark."

Mark nodded at Noell, then Katty "Bye, ladies. Have fun. Enjoy your drinks."

Was Katty mistaken? Had his smile changed when he looked at her?

Right. Who was she kidding? With a mom like his, she didn't have a chance with him. Anyway, she didn't deserve that kind of love. She was used up goods. She glanced around the store. Just like everything else in this place. Used up. Dried up. Just like that vase on that shelf—all chipped and faded.

And broken.

Bea ran off to play and even though there were several people at tables near them, it got very quiet at Katty and Noell's table.

"That was awkward." Noell relaxed her arms and slung her bag over the back of her chair. "She has issues."

Katty choked. Laughed out loud. She didn't know what to say. She herself had issues. But the minutes with Phyllis just now had been more than awkward. At some point, before today, she felt kind of like maybe she and Mark had a chance of at least friendship. But now, that chance had been burned down by Phyllis. She didn't know what to say to Noell in response.

Katty watched Mark hold the car door open for Phyllis. Katty had felt people's criticism and disapproval before. Even when drunk, she could feel people judging her. But just now, Phyllis had stabbed Katty in the back with an undeniable dagger that she'd never felt before. All from Mark's mom. "Yeah. Awkward." She would never be good enough for Mark's mom.

"You are being so nice, Katty. She was rude. She burned holes into us with her eyes." Noell turned and looked straight at Katty. "Into YOU." Noell started to sway on her chair. "But she has definite issues."

Katty leaned forward so she could see Bea. "You *said* that. What do you mean?" Katty thought awhile. "She's pretty."

"Dang. You're still being nice and I kinda get that. She's Mark's mom and there is definitely something going on between you and Mark. And she's pretty, alright." Noell picked up a small vase. "Gamma's." She hugged it. "When I shook her hand … well, let's just say she has issues."

Katty patted her chest. "*I* have issues. Drinking. Anger. Fear." She whispered. "Jail time." She blinked and met Noell's eyes. "Right? But how do you do that? You just shook her hand. How can you tell or feel her?"

"I don't know. If you want to get science-y, maybe her molecules rub off on me and maybe the molecules have the ability to accumulate voices and pictures and such. They store them until someone comes into contact with them and … what do I know? It's crazy."

"It *is* crazy." Katty shivered. "Don't touch me. It might kill you."

Noell started to reach for Katty like a lion, with a hiss. Grrr.

"Hello Noell."

Noell laughed and started to stand up. "Hi Mrs. Bertrand. Sorry. We were just kidding around."

"Gelda, Noell. Call me Gelda." She smiled. "I see that."

Bea happened to arrive at the table. "Gelda."

Gelda laughed. "See? She gets it. I hope you are enjoying our little store."

Katty nodded, as she scanned the place. "It's magical, Mrs. Gelda."

"You'll get there." She laughed then hesitated. "Are you Katty? Katty Randolph?"

Katty nodded.

"So, did your mom find you, Katty?" Gelda glanced behind at the other customers and smiled. She cleared trash from a table nearby. Back to Katty.

Mom? Katty's chest tightened every time she even thought of Mom, much less heard the word Mom in reference to her own. "My Mom?" She pointed at herself.

"Yes, she was in here asking about you, where you lived now —heh, *if* you even lived here. But where you lived and worked." She combed Bea's hair behind her ears. "I don't think she knows about your little girl, does she?"

Katty froze.

Probably not. Katty hadn't told her.

Katty never wanted to see her mom again.

TWENTY-THREE

Mark helped his mom into the car. "Is there more at home that you need to donate, here?" He glanced back at the store and his jaw dropped. Aligned through hanging frames in the front window of the store, was Katty. She was beautiful—enhanced by a gold gilded frame that just happened to be hanging in the window, on the one and only day he visited the store. He never stepped inside that store. Ever.

Phyllis was saying something and he missed it.

"What was that, Mom?" He leaned in to hear what she said.

"I was just saying that, there is more, I just have to go through it." She zipped her jacket and paused for him to close the door. "I want to go through a couple more drawers and see what's there. I found some things of your dad's in the back of a closet." She tilted her head and looked at him. "You might find some things."

"Well, I'll help when you need it." Mark made sure she was all inside and closed her door. As he stepped to the driver's side, ready to open his door, he looked up at the store again. Katty must have been watching him … er … them. She quickly looked away to where Bea was playing. He smiled. Her brown eyes remained in his memory from when she rescued him from dropping the box. Had they been five inches away from each other? Three?

Deep sigh. Open the door goof. Mom was waiting. Mom had been talking. One last look. Yup. She was watching him. She smiled this time. He nodded and smiled back. Yup. There was something going on.

He opened his car door and slid in. "Well, Mom. You want to go grab a burger somewhere? I mean there's not too much to choose from here in Osceola, but—"

"Not today, Son. I have stuff at home I can eat and I'm sure you have lots to do with your time off." She patted his arm. "Thanks anyway. I need to study for my ladies group, too."

"Okay. It would be my treat, though. You always cook for me." He pulled away from the curb, fighting the desire to check on Katty, one more time. Katty won out.

"Mark! Watch out!" Mom braced herself against the dash. "You almost hit her."

"Dang. And me a deputy." He waved at the woman as she walked by on the crosswalk. "Sorry. Yep. I must be a little tired. Long night last night."

"That was Tinnie's granddaughter. I can't remember her name. She's from Lincoln or Omaha, I think and she just finished law school." Mom almost clucked. "There are some pretty girls in Nebraska."

"Yup there are, Mom." He was sure that who Mom was talking about and who he was talking about were two different people. Always the matchmaker.

He pulled into her driveway and shifted the car into park. Before he could say good-bye, she turned to him. "I could get you set up with her. Tinnie is in my Bible Study. And you are right. She is a pretty woman."

"Uh. What? Um. Oh, you mean the woman I almost hit with the car?" Whew. Maybe he should ask Katty out. "Well, my work schedule is packed and you know I work evenings and nights." Saved by work. He put his hand on his door handle. "I'll come around and help you out."

She waved him away. "No, Son. I can get it. I'm not a hundred years old, yet." She opened her door and stepped onto the concrete. "Think about it. You need someone in your life." She smiled. "Maybe her." She stood and bent down to look him in the eye. "By the way, the little girl was cute and those girls are nice." She bit her tongue. "I just think you can do better. Start your own family."

Mark frowned. "Uh—" Like Bea wasn't good enough? Katty either?

"Bye, Mark. And thanks for the help. Love you!" And she slammed the door.

He usually watched her walk to the door to make sure she got in the house safely. But, today, it was more about shock at what she'd just implied. Bea wasn't good enough. Katty wasn't good enough in Mom's opinion?

He jumped into his truck and backed out of the driveway.

Car!

Damn! Slow down. He sucked in a couple of breaths, glanced at Mom's front room window—even though he couldn't see her, he knew she was standing there—and slowly backed onto the street. Shifted into drive and crept away.

Mom had the best intentions for him—she always had—but she could be very controlling. He remembered may times when she had barged in on his life and his plans. She had wanted him to play in the band at school and sing in the choir—neither were what he had wanted. He tried out, just to placate her, made it and fully hated it all year long. He never tried out again. He didn't like sports, either. She pushed him to go out for every sport: football, basketball, track. He hated running. He ran more now on his job, than he had back in the day for sports.

The more he learned about people, about counseling and

trauma, the more he understood what made Mom tick. A marriage to an alcoholic man had driven her to become the controlling woman she was. She felt she had to control so she wouldn't get hurt anymore. She had to protect Mark by controlling what he did or didn't do.

He didn't blame her, but he didn't want her living his life. He didn't want her speaking to Sheriff on his behalf. He didn't want her choosing his mate.

Kids on the street. Playing ball and riding bikes.

He needed to cast aside his frustrations and concentrate on the street and his driving. There. They pulled over at the curb and stood by with their bikes so he could pass.

Slow down, Mark. Focus on driving carefully and the rest would take care of itself.

Before he realized it, his thoughts returned to Mom and Katty and Bea. He didn't want to upset Mom, but he knew there were feelings on both sides with him and Katty. Definitely him and little Bea. His chest tightened and he white-knuckled the steering wheel without thinking about it.

Beep. Beep. Beep.

He checked his gas gauge. Yep. Thirty miles till empty. Thankfully, it was a small town and from Mom's house to his house took him almost by the gas station. Thankful there was even gas in this small town.

He flipped his blinker on and pulled in. Pizza for supper later. Sounded good.

He hopped out and scanned his card, removed the gas nozzle and flipped the gas on.

"Excuse me, sir." A woman's voice interrupted right behind him. "Would you happen to have an extra ten dollars on you?"

He didn't have to look very far away to find the source of the voice. Holy cow! She might have been pretty once. She was trying too hard at her current age. Tight, tight jeans which were the style, but still. Red lipstick. Black, black hair hanging down on her back and not hiding enough of her cleavage in front. If he didn't know better … she reminded him of someone. He backed away a step.

"Uh, I don't have any cash." Mark stepped away, patted his pockets, and shook his head. He checked around for someone he knew at the pumps. "There. Ask Milton over there. He might be able to help you." Mark pointed at Milton walking out of the convenience store, shoving his billfold into his back pocket. "Hey Milton. You got a couple bucks to help this lady out?"

Milton glanced at the woman, looked over at Mark, then his glance landed on the woman again. He pulled out his billfold, not taking his eyes off her. "Sure. I can help a pretty lady in distress."

The woman seemed to waver between Mark and Milton.

"Ma'am, if it's money you want, you ain't gitting anything from the deputy there. They don't get paid but shit." He pulled two twenties partway out, letting them flutter. "What's yer name, darlin'?"

She didn't seem too picky. Who knew what she wanted the money for and where she'd earned her money before. It almost felt like a sex deal going down. If he knew Milton, and maybe he didn't know him like he thought, but it felt like Milton was offering the cash in exchange for sex.

Or maybe it was the woman.

The woman smiled, her brown eyes back and forth between Milton and Mark. "Louise." She fluttered her eyelashes and stepped closer to Milton, eyeing the money. "I'd be so grateful if you can spare it." Her eyes back on Mark. "I don't mean to ignore you. Thanks for your help."

Playing both sides. If one won't, maybe the other will.

"No. No. That's okay, I didn't have any cash." And Mark didn't want to get involved with whatever else she might be selling. "No problem." There might be a problem, but it probably wouldn't show up until that night, when Mark happened to be on duty.

He finished fueling and replaced the nozzle just in time to see Milton holding the door to his truck open and Louise sliding in. Milton grinned at Mark and saluted him as he got in on the driver's side.

Mark walked inside as they pulled away. Pizza must have just come out of the oven. Smelled so good. "Hey, man, can I get a couple slices of pizza?"

"You bet. Just got it out." The guy slid a couple pieces onto the cardboard holders and handed them to Mark. "They're hot. Be careful."

"Thanks." Mark headed to the register. "Hot. Hot." He dropped the pizza onto the counter and pulled out his card. Only it wasn't there. He patted his other pockets, searched his shirt pocket. "I just paid for gas out there. Where is my card?"

The cashier looked outside at the same time Mark did.

"I pulled it out of the reader. I know I did." That was when the lady … Louise, or whatever … had approached him.

The cashier must have had the same thought. "That lady was in here begging for money. She must have sticky fingers. I noticed she had bright pink nail polish. You'd think it would be even more noticeable when she lifted your card."

"I have no idea when she might have …" He shook his head. She'd stood way too close to him, for his comfort. He'd turned away to pump the gas.

He picked up the slices of pizza and turned.

"Naw. Deputy. I gotcha." The cashier waved him back and pointed to the counter. "Put 'em here and I've got them." He literally removed his own billfold. "Ya want a soda, too?"

Mark growled and dropped his head to his chest. "Man. I can't do that."

"Naw. I've got it. Let me do this." He rang it up and paused, eyes on Mark. "So I rang up a drink—whatever you choose. Soda? Beer?" He snickered. "I'd be buying for a cop."

Mark shook his head and smiled. "Pizza is fine. I have stuff at home." A beer would taste good right now.

The guy slipped the money in and bagged the pizza. "Have a good night, Deputy."

Humbled. Mark nodded. "Thanks man. I'll get you back."

"You better call your bank, too, or you'll be buying the lady new shoes. Pink probably, to match her nail polish."

He pushed the door open. "First thing when I get in my car." He held up the bag. "Thanks again."

As he opened the car door, Milton's truck drove away past the implement dealership. Long, black hair flowed out of a window, almost like a salute.

He got in the car and there was his card, right on the passenger seat. What was wrong with him? He waved it at the cashier, inside and opened his car door. The guy ran around to the door and yelled out, "Nope. I got this."

"I'll get you back. Thank you." Mark started his truck and stopped. He slipped his card into his wallet and took off toward home. Only a couple hours before he had to be to work. Why was he so rattled? Why had he thought he'd lost his card?

TWENTY-FOUR

Katty jumped into her car. "We have to get back to your house, Noell. We need to pack up our stuff and find someplace to run to. Get far, far away from here."

Bea stomped her foot. "No, Mommy. I like it with Noell." She wailed and stomped her foot again. "I won't go. I won't leave her."

Katty shushed her. "Bea. Settle down." This kid really didin't want to leave. Her balled-up fists covered her eyes. Katty bent down, her hands on Bea's fists. "Baby Bea. You don't know how evil she is." Her hands were already trembling, as she pushed Bea toward her side of the car. She picked her up and opened the car door. "Bea. Shush. We'll be okay. You don't know my mom."

Noell stood at the passenger side, the expression on her face sympathetic. She slipped into the car and faced Katty and Bea. She reached for Bea's hand, as Katty buckled Bea in. "It'll be alright, Bea. You'll see."

Bea fussed. "But I don't want to leave. I don't want to leave you." She must have been distracted by something or someone at the store because she glanced that way. "I don't want to leave the store, or Mrs. Gelda. Or all the angels standing by the walls."

Katty smirked in the front seat and peeked at Noell. She was smiling, too, as she reached behind her to hold Bea's hand. "This is so weird. Mom'll go to your house first thing, Noell. She knows where you … or Gamma lived. Damn." Oh, for a drink. "We have to leave." Her mouth was so dry, she could hardly swallow. She'd even had something to drink inside. Just when she was trying to get her life back in order. Just when she almost felt sober. Damn. Damn. Even meeting Mark's mom was creepy. Phyllis hated her, she could tell. And now her own mom might be back in town.

Noell let go of Bea's hand and touched Katty's shoulder. "It's gonna be okay, Katty. It will." She glanced out the windshield and shrugged her shoulders. "What if she's changed? What if she is different … better?"

Katty licked her lips. "How could a woman like that change? That would take a … a mir-miracle." She glanced at Noell, then back to the street ahead. Visuals of Mom breaking her crayons, of throwing hot macaroni on Katty. Bruises that she had to hide to even go to school. Mom could never figure out why they used so many band-aids. The one time a family had taken Katty to church fueled a whole debate about whether Katty should be allowed to stay in the home with Mom. That kind of bruise. She glanced in the rearview mirror at Bea. God help.

She had to be a different mom than her own had been.

"Hey. Better slow down." Noell touched Katty's hand. "I know you're upset, but—"

"Oh, man. Wow. I went back to memories with Mom. Awful." Tears filled her eyes and she wiped her cheek. She slowed the car. "I don't want to be like her." She looked at Bea in the mirror, again. "Bea deserves better. Memories with Mom would make a great book title, huh?" She shook her head. "It'd be a horror story, for sure."

"Is a horror story like Daryl & Dumpty, Mommy?" Bea had been listening.

Katty sighed. Another deep breath. Slow it down. "No Baby Bea. Daryl & Dumpty stories are not horror. Horror stories are scary. Daryl & Dumpty are kind to each other and good." She snickered. "I've read every book and watched mostly every TV show. Believe me. They're not like living with my Mom."

They reached Noell's house and there wasn't a strange car in front or in the driveway.

Katty pulled in. "Whew. I thought she'd be here waiting for us, already." She unbuckled her seat belt and jumped out. No sign of her. It had been how long? Katty had literally run into her in the grocery store somewhere. Actually, Mom had run into her cart—just to be funny. So however long ago that had been. Oh man, she wanted a drink.

Noell appeared beside her almost like magic. "You okay?"

Katty jumped. "Yeah. As long as I don't see her. As long as she keeps her distance—like in worlds away." She grabbed her purse. "I just want a drink so bad right now." Eye to eye with Noell. "Just being honest."

Noell slowly nodded.

Bea scooted to the door. Unbuckled herself again. "A drink from those little bottles or a drink of water?'

"You are too smart, Baby Bea. A drink of water. Right?" Katty looked up at Noell again. "We met Mark's mom and she didn't like me at all. Now my mom might be back and who knows how that'll go." She fumbled with her purse, could hardly see through tears that threatened, and looked back at Noell. "And, I'm sorry but, your mom was probably the nicest and the best out of them all, and she … is … gone."

Noell blinked. Nodded. Sucked in a breath. Waited. "I know. Life doesn't seem fair sometimes. Mom might have been a bad mom, too. But I don't remember her that way."

Katty paused, then raised her arms to hug Noell. It was hard. Hugs were hard. Hugs were too close. But this one was different. Noell embraced Katty back.

"Hey. I want in." Bea pulled on Katty.

"Bea on the other hand, is a good hugger." Katty picked her up and pulled her in between herself and Noell. "Snuggly Baby Bea." She rubbed noses with her and smiled. "Bea, I love you. God help us find our way. God help us do the right thing."

"Mommy. You prayed to God. Just like Mrs. T." Bea patted her on the back. "Good job, Mommy."

Katty chuckled. "Well, that is a really nice complement, Bea. Thank you."

Noell stopped hugging and peered over Katty's shoulder. She tapped Katty on the back, then pointed.

Katty looked to where she pointed and saw a woman walking up the hill on State Street, toward Ridge Street—their street. She walked as if she didn't have any responsibilities, any problems, just bounced up the hill. It seemed like she might be a tourist, the way she studied each house, the trees, a car. She made sure to wave at whoever drove past.

Was that Mom?

Okay. Maybe.

On up to Ridge Street, she turned their direction. Seemed to be enjoying her day. Well, whoop-de-doo.

Katty took a step in her direction. "Mom?" She barely breathed it out. Strange and painful to say that word, after so long.

The woman walked up the sidewalk, to the house, like she knew where she was going.

Katty stepped another step toward her. This was her mom.

The woman stepped off the sidewalk onto the grass. She seemed to be smiling. Katty would have known Mom anywhere, and this lady looked like her. But there was something about her that Katty wouldn't have expected. She was dressed okay—jeans and a T-shirt. She didn't look like a grandma because she seemed in good shape. Her hair was dyed so she looked younger.

There was just something about her smile that stopped Katty.

The woman's mouth was spread wide with bright, red lipstick. Like it was forced somehow. Stretched like it was painted there. That smile was a horror story.

Her eyes, as she got closer, were almost the same as Katty remembered, except for the color. Katty had always remembered them as black. Now they were green. But people could do new things to change eye color … like contact lenses or surgery to insert colored lenses. They had always been black as far back as Katty could remember.

Had she changed?

When the woman looked up, directly into Katty's eyes, she shivered. Those green eyes pierced Katty's own, searched and penetrated Katty's very soul.

Katty gasped—almost caught her breath. Her mom's eyes pierced her like she was in some sort of x-ray machine and every cell of her being, every memory—painful and true—was being scanned and studied.

Made her feel naked. Vulnerable. It had been years since every nerve trembled and vibrated.

"Hello. Could I get a piece of that hug?" She had circled around the car and stood next to them, holding out her arms.

Bea bounced up, took one look, and pulled away. She hid behind Katty's legs.

Noell stepped away, too. She then grabbed Bea and moved away even farther.

Not hugging this woman. Never. Ever.

The woman dropped her hands. "Katty. Don't you know who I am?"

Nobody spoke.

"I'm your mom, for goodness sake."

Goodness? What? For goodness sake? She speaks a foreign language. For her at least.

Katty couldn't move. Her feet were stuck in concrete, buried in the ground. Her heart pounded inside her chest. Chills skittered up her arms. Even though her eyes appeared to be green, they were still Mom's eyes, with something stirring inside that wasn't normal. Horror eyes.

Noell didn't move toward her, either.

Bea hid her head in Noell's neck.

Mom moved closer to touch Bea. "Is this your little girl?" She touched her cheek.

Bea shuddered, screamed, then jumped down Noell's leg. She ran to the house and opened the front door. Peeked back outside, jumped inside, then slammed the door.

Katty stabbed a finger at Mom. "Don't touch her. Ever." Katty ran after Bea. She reached the door and turned. "Noell! You coming?"

Noell almost curtsied to Katty's mom, backed away, and ran to the house. "S-sorry. Gotta go unlock the inside door. Sh-she needed the bathroom before we drove up, so it's kind of an emergency." She turned and ran. Waved. "Have a good day."

Katty held onto Bea inside the enclosed porch and peeked out the window. Mom could probably see her, but she didn't care. What on earth? Why was she back? Probably just like the druggie guys. She was out of options.

As Katty watched from inside, Mom shook her head and faced the house. "You haven't changed a bit." Hands on her hips, she tossed long, black hair over her shoulders, and yelled it out this time, so loud that they could hear her words from inside the house. "You haven't changed a bit, you little slut. Whore. You always were a scab on my life."

"What's she saying? What's a slut, Mommy?" Bea tucked her head under Katty's chin. "Is she calling you bad names, Mommy?"

Katty nodded.

Noell stood behind them and covered Bea's ears.

Mom's back. Just like old times.

TWENTY-FIVE

Kadash stood in the corner of Mr. Grimes kitchen, towards the back of the house, his swords crossed in front of him. He had positioned himself in this particular corner, because he could see through the dining and living rooms, clear to the front door, in the natural world. Handy to see who the human let in. Even partway to the hallway, which he knew led to the bathroom, the back bedroom and up front to Mr. Grimes' bedroom.

There was a whole other layer or realm he had access to and saw everything in that one, layered over the physical world.

Humans weren't even aware of his world. Mr. Grimes might be able to see his demons. Maybe.

Kadash could see humans, angels, demons, and many other creatures in his realm. Interesting how some humans who wrote or created could actually describe them accurately, without having seen them.

From an angel's point of view, they might say he had an easy job—watching over Mr. Grimes as he did. And he guessed it *was* easy. The man never prayed to Jesus. He never went to church. He loved porn and was addicted to diet soda in a bad way. He didn't go anywhere unless he had to pay a bill or buy food. So, what did Kadash even do?

He watched over Mr. Grimes, to keep him safe. Kadash had done that since Mr. Grimes was a baby. Even before that while he was in his mother's womb. That always seemed like a very fragile time for a baby—inside the mother.

Angels had no say over what happened to the mother or baby. They were instructed to not interfere, except when Father in heaven released them to do so. They witnessed all that went on in the human's life, but did not judge. Ever.

Mr. Grimes watched the whole scene at his neighbor's house, snooping from his bathroom window. "Man, she's putting it to them. Doesn't look like it's directed at Noell Girl, but at the other one—the dark haired one." He sipped loudly on his straw in a can of soda. "Pretty little lady, too. Wears jeans nicely." He pushed aside his walker and stepped to the hallway, rubbing his hands together. "Mighty fine lady."

He walked to his computer in the dining room and refreshed the monitor. He watched it for a time—it was linked to his favorite porn site. He blew out a deep breath and walked back to the bathroom window.

As soon as he refreshed the website, a creature rose behind, its arms stretched on both sides of the desk, hissing. Demons actually. Dragon-like. Serpent-like. They writhed and spat, their tongues flicked sparks, as they wrapped themselves around the computer. When they caught sight of the filth that was playing on the screen, they laughed wickedly and licked the screen. Just like dogs to their vomit.

Kadash checked his sandals, scraping them on the edge of his sword. He didn't want any dung from this realm to drag into the throne room later. He nonchalantly watched the demons as he sharpened one sword against the other. They could see him and what he was doing. They continued hissing and flicking little flames of fire in his direction.

Kadash slowly shook his head.

Mr. Grimes walked through the dining room, then into the kitchen and opened the refrigerator door. "Hmm." He dragged out a chunk of cheese, salami, olives. He clapped his hands. "A true Jewish feast." Tilted his head. "Well, Italian, maybe. Doesn't matter."

The dragons hissed and smacked their lips.

Ring!

"Not now." Mr. Grimes had just set out a plate and started to slice the salami and cheese. "Not now, paper boy. Little Girl Scout." He hesitated. "Ooh cookies would be nice. He rearranged the snacks on the table to make room. "Coming!"

Kadash followed along behind Mr. Grimes as he walked to the entrance doorway. When he passed the demons behind the computer, one swiped his arm and scraped at him with its talons.

Mr. Grimes slicked down his hair and reached for the doorknob. He almost opened it, then stopped. He ran to the walker, turned it around, and drove it to the front door. He patted down his stomach, brushed his pants off and opened the door with a flourish.

The woman from Noell Girl's house. "Well, hello."

She fluttered her eyes at him. Two demons rose from behind her and reflected the late afternoon sunlight. Their scales seemed to have little lights in them. They locked eyes with Kadash and hissed. The woman definitely was lit up from something. Her skin sparkled for some reason, but the light in her eyes was mesmerizing.

Mr. Grimes blinked. "Uh. I don't believe I have met you." He offered his hand. "I'm Donald Grimes." He bowed. "And who might you be?" He retained his position, leaning over, probably not in honoring her, but in checking her out.

Kadash had seen him do this before with men and women.

The woman grabbed his chin and lifted his face up, so she could snarl in it. "I happen to be Louisiana Randolph. Nice to meet you, Donald Grimes." She dropped his chin and pushed her way inside.

TWENTY-SIX

It had already been a beautiful morning. The wind always seemed to blow in this part of Nebraska, but the sunshine warmed Noell's skin. Birds flapped in and out of the neighborhood trees, twittering their approval of the fine day.

Noell laughed as she slammed the front door. In fact she laughed so hard, that she dropped some of the mail. "I can't believe it." The door blew open again. "It's so windy." She pushed her backside against it. "There." She picked up the mail and walked into the living room. "I just taught that door a lesson."

"A lesson?" Bea didn't even look up from her coloring. "Like in a school lesson?" She picked up a blue crayon and scratched her head. "The door goes to school?"

Katty sat down beside her at the kitchen table and checked Bea's hair. "I need to give you a bath, before we go anywhere." She watched Noell sort the mail. "Is that okay? In Gamma's tub?"

"Sure. Anything. Snoop for anything you need." She breathed in and out, then peeked up at Katty. Than back at the mail. Back at Katty. "I'm glad you decided to stay last night. It had to be hard to see your mom and not run."

Katty nodded slowly. "Yeah." She visibly shuddered. "When we saw her walking toward us, I at first thought—hoped—it was somebody else. Not really Mom, just someone who looked like her. And really? She looks good." She hesitated, possibly remembering awful stuff, because her face contorted into a grimace, like she might burst into tears. She visibly sucked in a deep breath. "But the minute she opened her mouth." Katty blinked. "There was no question." She shook her head, hugging herself. "None at all."

Noell organized the mail. Bills in a pile. Junk in another pile. "So … are you staying?"

Katty glanced at Bea, who seemed to be in her own little world coloring and humming. "Where would we go?" She glanced out the window. "I want to run, but." She tipped her head in the direction of Gamma's bedroom. "Something in there pulls at me, draws me to find … to—"

Noell reached for her hand. "Me, too. Something in Gamma's closet pulls at me. She packed all of that in there, probably for her, but for us." She gathered the junk mail, tossed it in the trash, and sat back down. "There is something in there that we are supposed to find, but to learn. If I know Gamma." She swallowed and almost whispered. "If I knew her, she still has something to say—to teach us."

"Yeah." Katty picked up a crayon, tapped it against the paper, and seemed to ponder Noell's words. "Yes. I feel it too." Her eyes as she looked back at Noell appeared wet. "I need to stay and learn from Gamma … and you. But I can't stay with Mom here now."

Noell tore open an envelope and pulled out the contents. As she pulled the letters out, she sucked in a breath. She'd received these before from an investment company that Gamma had done business with. Every once in a while, a check arrived in the mail for thousands of dollars. And now that she was Gamma's beneficiary or heir, they were addressed to her.

This check was different. From the same investment company … but … it was signed … by Gamma?

How did that happen? A check signed by Gamma?

She shook her head, flipped it over to the back, and then to the front. Gamma was gone—dead. The date was recent, but had it maybe slipped through the legal system? Probably just something that had been detained. It hadn't been that long since she passed and Clarence had helped set everything up. She glanced around the house. She was sure that it was possible to miss something in this mess.

Bea's humming became louder with words to a song.

"Shh, Bea. Noell's busy." Katty shushed Bea and picked up a crayon. "She has lots of mail to go through."

Bea mumbled something.

Oh Gamma. What to do? *I miss you so much.* This house. Noell was thankful. Especially now. Hopefully Bea and Katty stayed. But how do deal with it all?

The mess overwhelmed her.

She owned the house, the property. She had no clue as to what to do with these checks. Each time she received one, she walked over to the nursing home and talked to Clarence. She needed to make an appointment, now that he had the agency. He always listened and helped her decide. How could having lots of money and property be so difficult and time-consuming? If she had so much money, why couldn't she make her nightmares go away?

"What did you say when you came in? You were laughing." Katty colored a spot on Bea's paper, chose another crayon but dropped it again. "What can't you believe?"

Noell glanced up. The minute she had thought about the nightmares, a wave of water crashed into the room, floated the stacks of totes from the wall, and flooded the kitchen floor. If the dream or vision had been real, the totes might have slammed into Bea at the table. Sometimes they were too real. Her shoes had become soaked, or her bedding and pillows drenched more than once.

Breathe. What had she been laughing about? "Oh. When I got the mail out by the street just now, a man and a woman walked by and stopped to chat. Nice people." She slipped the check back into the envelope. "Really nice." She glanced toward the street. "I've never seen them before. They asked me about the neighborhood, the park, even Osceola, and especially the house over there." She pointed. "Mr. Grimes, the guy we were talking about the other day?"

Katty nodded. She picked up another crayon and put it right down again.

"Well, I told them his name and they interrupted me. They got really excited. They do what they called … prayer walking? I guess they walk all over Osceola, or some town, down every street that they can get to. And when they walked by the other day—I don't remember when they said—they were praying in front of Mr. Grimes' house." She dropped the mail onto the table and folded her hands on top. She leaned toward Katty. "They said it was like God called them to that house. When they stopped there, they kept sensing something bad was going on and they asked angels to break down the strongholds there."

"What's a stronghold?" Bea scratched her chin. She had obviously come out of her little world and was listening.

Noell glanced at Katty. She looked perplexed, too—like she didn't understand. How would Gamma have answered that question? "A stronghold. Uhh … it might be like in the war, either … wait." She grabbed her phone and tapped on it. "Okay. Here it says it's a fortress, or a strongly fortified structure for defense. So … if it was winter and we had a bunch of snow outside, we could build a wall of snowballs."

Bea's eyes widened. "Ooo! Okay!" She was fully engaged with their conversation, now.

Katty chuckled. "Hard to tell what she's thinking, right?" She shook her head.

Noell laughed and stood. "Right." She pulled a couple of totes to the center of the room and stacked them. Topped them with boxes forming a wall of sorts. This was fun. She stopped. Gamma used to do this all the time. She did it to explain how a bridge had been built once, and how David had gone up against Goliath, among other things.

Bea stood up, scattering crayons on the floor. "So are we having a snowball fight?"

This kid. So good to laugh. So good to have them here. Them living here for however long they could, made her realize how lonely she had been for the last … since Gamma died. Thankful they had stayed.

Noell stuck her tongue out at her. "You are silly!" She added another tote to make a wall—at least a Bea-sized wall. "This is a wall so we won't get hit with … snowballs, or other things that are painful and dangerous." She peeked into one box on top, rolled her eyes, then closed the cardboard flaps. So much to do— so many boxes.

Grabbing a letter from the trash, she folded the paper into an airplane. She was becoming Gamma, and it felt totally right. She pushed Bea down to hide on the other side of the wall and flew the plane over it. "Did I get you? Are you hit?"

Bea laughed. "No silly. You can't even see me, it … the wall, or the strong wall is too tall." She peeked around the end. "Here I am. Peek-a-boo!"

Noell flew another airplane at just the right time and hit Bea in the tummy.

Bea gripped her chest. "You got me! You killed me." She rolled onto the floor, still holding her sides. "I'm dead."

Katty shook her head and laughed.

Noell folded a newspaper into a nurse's hat and put it on, as she rushed to Bea's side. "Ding, ding, ding. I'm the ambulance."

Bea giggled. "No. You're the nurse." She fell back onto the floor. "I'm bleeding and dying." She closed her eyes then quickly opened them again. "You gonna save me, or what?"

Noell stopped. Something fluttered inside her just now. What was the first thing Gamma had always told her to do? Not run to the doctor. Never run to the hospital. She swallowed. She had forgotten what was probably the most important lesson Gamma ever taught her.

Gamma had always told her to pray first. Doctor later. Pray first. Hospital later.

When she couldn't find her keys—pray. When she got hurt at school—pray. When she had a nightmare—pray.

She slipped the nurse's hat off and knelt on the floor beside Bea. Folding her hands, she closed her eyes. "Lord. Please make Bea get better. Please heal little Bea. In Jesus' name, Amen."

A tiny hand tapped her on her knee.

She opened her eyes and Bea climbed onto her lap.

"I'm all better. Thank you Nurse Noell."

Noell shook her head and hugged Bea hard. "And thank you, Jesus." She wanted to cry. Gamma was here. Gamma used to pray with her all the time and she might have prayed *once* since Gamma died. Once. Now, maybe twice. "Oh, Gamma."

Bea's head popped up. When she saw Noell's face and tears, her expression crumpled and she burst out with a wail.

"Gamma, I'm sorry. I forgot to pray to Jesus." Noell's heart broke. "You always taught me to do that and I forgot." She pushed Bea's hair out of her eyes. "I know it was just playing— making our stronghold, but God was teaching us something."

Bea's eyes grew wide.

Katty scooted onto the floor beside them.

They all sat in a huddle. "God, please help us. We were just playing that Bea got shot, but please help us remember to pray to

You ... for everything. Please help us live together like You want us to. Please give us peace. Please help us know you more. In Jesus' name. Amen."

No sound. No one talked.

Bea stroked Noell's thick, blond braid that trailed around her neck, onto her front.

Katty rubbed Bea's back and wiped away tears from Noell's eyes.

Noell glanced up at the stronghold. "Sooo that's a stronghold. If we stay behind it, it protects us. Right Bea?"

Bea nodded.

Katty tilted her head. "But what did those people mean by a stronghold at that guy's ... uh, Mr. Grimes' house?"

Noell looked up at the wall they'd built. "Wait. That's a stronghold at the bad guys." She glanced toward Mr. Grimes' house, down the street, and zoned for a minute. Too many visuals played in her mind—she'd been in his house when she was younger, she knew the truth about him—both in his faking needing a walker and in the evil intentions of his heart. She'd even seen a demon rise up behind him as he had reached for her.

Katty gently touched Noell's arm. "Are you okay, Noell? Your face ... it—"

Bea broke in. "It looks scared." She cupped Noell's face in her little hands, making her look into her eyes. "You are scared, Noell."

Noell blinked and looked at Katty. "How old is this kid? She's always so mature for her age. She's like an adult right now." Back to Bea, then Katty. "If I remember right, Gamma talked about strongholds ... like when the enemy—"

"The emeny? Enemy? The bad guys? Like in Phil? He's my emeny ... en-em-y." Bea rubbed her shoulders. "He hurt me. He threw me." She looked at Katty. "Threw me against ... the wall?"

Noell guessed that Bea could fake a lot—like fake wanting a

nap when they needed to go to a doctor's appointment, or fake a pout to get her way.

But right now, Noell knew for sure. This little kid had been through terrible things already at her age. How to explain this? She traced Bea's arm. "You know what an enemy is, Bea?"

Bea nodded, her face very serious, her mouth almost quivered. "An enemy is someone who wants to hurt people." She sucked in a deep breath—almost a sob. "Phil tried to burn me on the slide. He threw me against the wall." She pointed at the wall near them. "Not that wall. The wall at our trailer house. That wall."

Noell stole a look at Katty's face, who was nodding at her.

This was for real.

She slowly shook her head and tucked Bea's head under her chin. "Yes, Bea. Phil might be your daddy, but right now, he's your enemy. And sometimes that enemy tries to steal us."

TWENTY-SEVEN

Kadash moved back to the kitchen. It was getting crowded in the entrance. Very interesting. Katty's mother came to visit. He and the angels knew Katty and Bea. They had fought battles on their behalf many times and if this was Katty's mother, then she was welcome here. Kadash didn't have anything against her.

As soon as she and her demons floated inside, another couple demons flew to the living room. Extra help. Evil drew in evil. Several more positioned themselves outside the windows as if to guard the humans or to prevent anything outside from seeing inside.

It didn't matter. Kadash was inside and he could see.

But he was always locked into never interfering with the humans. Ever.

He was outnumbered, for sure—the only angel on the property. There must be a sign outside that welcomed every hissing demon covered with scales.

Mr. Grimes turned to follow Louise into the room. "Well, well. Okay then." He picked up her hands in his and looked into her eyes. "I just laid out a banquet of food in the kitchen there. Would you like to take part, or do you have other plans?"

She wiggled her way into the kitchen and clapped her hands. "Oh, lovely! This looks delish."

He followed her in and dropped a napkin over her arm. "This is only a beginning of wonderful banquets, my dear." He stepped closer. "Potential for … other delicacies to satisfy the appetite live just down this block."

Her eyes met his.

Something clicked between them and Kadesh blinked. He had seen the whole gamut of evil, from the very beginnings with Lucifer, when he was kicked out of heaven. He'd heard of Lucifer's transformation from Michael. Kadesh had never even imagined anything so vile could ever be thought of, by this race of humans or otherwise. And he knew of many different creatures or beings. Probably every kind.

But, Lucifer, now Satan, had developed a whole different range of evil. From very subtle and almost innocent, to very blatant and gruesome. Vile.

What appeared to be growing between this male human and female human bordered on the worst evil he had ever seen—the abuse and desecration of a pure heart. They'd just met. How could this possibly … it was the plan of the enemy … Satan himself.

Louisiana's demons had followed her as had Mr. Grimes' demons. They were all panting—for whatever reasons—as Mr. Grimes and Louisiana offered each other bites of cheese and meat. They had all lined up side-by-side behind the humans—his and hers demons.

The more these two humans interacted, the more the demons manifested. Their eyes widened and turned black. Scales that trailed down each back to a tail, rose and fell, almost with each breath. Putrid smelling mist rose from each demon, a dark cloud cloaked each one.

Almost gave Kadesh shivers to watch, except he knew their real Master.

This might be his only chance. Kadesh stepped forward, positioned himself, and swung his sharp sword, slashing the tails off the demons.

The demons howled. Fire erupted from each mouth and ignited everything on the table.

Any chance for love and sex was gone.

Food was completely consumed.

Human fire was doused with demon tears.

Evening ruined.

TWENTY-EIGHT

Mark was innocent. This time.

Chantelle radioed him about some people causing a ruckus in the north part of town. A legitimate reason to drive past Noell's, where he knew Katty and Bea were staying.

But the radio message had been odd.

"An older man and an older, but fairly attractive woman have been seen running down the street." According to the report, they had been dressed, but not fully. They were probably drunk and evidently very loud.

That might fly on a Saturday night, but it was morning where Mark lived and where the complaint had been filed.

Mark shook his head. For some reason, when he heard the information, he immediately thought of the woman at the convenience store yesterday who had been begging. Well, she was begging. She'd asked for money from him and several others. She was attractive and kind of fit the description.

He stopped at the sign by the convenience store and checked cars parked there as always. License plates were all familiar except one, and he guessed other people were allowed to stop for gas or a rest break.

And there was Guy with his family. Good. The man deserved a day off. Time with a man's family—especially a cop—was well deserved from the deputy's point of view *and* from the spouse's point of view. His wife, Steph, was a one class act. Beautiful. Two kids were way over Mark's goal for number of kids. These two might be okay. He stretched to see them. Jackson, the boy, waved at him and started to unbuckle his seatbelt until his mom caught him.

Guy glanced up from the gas pump and stuck his tongue out at Mark. If Mark hadn't been in a squad car, or his uniform, he would have flipped him off. He pulled in beside Guy's car. "Hey. Whatchu up to? Going places?"

Jackson piped up. "Hi Mark! We're going to the zoo!"

"Mr. Mark to you, Sir." Guy corrected him.

The little girl, Kendall, jabbered a response. So beautiful.

Mark chuckled. "The zoo? I haven't been there in years." Too many trips there when he'd lived in Omaha and his so-called friends from the theater he worked at thought it was funny to do drugs, then tease the animals. He never did it, but he never stopped them, either.

Both Jackson and Kendall got so excited they pulled on their car seats. "Come with us, Mr. Mark. You'd have fun. We'll get hotdogs. Cotton candy."

Steph laughed. "Settle down, guys. He has his uniform on and he's driving what kind of car?"

"Quad car." The little girl pointed. "Mr. Mark working."

Mark nodded. "Yep. Darn. Maybe next time I can. Okay?"

"Okay." They both yelled. They were wound up tight.

Guy stepped closer. "What's on the agenda for you, today?"

Mark pointed up the hill. "I get to check on a complaint that a man and woman were romping in the street up on Ridge Street, scantily dressed, and making a spectacle of themselves just now." He laughed and saluted Guy. "Gotta go."

Guy saluted back. "Be safe. See you tomorrow." He tilted his head that direction. "Uh, that wouldn't be the direction where Miss Katty and Little Bea are staying?"

"Shut-up." Mark configured his hands on the steering wheel to where no one else would figure out that he was flipping Guy off.

Guy laughed. He didn't miss a thing.

Mark waved at the kids and Steph and drove off. He waited at the stop sign for a semi and pickup to pass and drove on up the hill past Hillcrest and the park. At Ridge Street, he checked both ways and turned right, not left, to not be too obvious.

Noell's house was left.

Ridge Street seemed pretty normal so far. He knew almost every car, house, tree, so he might know if things were out of line or different. The only thing that made that difficult, was that he'd driven on this street or every street so many times that a person could become complacent or blind to something different or suspicious. Or like just now, how long had that tree been gone?

The railroad tracks and the highway stopped him and he turned right onto the highway. He hadn't seen one human along that end of the street. Not even one dog or cat.

The street between Hillcrest Nursing Home and the park was always so picturesque, driving from the highway on up the hill north. A bridge allowed the creek to flow through both properties. Huge trees grew in the park, their bark was rough and layered, speaking of the years they had ruled over this ground—probably back to Indian days.

The stories they could tell.

Mark had no doubt that many little kids had climbed the branches.

Back up to Ridge street. Huge old victorian house at the very head of State Street. He'd only been called there once to check on an old dog that had been harassing the neighbor's cat. The dog couldn't have done much damage—he was blind and almost deaf—but the neighbor was sure her cat would be attacked. Poor old dog.

Now left. Things seems quiet until he heard screams through his open window, behind him from the direction of the park.

He didn't even get to drive past Noell's house. He pulled in the driveway of the victorian house and backed into the street, going the way he had come. Down State Street to the park entrance.

Where had the scream come from? It wasn't just a little kid playing. The scream sounded older, terrified. Or worse.

There. The old slide.

A man slid down. At the bottom, when he stood up, he only had his underwear on. Burn marks from going down the slide were visible on his torso and legs.

Mark pulled in at the picnic building and watched. Where had the scream come from?

A woman—that same woman from the convenience store— slid down next. She just had her underwear on, too. At the bottom of the slide stood a little boy, possibly traumatized by the man and woman. His eyes were wide open and he seemed to be crying. The man had hold of his shirt collar and when the woman landed at the bottom of the slide, she stepped over and grabbed the boy's arm.

Mark called in to Chantelle. "Hey, I found the man and woman. They are at the park and I'm getting out. Might be drunk or high. There is a little boy that they seem to be hanging onto. Did the caller say anything about him?"

"No. Are there any visible weapons? Be careful. The complaint was specific about the fact that they might be danger-ous." She paused. "There isn't a little boy." Her mom instincts rose up. "They might be kidnapping him."

Mark went on alert. "Right." He snickered. "I don't think there are any weapons. They are both in just underwear, so I'd be able to see a gun."

Chantelle paused. No response. Then. "You … you mean like he's in his skivvies? And she's in her—"

"Yup. That." He opened his car door, timed with the couple's laughter, so they might not realize they were caught. "Send back-up, please."

As Mark walked toward the couple, the little boy saw him first and jumped. Instinctively, Mark had his hand on his gun. The little boy screamed, wiggled out from the woman's grip, and ran up the hill. Maybe he lived nearby. Hopefully he would find his way home. After Mark detained the couple, he'd have to find out where the boy lived.

The man had climbed up the ladder and begun to slide down when he finally spied Mark approaching. What a picture of an old bull. He tried to stop himself by sticking his legs out over the edges but one foot caught on a support bar and twisted him over the edge. He fell in the weeds on the ground with a groan.

"What'd you do, Stupid? Can't go down a slide by yourself anymore?" The woman slapped him on the butt and laughed.

Didn't this guy usually use a walker? Mark had seen him many times and many places using one and acting like he was an invalid. He might just be one now, after falling off the slide. His walker might end up being legitimate.

And wasn't this the woman he'd seen at the convenience store begging? She seemed to show up many places. And evidently Milton hadn't pulled his weight or made the right donation, because here she was with a different man, altogether.

Sheriff Dennison pulled into the park beside Mark's squad car. Good. The top dog was back-up.

The woman slapped the man again and tried to drag him to his feet when she saw Mark and the sheriff. She dropped the man and tried to run, except he caught her by the heel and she fell down beside him.

"Hey, Mr. Grimes." Dennison pulled his beat stick and whapped it again his other hand. "Where's your walker? You get healed from your diseases, your disabilities?" He glanced at Mark.

Yep. Get them handcuffed.

Mark grabbed the woman's hand before she could get away and pulled it behind her back. She kicked him, missed his groin, and lost her balance. Dang. Her underwear slipped as she struggled to get free, exposing more skin than he wanted to see. Mark clicked a handcuff on one wrist and avoided her slug from her other fist. He grabbed it as she swung and clicked the handcuff around the other wrist behind her back.

She kicked him, only this time he caught her foot and yanked it sideways, making her fall into the sand. That couldn't feel good on bare skin.

"Had enough?" He yanked her upright and dragged her to his squad car. She kicked Mr. Grimes as they passed him. Dennison had rolled him to his stomach, his face in the dirt and handcuffed him.

Mark pushed her into his squad car, holding her head from bumping it as she clambered in.

"You don't know who I am." She struggled against him as he reached across her belly and buckled her in. She bit his arm as he leaned in.

"Ouch! No I don't, but I'm pretty sure we will, in a couple minutes." He checked his arm. Blood. He'd have to swab his car seats with Pine Sol and his arm with alcohol or maybe Chantelle would have a suggestion.

"I'm cold. I need a blanket."

Mark snorted. He'd been trained to always respect the prisoner—they were innocent until proven guilty. But he could tell she was up to something; she was trying to distract him and escape. "You should have thought of that when you and your ... your boyfriend there ran outside half-naked." Or distract him to get money, like she had at the convenience store. He guessed Phil, Bea's dad, wasn't the only evil one.

Dennison walked over. Mr. Grimes was locked in his squad car. "Hey, let me take her, too. Tyler can help me unload when I get back to the department. You go on about your rounds and I'll see you back there."

"Okay." Mark helped Dennison transfer her to his car. "You sure? She's sneaky." He blew out a breath and smiled. "Not that you can't handle it, I just … she's just—" He glanced at his arm.

"She do that to you?" He pointed at Mark's car. "First aid. Splash some peroxide on it before it gets infected. There are stories, people have done strange things. And I know. I've got her in leg restraints and handcuffs. The man is so possessed that he tried to talk me out of restraining him. He has double-locked leg restraints, plus waist-belt chain restraint and handcuffs." Dennison glanced back at his car. "I think they're restrained."

Mark chuckled. "I should have never questioned you, Sheriff." He turned to go.

"This may sound crazy, Mark, but I want you to drive by Noell Carpenter's house and check on Katty and Bea."

"What?" Mark was sure he'd heard Dennison wrong. "I'm sorry. What'd you just say?"

"Those girls have been through a lot—both of them—and we need to follow up and make sure they're okay and recovering well." He glanced at his squad car. "Something about those two …." Back to Mark. "Just check."

Mark blinked. He stared at Dennison. Was he teasing? Was he serious?

Dennison stepped closer to Mark, checked the prisoners over his shoulder, and stood facing him. "I'm not teasing and I'm not making fun of you." He visibly swallowed. "I see something between you two—you three—and God only knows the future, but nurture what might be developing there."

A face morphed over Sheriff's. Uncle Ted? Sheriff's voice even took on tones of Uncle Ted's voice.

What? Dennison seemed to be talking double talk. Or like a

grandpa talking to a grandson. Mark swallowed. Or like Uncle Ted, who became Mark's rehab mentor—and father, and grandfather, and brother.

Whew.

"Okay. I'll check on them."

TWENTY-NINE

Mark tapped the steering wheel. He blew out a deep breath. Blew out another. He wiped the beads of sweat gathering on his upper lip. It wasn't summer anymore.

He watched Dennison drive away. Those two prisoners were the unsuspecting troublemaker kind. They didn't drive loud vehicles. They didn't throw loud parties or invite high school kids and give them booze.

They might even be more dangerous than the usual suspect who walked into a shopping mall with a gun and opened fire on the shoppers loitering there. Those people were dangerous— horribly so. Or the terrorists that were always in the news— which made them seem very dangerous, but very far away and not in the local park.

The guy was for sure the man Mark had seen using a walker. Where had he seen him from time-to-time? Post office probably. Most likely. The post office was right next to the sheriff's department, so that might be where.

He probably abused every disability insurance, each parking handicap sticker or tag, every natural kindness other people bestowed on handicapped and disabled people. But now he was no longer eligible. Mark had seen him bounce from the slide and run up the ladder to go down again.

Busted in more ways than that.

The two of them had to be on something—some drug. They didn't seem drunk, just wired and without good judgement of any kind.

Duh. Running almost naked in the park.

Sheriff was long gone and Mark still sat at the park, tapping the steering wheel. He shifted into drive and slowly drove through the rest of the park to the exit—which was the entrance, too.

What if she wasn't at Noell's anymore?

What if she didn't want … wait. Sheriff had told him to check on them. And just the other day—yesterday—he'd seen her, Bea, and Noell at Mrs. B's. She had seemed interested then.

It was official police business.

He turned right out of the park and on up the hill to Ridge Street. The house at the top of the hill was a huge, Victorian home full of the history of Polk County and of Osceola. Many people had lived there and it had stood time and many renovations.

Left on Ridge Street. Noell's house could be seen from the corner where he was now.

Quit being such a chicken.

Go check on them.

He wiped his forehead and pulled over to park in front. Nice house, too, although not as large as the big Victorian. Noell had lived there most of her life with her grandma, but Mark didn't know much else. It was said that the house was full of stuff, like a hoarder, but he didn't know for sure.

He walked up the sidewalk and rang the doorbell.

Nothing. No response.

He knocked and waited.

No one came. Katty's replacement car was there in the driveway, so maybe—

"Hi Mr. Depdy, Sir!" That little voice. Bea. She didn't open the outside screen door. She'd been warned.

"Hi, Bea. Is your mommy home? Or Noell?"

She nodded and grinned. "What are you doing here?" She crossed her arms over her chest. "Are we 'rested?"

"Rested?" He shook his head. "Oh. You mean arrested?" He laughed.

Footsteps tapped on the porch floor and Katty appeared. Noell right behind her.

"Mommy. Mr. Depdy is here." She pointed at him. "He's going to 'rest us."

Katty frowned. "Rest us?"

"Yeah. You know. He has to handcuff us and take us to the … the—"

"The Sheriff's Department?"

"No. The jail."

Katty's eyes blinked and connected with Mark's.

Oh my. Reality was … jail time. Too close to reality and recent situations. Too recent.

Noell rescued Katty and Mark. "Can you come in? We have—"

"Orange juice." Bea jumped up and down. "We have orange juice."

Katty picked her up and laughed.

Oh, such an awkward moment.

Noell pushed the screen door open. "Come on in or the neighbors will think you really did arrest Bea."

"We are cleaning out Gamma's closet … or going through her things and we are … finding some interesting things … in there." Noell motioned for Mark to come on in. "She must have had a leaf collection or something. Very interesting."

Mark stepped inside and immediately his training kicked in.

He gave no indication of what he might be thinking in response to all he saw. Just assess. Only observe and assess. Nothing had prepared him for the state of the inside of the house. Stacks and stacks of totes and boxes lined each wall of the small entry porch.

Whew.

Noell chuckled. "I know. It's startling, right?" She walked on through another door into a living space and dining room. The only thing that helped him decide that was a huge beautiful red leather sofa along one wall to his right. Otherwise, it just held boxes and household things all around the rooms. He followed on through the dining room into a kitchen.

Ahh. This really looked like a kitchen. Still littered and full of books and some totes and boxes, but not at the level of the previous rooms.

"Have a seat, Deputy." Noell pulled out a chair.

Katty and Bea followed. They were very quiet all of a sudden.

"Need something to drink?" Noell was on it. She didn't let the fact that a deputy had just entered her home make her nervous. She stepped to the refrigerator and opened it. Interesting. She seemed to wince but recovered quickly.

"No. No. I just stopped by … uh, Sheriff asked me to stop and check on you, Katty. See how you're getting along, after … we saw you last." Bea's ears were always flapping and open. Had to be careful what he said around her. She was a smart little girl, too. She picked up on vibes around her.

Noell smiled. She sat in the chair opposite him. She glanced over at Katty and Bea. "Yeah. We were just cleaning and going through some things in Gamma's closet. She was a collector for sure." She swept her arm around the kitchen and then pointed to the rooms they'd just walked through. "As you can see."

"Yeah. But you should see Noell's room." Bea pipped up. "Just a bed."

"Yeah. That's me. I am very much a germaphobe, living in a hoarder house. Gamma wasn't always that way, but since Gramps died, I guess she still went to sales and thrift shops and couldn't part with anything that maybe he might have liked or used."

Thankful for Noell. She saved the moments. Good go-between.

"We all keep too much stuff." Mark tried to help her soften the awkward situation. Katty wasn't entering in the conversation at all. No help at all. "This is a great house, though, Noell." He nodded. "Nice of you to open it to Katty and Bea."

"Well, they're family."

"Wait." He pointed from Noell to Katty and Bea. "You're related?"

Katty was clearly blushing.

Bea nodded. "Yep. She's my … she's my …."

Katty snuggled into Bea. "Noell is our cousin."

At least Katty was talking.

"Cousins. That's awesome. I don't have any cousins." That he knew of. He definitely knew how family lines went and how people could pop up and claim they were related and might even actually *be* related. "I don't even have a brother or sister."

Bea lowered her head. "I don't, too. No brother. I have Boy." She shook her head. "No sisters."

Nobody said anything. All quiet. Nobody stepped up to save the awkward moment.

"Well … I guess that's what we have in common, Bea." Mark reached over and stroked her hair and tweaked her nose.

She looked up at him from under Katty's arm. "In common?'

Careful Mark. She picked up on everything. "Yeah. I don't have brothers or sisters and you don't have any either."

Bea thought a minute, gazing at him. "Like … we're the same."

Mark swallowed. Katty and Noell didn't help at all. In fact, their faces in his peripheral appeared to be no help. Noell bit her lip. Katty buried her face in Bea's hair. He couldn't even see her face.

Chickens.

It was just Bea and him.

"Well, kind of." He smiled and took her on his lap. He shouldn't be doing this. She didn't hesitate at all. She almost helped him by giving a bounce as he lifted her. "Yeah, see. Even though I'm a guy and you're a girl." He swallowed. Dang. The sex conversation about cats a few weeks ago. "That makes us different, right?"

She nodded.

Before she could answer, because he was terrified of what she might say and how he'd have to answer her, he jumped in. "But we are the same in ways, too."

She nodded. Her eyes were locked onto his. Dang. He wanted more of this kid. He wanted to be free to love her and talk to her. Tuck her in at night.

Gulp.

"Well, how are you liking living here at Noell's?" Sounded like an interview. He tried to keep this conversation and visit to business but Bea made it hard. He didn't want to say too much, but he wanted to say more. He'd rather play and laugh with her, than think about how they might be doing after her mommy had been in jail. That was important, too, but he wanted more—he wanted to ask her what she wanted for lunch and fix it for her, for them. How did they like their steaks cooked? Did they like to go boating? He didn't even have a boat, so where did that come from?

Why had Sheriff even sent him here? They were fine. This didn't need to happen.

Except …

Katty finally lifted her head and looked him in the eyes. "It's awesome here." She met Noell's gaze and then back to him.

"And yes, we are related. Noell is my cousin. Her mom … " She stopped and checked with Noell.

"It's okay, Katty." She turned to Mark. "Katty's mom is my Gamma's sister. But we didn't get too much time together because—"

"Because my mom was brutal and didn't let me play over here. For some reason, Noell's Gamma was nice, creative, religious." Katty lowered her eyes to the floor. "And my mom went … evil."

Mark tried not to respond. Evil? A face morphed over Katty's own. That woman in the park. No way. Couldn't be her mom. Just a resemblance. He thought of the woman in the park just because he had just seen her, just arrested her.

Damn.

THIRTY

After Mark left, Katty stayed seated at the kitchen table.

Mark.

And Baby Bea. She'd followed him to the front door with Noell. Bea loved him.

Sigh. Katty blinked and squirmed on her chair. The creak of the chair seemed to talk to her—convicting her. Maybe she loved him, too. Or at least she was attracted to him. But who was she to be loved by a man like Mark?

Mom was back. Katty's chest caved in on itself and she could hardly breathe. The stuff Mom had just screamed at her was still true.

Something she hadn't felt in a long time crushed her heart. An undeniable need to run away from Mom, even from Noell—everything, everyone. Maybe even Bea. Fear enveloped her. Strangled her. Chained her. Those words wrapped around her and choked her. "You are a slut. Whore. You always were a slut."

Choked her once more.

She was right back to when she was four years old, or eight—a little girl. Or sixteen. Yeah. She'd lived out those words. Intimidated. Terrified.

Katty shivered, as memories crawled in.

Broken crayons.

Bruised arms.

Burned legs.

Broken heart.

Oh, she wanted a drink. Tears threatened. She patted her pockets. No little bottles. She'd been sober for what—a couple days, a week? Not long enough to build the strength and determination she'd seen in people who'd been free for years.

Why did Mom have to come back?

Noell's words still rang in the other room. Other than Mrs. T, she'd never heard anyone pray. Oh, she'd heard little Bea. Her "Daddy" prayers were cute. But maybe—after hearing Noell's prayer just now—maybe they were more than just words—more than cute. Maybe Bea's prayers were grown-up or … more real and powerful than a preacher's prayers.

Definitely more powerful than her own.

She glanced out the window to the back yard. Those words, "Help us live together like …" She'd already forgotten the exact words, but they were close to … like good people. No. Like God wants us to live together.

What did that mean? What would God say to her now about how to live? Mom always told her she was a slut and she probably was. Absolutely had been one. Always had been and always would be.

But …

"Mommy?" Baby voices.

"Oh Bea—not now."

How would God want them to live? How could she even know anything God wanted?

She didn't have any idea.

"Mommy?" Whispered voices.

But Bea did. Bea already knew about God. She knew Him like He was real. Like He was actually sitting right beside her.

The times Katty had quietly hidden outside Bea's bedroom door and listened.

"Mommy?" Bea started to run into the kitchen, but Noell caught up with her and stopped her.

Katty shook her head, swayed back and forth. The tree branches and leaves outside swayed almost along with her. How could God be real? How could He give them peace, like Noell had asked?

How could she be different than a slut?

Had she ever felt or known peace? The only place of solace, or place of peace, or refuge she had known, other than booze and drugs, had appeared recently—Gamma's closet.

No. There was her treehouse—back then—as that little girl. That had been her refuge from Mom's abuse, her words. Even though Katty didn't know who had built it or who had played in it before her, it was a place of quiet solitude where she could be herself, where she could find herself in her childhood art.

She wiped her eyes, ignored all around her. Bea clamored for attention and Noell tried to contain her.

Something stirred in Katty.

She jumped from the chair and ran from the room.

"Mommy?" Little clouds floated in behind her. Oh no. The babies.

As she rushed through the dining room, a mist seemed to surround her. At first she thought it was her imagination or was it smoke? Smoke terrified her, so she stopped and sniffed. Just Noell's house smells—not smoke. She'd seen fires destroy whole houses. The cloud seemed to grow, rise like a fog, from the corners of the room as she rushed through.

But when she reached the living room, the cloud expanded into the whole room. It followed her. Voices behind her became louder. "Mommy. Mommy." Bea's voice was discernible, but there seemed to be other voices mixed in—like a little kid choir —all crying, "Mommy, Mommy."

The baby voices had followed her here.

Was that allowed? Shouldn't those baby voices stay where they belonged at the trailer, or at least where they started harassing her? Why? How could they follow her here? Shouldn't they have stayed where they first appeared? At the painting on the wall back at her trailer? Weren't there rules?

Noell, still behind in the dining room, shushed Bea. "Maybe she has to potty, Bea."

God bless Noell.

Crazy. God bless Noell? God bless anyone? Katty had never entertained that thought in all her life. "God bless her." Hearing the words out loud right now startled her. Crazy. Crazy. Baby voices following her everywhere and clouds appearing inside a house. Crazy. She'd assumed that baby angels and voices and wild things happening would not follow her here to Noell's house. That evil belonged back at her trailer house, not here. It had been the booze.

But, she was wrong.

As she reached the doorway to Gamma's room, the mist divided into shapes. She stopped short. Her throat locked up. A scream wanted to burst out, but something choked her. Belch. She swallowed. No!

Her legs trembled beneath her. She almost collapsed, but something touched her shoulders, supporting her. Open her eyes —close her eyes—keep her eyes wide open. Terrified if she saw what it was. Terrified if she didn't.

The shapes morphed into pillars or tall columns of clouds. Behind her, several rose in the living room, in the dining room. Many tall pillars or statues lined the walls of each room. The pillars grew taller, as big as the pillars on the front of the court house, downtown. Through the ceilings in each room. What might have been heads rose through the ceiling and through the roof to outside.

Horror story in Noell's house.

Pressure at her back seemed to push her into Gamma's room. She stumbled over the threshold. The closet door was open and the light was on. Had she left the light on? Or wait. The lightbulb was off, but light filled the little room. What? Where was the light coming from? Now it appeared to be more than a closet—it had expanded into a room somehow—a room big enough to be another bedroom. Only it wasn't a bedroom. Packed shelves, journals everywhere, framed art filled the room.

But the room had expanded with wall space in between the shelving. Blank walls.

Wait. One had strokes of blue about halfway up the wall, from side-to-side. The wall space was only four or five feet wide and floor to ceiling. But there was a wide swipe of blue halfway up the wall … that almost … appeared to become wider, thicker, the more she looked at it.

Like someone was—

"Mommy!" That was Bea. No question. "Did you go potty?"

Bea stepped into the room, then to the closet.

Noell was right behind her. "I tried to catch her, so you could have some …." Her eyes widened as she glanced at the closet. "Gamma's closet." She seemed to freeze in the doorway. Her eyes grew wider as she scanned each wall, her mouth hung open.

Katty turned and nodded. The pillars were still there in the bedroom, only now they had taken on definition. They were still as huge, but they resembled … men? Lining each wall?

Katty froze. Like the man she had seen in her trailer house. Had Bea called him her angel? These guys were almost the same. Their eyes were soft, tender. Loving. But each one was just as muscular as the one in her trailer. A sort of light emanated from them.

Some wore creamy-white robes with beautiful leather brown belts around their waist. Various things dangled from the belts— little leather-like bags, daggers maybe. One dangled things that resembled instruments—stringed wooden things that Bea would love to play with but that she would also break.

Swords—Katty took a step back.

"Mommy what did you do?"

Bumped into Bea.

"Katty, what happened? How did the closet get bigger?"

Noell.

Katty swallowed. She wiped her eyes, looked at the wall, then wiped them again. The blue on that wall had darkened and widened.

Her knees buckled and down she went, landing on a fluffy, cushy rug that she didn't remember. Beautiful. Soft. Colors of green, blue, purple, colors she didn't recognize. The fluff went deeper than any rug or blanket she'd ever seen.

"I … I don't know."

Bea snuggled close onto Katty's lap. "Mommy, who are the big guys?"

Katty blinked. "You can see them, too?" She started, then stared at Noell. "Honest. I haven't had anything to drink … except what you give me. Except what you have here in your house."

Noell slowly knelt beside Katty and Bea. She stared at the walls, at the shelving, the art, the journals. She met Katty's gaze, but then her eyes jumped right back to the walls. Her arm slowly rose, a finger pointing at the wall closest to her. "The walls. The shelves." Back to Katty. "I've never seen any of this." Her chin quivered. "I never knew this was here. I never saw the door there." She reached behind her, pointed at the door, but in her obvious confusion missed it. "Gamma never showed it to me." Noell shuddered and tears streamed down her cheeks.

Katty just about replied to her, but a stripe of green appeared on the wall, just below the blue. Another swipe, wider. It seemed like someone was painting it as Katty looked on.

"Mommy. Pretty." Bea stood right in front of the wall, facing it.

Another swipe of green.

Bea pointed. "Mommy. Did you do that?" Bea pointed again, then turned to Katty. "That's like your paintings at home. On the wall at our house." Bea faced the wall again.

Another stripe of green.

The more they watched, the more the wall sported different paint. More stripes appeared.

Katty shivered and glanced around the closet and the room. The men were still there. In fact, there were more than before. Behind and between the ones who had already been there. More than before. Almost frightening.

Except … Bea could see them.

Katty pointed at the men. "Bea? You can see them, too? Those men?"

Bea barely took her eyes off the painted wall to glance at the men, like she saw them everyday. "Yeah, Mommy. They're always there."

What?

Bea stared at the painting taking shape, then back to the men. "They're called angels, Mommy. An-gels." She said it slowly and deliberately. "An-gels."

One waved at her and she waved back.

Katty gasped and fell backwards.

Noell jumped and caught her. "What, Katty? What happened?"

The room spun, like she might black out. That had happened plenty of times when she had been drinking. Drunk. Now sober? Still learning the difference. But this was different than drunk. She'd been sober for a few days. Maybe not completely healed, but able to function.

"I … I don't know." She drilled Noell's eyes. "Can you see

the closet?" She pointed in the bedroom. "Can you see those guys?"

Noell's eyes bounced around the closet. "Yes. No. Men?" She checked around again and then back into the bedroom. "But this doesn't make sense." She pointed at the corners in the closet. "It's too big. It shouldn't be this big. This part of the house doesn't stick out this far outside." She rotated. "This doesn't make sense."

Katty was in a fog, herself. She nodded. "It wasn't like this before." Her eyes met Noell's. "Was it? When we were in here before? It wasn't this big." She jumped up and pointed at the painting on the wall. "Can you see that?"

"What?" Noell glanced where Katty pointed. "That painting?' Noell sat beside Katty and Bea. "It's beautiful. The sunset or sunrise—either one—the reds and blues and purples—are beautiful."

Katty stared at Noell. "Reds? Purples?"

"Yeah. And the tree is amazing."

"It's like the tree on our wall, Mommy." Bea tapped Katty's arm. "Like the one you painted on our wall." She peered closer at the wall. "Mommy, there's a bird in a nest." Bea stepped closer and touched the wall.

Katty jumped up. "Don't touch, Bea. It's probably not dry yet. You might smear it."

Noell stepped close to the wall and touched it, too. "It's dry."

Katty wiped her eyes, her cheeks again, and pointed. "But … the blue and green are just going on." She gulped. "There's no other—"

"Just going on?" Noell touched it again. "It's dry. Like it's been finished for a long time."

Katty shook her head. "No. There goes another stripe of green." She waved her hand back and forth, following the flow of the paint. "And now there's a blob of purple above the blue."

Noell shook her head and gently let her fingers follow the

wall. "No, it's dry. It's finished." She stepped back. "It's beautiful."

What? Noell saw a completed painting—even Bea saw it—and she herself could only see stripes of paint actually going on?

Wait. She was literally watching a painting happen right now.

Impossible.

Who was painting it?

It was still freaking her out that there were rows of men or, according to Bea, angels still standing—no, lining each wall.

"Noell. I can only see the purple." Her chin quivered, as she stood. Another stripe went on the wall. And another. Now orange. She stepped closer and shook her head. "I am literally seeing it get painted as I stand here. I can't see a brush or hand, but it's ..." Her face crumpled. Tears dripped. Weeping, she pointed at the painting, following each stripe with her hand as it happened. "More there now." Wiped her face. "Orange. Red."

She turned to Noell. "You see the full dried painting." She checked the wall again. A stripe of brown made what appeared to be the trunk of a ... tree. "And I see it being painted?"

She stared at Noell's face and promptly sat back down on the fluffy rug on the floor.

Bea snuggled on her lap.

Noell stared back, then sat beside them.

Who else was here?

THIRTY-ONE

Jasper stood guard over Katty, Noell, and Bea in what was known as Gamma's room to the humans, but as Command Central to the angels. This battle required more than the usual battalions and weapons.

Every wall in the bedroom was lined with beings: pillars of light, humans who had lived on this earth before but had gone to heaven, and every kind of angel in the Kingdom of God. There were angels of gold—all gold from head to toe—who carried lines or strips of golden pipes in each hand. Humans might laugh to think of those pipes as weapons, but Jasper had witnessed first-hand how effective they were.

Huge, muscular angels stood in line with beings of light, with tiny baby angels. The wall of beings became a rich tapestry of colors: gold, white, red, orange, brown, green, blue. More than Jasper could name.

A beautiful sight to see. More than just the paint that the humans might be seeing. Very few humans had ventured beyond their human ability to see into this realm of the Kingdom.

Bea's eyes were wide open.

He grinned at her.

She blinked and chattered, pointing at him, at this being, at that angel. A golden glow surrounded every part of her. Outlined her.

Jasper had seen it all from earthly standards *and* from a kingdom point of view. This was the most beautiful picture—a visual of light from a pure heart. Someone was praying for this child, for this family and it was visible in the light around Bea and from her eyes.

Jasper shook his head, as a deep breath escaped his chest.

Katty just shook her head. She didn't see—yet.

Noell had a very deep sense of what might be going on around her. She had an unusual gift. Molecules deposited from another human's hands or body onto any physical object spoke to her, giving her flashes of their life, words spoken by them. She visibly saw parts of that person's life—bad and good.

As Jasper surveyed the property, an interesting mix of spiritual beings appeared in the neighborhood around Noell's house, at the boundary line. Boundaries were very important. A boundary declared ownership—where it began and where it ended.

Jasper had called in several more angels when Katty's mom came to visit. Not in fear. Never that, but because the demons with her mom needed to face reality. They needed to know that Katty was under the Father's care and no longer free for them to harass or to draw her into the enemy's camp.

She was no longer theirs.

Unless.

The humans had free will.

Prayer made all the difference.

But Father had always demanded that no angel could tamper with human will.

Seeds had been planted, as in Katty hearing Noell's prayer and pondering the words and how God wanted humans to live. Those seeds began to sprout tiny roots in her heart.

Prayer warrior Mrs. T prayed without ceasing in her rooms at Hillcrest. Many of the tasks that Jasper had been sent out to do were directed by her prayers. Prayers that she knew and directed as a daughter of the Most High God, but many, as she prayed in her prayer language, were directed by the Father's heart.

She'd sit in her chair after returning to her rooms from physical therapy, or a meal and mumble her prayers. If Clarence had clients, she'd close the door between the rooms and pray through the appointment as the client and Clarence talked. Sometimes Harold Dexter would join them as the other member of the agency. All got prayed for.

The enemy didn't have a chance against the kingdom of God with prayer warriors like Mrs. T.

More angels flew into the area around Noell's house and neighborhood.

Jasper nodded to each one as they passed him. They nodded back and shook what they carried—heavy golden chains. As each angel shook their chains, the sound echoed all across time—maybe even some humans who had learned to quiet their souls heard the rattling, the clunking. That sound stirred the battle cries of millions of intercessors. The sound of chains rattling and clattering meant the enemy would be bound.

It also meant the followers of the Lord Jesus Christ would be freed.

Katty would be freed.

It was all a process in the natural world, the physical world. But in the Kingdom of God, it was finished. The Great Commander Eternal One had spoken. He had given His life for their freedom.

Each angel flew deep into the realm, under layers of sin, uncovered hidden generations of bondage, stirred up a horrid stench, pushed aside blockages and carnage until they reached the underlying roots.

Each angel flew out from the muck, their chains circled around every part of a demon—a prisoner bound.

These demons were unusual from what most demons appeared like—the usual talons, horns, scales and mostly upright in stature—different than what humans or others might think of.

These demons were long and threadlike, fibrous beings that were very difficult to fully capture, for they were long and snakelike, branching out. An angel might tie up what he thought was the demon, to have an arm or leg part slither and pull away. Slimy buzzards. Slimy and slick. Just when the angel might think it had captured one, the end of another slithered out of the angel's hold on it.

The head itself was strange. Almost cat-like but longer. Very fibrous, stringy. It's eyes appeared like slits between fibers.

Just like a vine might grow, arms and legs and other extremities grew out of the main root-like body, again making it hard to contain the creatures. Also making it easy for the demon to root into a human's life, into a human body. All it took was one hair-like tendril of an arm or leg to root into a human's thoughts or emotions, or for the human to open their minds to thoughts of fear, selfishness, or anger. Then a tiny root would slither into that open gateway. If the human didn't know The Eternal One, Jesus Christ, and didn't recognize the evil presence and cast it out, the demon could probe deeper, bury itself and root its tendrils into the mind and heart, the life of the human until that human was fully under the control of the enemy.

Jasper watched, as Katty entered the closet again, this time with paints and brushes. She pulled a brush out, dipped it into the blue blob of paint on the palette, and touched it to the wall.

At exactly the same moment, Gamma appeared with her paints and brushes and gently daubed her brush into blue paint and knelt up to the wall, her brush poised to paint.

Gamma over Katty or Katty over Gamma.

As one.

THIRTY-TWO

Bea watched as Mommy dipped the brush into the blob of blue paint and held it to the wall.

"Noell, are you sure it's okay if I do this?" Mommy lowered her hand and turned to Noell. "Is it okay if I paint on your wall?" She shook her head and waved her hand over the wall already painted. "Not over that painting." She moved to a blank wall. "Here. Is that okay?"

Bea held her breath. She already knew it wasn't okay to draw on the walls in her own room, back in their trailer. Even worse to paint on somebody else's walls. Mommy might get in trouble with Noell and Bea loved Noell.

Noell smiled and stepped closer to Mommy.

Oh-oh.

All Bea had ever known was hitting. Was Noell—

Noell hugged Mommy. She pulled away to look at her face. "Of course this is okay. This is your house, in a way, too. Gamma was your aunt, but will always be your Gamma. She was so much older than your mom, so she's kind of like your grandma." She tilted her head.

Bea blew out a breath and picked up a book from the bottom

shelf. It had a black cover, nothing on the front. She flipped it over. Nothing on the back. Just black.

She could still hear Mommy's words from earlier. *Be careful with Gamma's stuff, especially her notebooks and stuff.*

She slowly opened the book, only it was upside-down. Everything was upside-down. Okay. She closed it and turned it over. She opened it again and words flew at her. At first Bea gasped, but as she watched, she wanted to draw everything. "Pretty." Pictures and drawings flowed off the pages. Letters of the alphabet—most she knew—flowers, trees, rainbows, birds and kitties. Musical notes—one of her favorite Daryl and Dumpty books was about music. Everything hovered above the book, sparkling, dancing.

Bea touched the drawing softly, carefully. Colors. Gamma must have liked colors, because as she flipped through more pages, colors spilled out. Every color. Gamma liked every color in Bea's crayon box.

Certain words Bea could read, like baby, or love, or stop. She knew stop from reading the stop signs along roads. At street corners.

Other words, not so much. Gamma had a funny way of writing, all pretty, all curvy lines. Mommy wrote in squares or lines or boxes. Gamma wrote words like plants grew—all running in lines together.

Noell had taught Bea, just yesterday, about plants growing right outside the house. Some Noell liked and wanted to grow— they had pretty pink or yellow flowers. But some she didn't want to grow and she showed Bea how to pull them up. Some of those plants had wound around the plants she *wanted* to keep and those they had pulled off and out of the ground. Weeds, Noell had called them.

Bea shook her head even now as she thought about it. The plants they had pulled out of the ground had flowers, too. Tiny white or pink flowers shaped like little bells. But those were the plants that Noell didn't like or didn't want to grow in her flower beds.

Flower beds.

Bea glanced up at the bed she and Mommy had been sleeping in. Gamma's bed. Beds for sleeping. Beds for plants. Beds to let plants grow in or beds to pull weeds out of.

One bed was comfy with sheets and blankets and Daryl & Dumpty bedspreads and every morning she and Mommy pulled up the covers to the pillows and made the bed—at least they did that at Noell's house.

The other bed was all made of dirt where stuff could grow. Or not. Or be pulled out.

Bea shook her head.

"What Bea?" Noell leaned down, then sat beside Bea on the floor. "Why are you shaking your head?" She combed Bea's hair out of her eyes. "Something in Gamma's journals that you don't like?"

Bea blinked. "Gamma's journals?"

Noell chuckled and tapped the book in Bea's lap. "These are called journals. They are books that Gamma wrote her thoughts down in." She pointed to words. "Here. Or she painted in them. So pretty."

Bea nodded slowly and glanced at the bed. Adults were so confusing. "Is this a painting of her flowers?"

Noell nodded. "Remember when we were outside yesterday and we talked about her flowers?"

Bea nodded. "And we pulled some up."

"Right." Noell stared at the painting of flowers in Gamma's books, her journals. "It's kind of weird to pull some up and leave some."

"Yeah. They all have flowers." Bea pointed to a flower in the journal. She glanced up.

Mommy was painting on the wall. A huge tree was forming,

like it was growing there. "Mommy, is that like the tree you painted on our wall at home? Is it gonna have leaves?"

Only Mommy didn't answer.

Lines of brown flowed from Mommy's brush onto the wall. Branches appeared. They almost grew out of the wall from the paint brush. Large trunk. Bea knew the parts. Then big branches. Then smaller branches, called sticks. She'd also helped Noell pick up dead sticks from the grass and throw them in a bin out back by the shop.

Mommy changed colors to green and leaves grew out of the wall. Pretty green. Some yellow. Blue sky behind. White clouds touched some branches.

Fun to watch Mommy's hand move. She dipped the brush into the paint blobs and touched the wall with the brush and made lines on the wall.

Back and forth.

Again and again.

Deep breath. It was so quiet in Gamma's closet. Safe. Nice.

As Bea stared, another hand painted along with Mommy's. Pretty. Two hands painting. Two brushes painting. Two stripes of brown paint on the wall at the same time.

Another deep sigh.

Two arms moving. Mommy's and another arm. Both painting.

Bea smiled. This was better than watching Daryl & Dumpty on TV.

Another head beside Mommy's, only this head had grey hair and Mommy's was black—no, brown. Mommy's hair was longer.

Another body, legs, and feet slowly appeared. Pretty white dress with all colors of flowers splattered over it: blues, greens, purples, and oranges. All kinds of colors. All kinds of flowers.

Bea leaned forward as the head turned toward her. The lady smiled at her, then turned back to the wall to paint again.

Mommy was still painting the tree and now leaves. The lady painted the same leaves right with Mommy.

Someone was singing, too. Not Mommy. Mommy never sang.

The lady turned her head to Bea again and sang pretty. Some words that Bea didn't know but reminded her of Mrs. T's baby talk when she prayed. Only this was a song.

Bea's heart was happy and full. Pretty lady. Pretty song.

Wait!

Bea jumped and pushed Noell away. Where was that picture?

"What's wrong Bea?" Noell stood with her, catching the book from Bea's lap.

Where was that picture? Every wall in Gamma's bedroom had pictures. Bea had studied each one. Not that one. Not this one.

"Bea. What are you doing?" Even Mommy stopped painting.

The lady didn't stop painting or singing.

"The lady that's painting with you. She's singing, too. She's in a picture … somewhere."

"Lady painting with … me?" Mommy shook her head and glanced at Noell. "There's no one here but you, me and Noell."

Next room. The dining room. Pictures were all over the room, even behind stacks of boxes. Not in the room with the big red sofa.

Bea ran into the kitchen, with Noell and Mommy following her. "There!" Bea climbed up on the chair, then the table and sat on it, pulling a photo from off the wall beside the table. That picture was of the lady who was painting and singing. She had on a different dress though than today in the closet. "That's the lady in the closet right now. She's standing beside Mommy. I know beside—what it means. I know above. She was almost with Mommy. She was painting and singing." Bea turned to make sure Mommy and Noell were there. "That's the lady in the closet."

Noell leaned closer. "That's Gamma." She shook her head. "You saw Gamma in the closet painting?" She looked at Mommy. She didn't believe Bea.

Mommy didn't either. She shook her head. "Bea. That's impossible. She's--"

"She's dead. I know."

Noell picked her up and showed her other pictures on the walls. "See here? This is the same lady, only she's—"

"She'd dead. I know."

"Bea. You need to say it nicer. That's Noell's Gamma." Mommy sat down.

Bea lowered her head. "I'm sorry, Noell." Her head popped up again. "But she's in the closet now and she's painting with Mommy." She visibly swallowed and peeked at Mommy. "She's painting with *you*, Mommy. She's painting the tree and leaves too." She slipped down out of Noell's arms. "And she's singing funny words in a song.

Noell's face changed. She sat down beside Mommy.

"And she has a pretty dress on." Bea started to dance and swirl, the picture still in her heart. "It's white." She stopped and looked directly at Mommy and Noell. "I know my colors. It's white with blue, purple, green. Maybe orange too. Big flowers all over that white dress." She clapped her hands. "It's so pretty!" She swirled in a circle and stopped.

Mommy's and Noell's faces were funny. Their eyes were big and their mouths were open. They didn't stop looking at her.

Noell jumped up from her chair and ran out of the room.

"Now you've done it. Bea—"

Noell ran back in the room, her hands pushed out. "No. No. She's fine. I just have to find something." Her eyes were even bigger now. Back into the living room.

Bea swallowed. She was in trouble. Again.

Noell yelled from another room. "Bea come here and help me."

Bea shuffled out of the kitchen, her eyes on the floor. Mommy shook her head. Bea was in trouble.

Noell pulled a box off a stack in the dining room. And another box. She turned as Bea came in the room. "I know what's in these boxes, because I've gone through them and repacked them." She opened one and dug through it.

Bea stood a few steps away from her and tried to calm down. She couldn't stop thinking of times when Mommy had told her to go to her room and she was going to get a spanking—or worse. She wiped her eyes.

Mommy was right behind her.

Noell turned to them. "This is crazy." But she stopped. "Why are you crying, Bea?" Noell reached for her, but Bea pulled away. "You're not in trouble."

Noell was acting funny. Like she had found—like she remembered, or like Mommy when she found her keys. She always screamed. Happy screams.

Noell hugged Bea and took her hand. She pulled her to the cardboard box and closed it, flap over flap. She pulled down another one, opened it, and handed some clothes to Bea. Lots of clothes, dresses, shirts. Lots of colors. Bea sat on the floor and scooted away.

"Bea. You're still not sure. You don't trust me?"

Bea just sat, buried under the clothes.

Noell shrieked and slowly pulled something from the box. "Bea. Look."

It was the dress. The dress the lady, Gamma had on in the closet. Bea reached out for it. Was it real?

Noell brought it to Bea and knelt in front of her. She turned to Mommy. "Katty. This is Gamma's dress."

"That's it!" Bea raised her voice. "That's the dress." She pushed the other clothes off of her and held the dress to her chest. It was the dress that was on the lady in the closet painting with Mommy.

Mommy sat down beside them. "Is she saying … did she see your Gamma—"

Noell shook her head. "Our Gamma."

Mommy nodded and touched the dress in Bea's lap. "She saw Gamma in there—"

"I saw Gamma." Bea swallowed. She still wasn't sure if she'd get a spanking, but she said it all anyway, in spite of tears. It was what was there. She'd seen her. "She painted with you, Mommy."

She checked Mommy's face. Bad Mommy wasn't there, so she pushed on ahead. "She painted a line the same color as you did Mommy. The same time as you." Bea lifted the dress. "She was wearing this dress and singing a funny song."

Noell and Mommy looked at each other, then back at Bea.

THIRTY-THREE

Mark tapped the steering wheel on his personal vehicle. It was an inheritance from Uncle Ted. He'd made sure in his will that Mark inherited his truck—a nice crew cab.

He smoothed his hands over the console beside him and scanned the rest of the truck. It was a used one, but better than anything he'd ever owned. He guessed Fords were okay and it was just the right size for anything he'd ever need.

His thoughts immediately blinked to Katty and Bea.

He whistled out a breath. What if. What if they did become a family? He closed his eyes and tried to push down emotion.

He'd been hurt before. If he took a chance on even dating Katty and if it didn't work out, he wasn't sure he could live through that—that he'd ever take a chance on a woman again.

Mark opened the glove box and pulled out Uncle Ted's papers for the truck and other stuff. Among those items was a Bible. Seriously? He'd kept a Bible in his truck?

Uncle Ted had lived as a bachelor after his wife died. He had told Mark once that he cried everyday since she passed. She had been a nice woman, but what did she have to make him miss her so much? He always told Mark that he wasn't perfect and neither was she. So what made the difference?

His own parents had divorced, but the reason behind that as far as Mark could see was alcohol. After that, Mom had joined a Bible study and that seemed to help her get through, but there had been many times when Mark was still at home that she flipped out in anger just remembering the stuff she'd experienced. Dad's drinking. His abuse. Had he really abused her?

Mark definitely knew through his job as a deputy that it happened.

But his own dad?

He figured every person had their own crap, their own baggage as the therapists seemed to term it nowadays.

What had Uncle Ted learned back then?

Mark continued to dig through the console. The usual. Old napkins, keys. Mark matched the keys to the ones he knew to be for the truck. One matched. He looped it off the key chain and onto his own. Might as well keep them together, until—

Buzz.

His phone vibrated. It had been too quiet too long on his day off.

"Mom. Good morning!" He checked the time. "Is it still morning?"

Mom laughed. "Yes it is, Son. But almost lunch time. What are you doing for lunch?"

"How'd you know it was my day off?" He chuckled. She probably went to the department when he wasn't there and asked Chantelle. Knowing Mom, that might be it.

"I just guessed. You worked last night, right? So just hoped it was." She cleared her throat. "So, back to my question. What are you doing for lunch?"

She always had a motive. Can you help me with the bathroom fan? Could you haul stuff to the dump—usually after a major clear out of Dad's stuff. Help me box up stuff to take to Mrs. B's store?

"I'm … I'm free. What did you have in mind?" He knew she always had something in mind—whether it was match-making or cleaning or rescuing him from the perils of this world.

"Well, I made lasagne on purpose to have leftovers. I'm having Bible study ladies over." She paused. "Sound good?"

"Mom, you made all that just to have leftovers?" He licked his lips. "My mouth is already watering." He should do that—fix something—even a roast to have leftovers. It was easy to do. Uncle Ted had shown him how. "What time?"

She chuckled. "How about now? Or whenever you can. It'll keep till—"

"No. Now is fine. I was just cleaning out my truck." He dropped Uncle Ted's stuff back into the console and picked up the Bible. "Yeah. I can come over. Is there anything I can help with while I"m there?" Save her asking. She hated to ask. In fact, she should ask more, instead of climbing up a ladder to change a light bulb.

She laughed. "As a matter of fact, there is. But it shouldn't take long. We can eat first."

"Okay. I'll be right there." He opened the Bible and a piece of paper slipped out. Uncle Ted had always taken notes, writing sermons down, quoting Bible verses. He unfolded the paper revealing Uncle Ted's handwriting. It wasn't scribbled notes at all. In fact, it was addressed … to Mark.

Dear Mark, I hope and pray that my plans for this truck to be yours were carried out and you are sitting in it right now as you are reading this.

Mark glanced around at the truck and shook his head. He read on.

I am so grateful for the time I had with you. I know I was very hard on you—probably mostly due to my military training— and I'm kind of sorry for some of it, but some of it you deserved.

Mark wiped his eyes. Rightly so, Uncle Ted. He deserved every bit of military discipline Uncle Ted had dished out.

My prayer for you and for your life is that you will find your way to Jesus.

Mark could no longer breathe. His eyes were wet, and something pressed on his chest. He shook his head. He closed the note. Not going to Mom's all messed up. Why was he getting so emotional?

But he couldn't not read more.

Son, you have been through some hard times—with your Mom and Dad, but with other people, too. You yourself have made some bad decisions. We all do.

Why had Mark waited till now to dig through the console. He'd washed the truck many times. Vacuumed it out several times. Definitely changed the title to his name and all that legal stuff. He paid his insurance every month.

He'd never taken the time to pull everything out. He'd opened it. Seen it stuffed full and closed it right away, figuring he didn't have time at that moment.

But now.

I'm praying for you to wait for the right woman. Don't let that testosterone level rule your decisions. Mistakes are made as a result of lust and not reigning in the ... well, you know what I mean.

Mark blinked. Uncle Ted had always spoken truth and never minced words. He shocked most people but he never cared. He was always to the point and honest.

Wait for her.

Mark breathed out slowly.

And yes, I love you like I fathered you, like you were my blood son. But I did, in a way, father you as best I could and with the time I had. Long story short: Jesus and the right woman. After that, it all comes together in the right way for the best life.

It's never easy and as you know, there are some hard times. You've seen me break down.

Mark looked around him. No neighbors outside. He covered his face with his hands and leaned onto the steering wheel.

He wiped his eyes again.

But it's all worth it with Jesus and His choice in a woman for you. You're a good man, Mark, and I love you like my own. Uncle Ted.

Salty tears ran into his mouth. Snot smeared on both cheeks. He opened the Bible again. There were lots of highlights and underlined verses. That's where he could start.

It was time.

Better go back inside and wash up. Mom would know he'd … a sob burst out again. He opened the truck door and made it to the bathroom.

Uncle Ted.

Right out of the bathroom, Mark stopped. He should get to Mom's. But she'd be all over him. *Why are you late? Are you okay? Have you been crying?*

But he had to. He knelt on the floor right outside of the bathroom. "God? I don't know what to say. I should know with Mom always … Jesus, please live in me. Please forgive me. Please. Please be in me what You were for Uncle Ted." His face was all the way to the floor. "I hope that's " But he knew. A presence filled him, a peace overpowered him.

He was gonna be late.

THIRTY-FOUR

The painting stopped.

It had been several minutes. The tree was beautiful. Brown trunk and branches. Beautiful realistic leaves seemingly fluttered in light from somewhere. Blue sky behind. Green grass and colorful flowers.

Katty leaned forward and touched the wall. Still wet. Orange paint came off on her fingertip. Wha?

She held her finger up to Noell, shaking her head.

Noell frowned and touched Katty's finger. Her own finger now had orange paint on it. She stood up and touched the wall with her other hand. "But … it's dry." She touched several other areas—the orange especially— and turned her finger toward Katty to see. "It's dry."

Katty scooted closer and touched another area. Wet. She showed Noell. "Why is it wet for me and dry for you?"

Noell sat beside the wall and wiped her eyes. "I-I don't know. It's impossible." She stared at the wall for some time, slowly shaking her head. "*You* see it getting painted—like someone—like Gamma is here actually painting it right now." She frowned. "And I see it totally dry. Done. Like it was painted years ago and all dry." She looked back at Katty. "This is impossible." She examined her finger.

Katty had been so engrossed with her own experience, she barely noticed Bea's reaction. Bea's head turned and tilted between Katty, Noell and the wall. She sat quietly, seeming to listen and watch her mom and Noell. Super unusual. She was a little artist—what was she thinking?

But now, Bea stood up. "Mommy. There's a hand on the wall again. It's still painting."

Katty gasped. It was really there. A hand appeared to be holding a paint brush and smoothing on paint. A tiny brush added detail to the leaves with various colors of green and blue and yellow—even orange. Brown. White. The hand dipped the brush onto an artist's palette and moved to the wall. At the same time, leaves fluttered, as if a gentle breeze was blowing through the closet.

Katty rubbed her arms. No breeze. Just goosebumps.

At that same moment, a visual of Mom appeared, morphed over Gamma fading in the background. Mom looked like she had when Katty was little. Her black eyes appeared, too close. She grabbed a colored pencil and snapped it into two pieces.

Katty jumped at the sound—louder than it should have been.

Mom's raucous laughter made Katty shudder.

Then Mom disappeared. Gamma, too.

She reached for Noell. "Did … did you see that? See Mom?"

"What?" Noell stared at the wall—not appearing to hear.

The painting—clouds billowed in the blue sky and floated across the wall. Flowers at the base of the tree danced gently. A petal dropped to the ground.

Katty shook her head and squinted. This couldn't be. It was like a movie, only in real life. Like someone yelled, "Action!" She stopped at that thought. This? Real life? This was living in a fantasy novel or a movie.

She glanced at Noell. "Do you see this? The leaves are fluttering and clouds are really moving." She pointed at the flowers. "These petals just moved and one dropped. Do you see this, or am I in a dream? Am I crazy? I'm not drunk." Deep breath. "And … and … I smell them, the flowers. Smells like flowers in here." Oh, dear Lord, she wanted a drink.

Bea patted Katty's shoulder. "Look! A baby crawled to the flower and bit it." Bea stood closer to the wall. "No, no, Baby. Don't eat the flowers. It might poi … make you sick. You can't eat flowers."

Noell sat still on the floor, her eyes unblinking and mouth open.

"Noell?" Katty tapped her on the arm. "You okay? You seeing this?"

Noell blinked and slowly turned toward Katty, but immediately turned back to the wall. She appeared to be holding her breath and slowly raised her hand to point. "It's a-alive. It's moving." She glanced down at Bea. "And I see the baby crawling along the green grass." She shook her head, her forehead wrinkled. "What the heck?"

Another vison popped into Katty's mind—of Mom pouring boiling water on Katty's plastic bucket full of beautiful crayons and melting them all together.

The vision faded, but Katty didn't want to move. If she didn't move, Gamma might come back. Were they all three in a dream together? Or a vision? Was Katty in her own personal hell? Had they all floated into another dimension. She used to watch movies when she was with Phil. Some were awful and scary, but some provoked her to think about her own reality, where she had come from, and how she had landed on this earth, about the possibility of other dimensions. She knew about babies being born. She'd given birth herself, but were there other worlds or places? Movies called them realms or dimensions.

This painting thing was startling enough to be somewhere else.

But it wasn't creepy. It wasn't scary, even though both she and Noell had jumped and screamed, startled by what was appearing, by what was moving in the painting.

Paintings didn't move, unless it was a video. This wasn't a video. It wasn't digital. It wasn't anything like the technology of this earth.

Katty examined her finger again. The orange paint was drying. This was just paint. Real paint. Not make-believe. Not fake. Real paint that she could smell and feel and touch. Noell had touched it. It was real.

The hand moved again, the small paintbrush daubed green on a leaf and the leaf fell to the ground. Only this time, it fell to the floor. The floor inside Gamma's house, her bedroom, her closet. It fell to the floor to inside where Katty, Noell, and Bea were sitting.

They all three saw it flutter out from the painting and noiselessly float to rest on the wooden floor.

They all paused for a split-second, then all three moved toward the leaf. Bea reached it first and gently touched it. She was so gentle. She picked it up and cupped it in her small hands. She held it out to Katty and Noell. She seemed to know how astonishing and unusual it was. It was stuff dreams were made of —not an ordinary day.

"It's a leaf." She glanced behind her at the wall.

Another leaf floated off the tree just as the hand added the last bit of detail.

Noell caught it in mid-air. A gasp escaped from her mouth. She blinked, her chin crumpled, and she raised her teary eyes to Katty's. "What?" She visibly swallowed. "How can this be happening?"

Katty stared at the leaf in Noell's hand, then at Bea's hands. Then back up to the wall, where the hand was still painting. Several more leaves fluttered off the wall and onto the wooden floor. Green, yellow, with daubs of blue and orange and brown.

On the wall it looked very realistic, but as Bea handed Katty another one, it was real. A real leaf.

Katty glanced through the door at a window in the bedroom.

Those leaves.

Real leaves.

Like from a real tree. Only … the tree wasn't real. It was a tree painted on a wall in a house. A tree, but a painting of a tree. But as she watched, more details emerged. The paintbrush had brown paint on it and the hand swooped a length of it into the tree.

"What is that?" Bea sat beside Katty and snuggled into her. "What is … the brush doing?'

Katty shook her head. She couldn't take her eyes off what was happening on the wall. Or in the wall. In this closet. In this, what now looked like a whole room, a room almost the same size as Gamma's bedroom, in a house that didn't appear to have an extra room here. She shook her head again. "I … don't know." She uncrossed her legs and gently pushed Bea off. If she stepped closer to the wall, to the hand and paintbrush, would it disappear?

One step.

Still there.

Another.

The hand seemed to be even more determined to paint with a purpose—laying down another brown stripe and another at an odd angle. Another and another. A building. In a tree?

Another step closer. The hand was directly in front of Katty's face. Still it painted—now with a lighter color of brown—seemingly for emphasis or definition. Highlights.

Now a darker color of brown defined the brown stripes.

As Katty's eyes traveled across each brown stripe, she gulped and stumbled back against the far bookcase. The bookshelf vibrated and shook when she bumped into it. A small donkey cart planter startled her when it fell into her hands.

The hand didn't stop painting.

Katty didn't want to stop watching the hand to examine the planter, but from where Katty now stood, the brown stripes made sense. It was a structure. A building.

She gasped.

No.

A tree house.

Her old tree house.

She slumped down against the bookshelf. Tears quietly slipped from her eyes. She reached out and pointed at the wall. "That." A sob escaped. "That is my old tree house."

Noell jumped up and ran from the room.

THIRTY-FIVE

Noell shook her head, her back against the closed door, and studied her room—her space.

She knew that Katty and Bea wouldn't follow her and barge in on her in her private space, but maybe she wasn't keeping them out, as much as she was trying to protect herself from what was going on down there in Gamma's closet.

No, maybe she was trying to guard against her own fears. Seeing what was possibly Gamma's hand painting on that wall downstairs made her miss Gamma all the more. But just as much as that, the mysterious appearance, the fact that Katty could see the wall painting wet and Noell knew it was dry.

Until the hand appeared. Then time seemed to mesh, to morph into the same second, the same nanosecond. Before, Noell was in her regular time, right where she had lived all her life. But when Katty started talking about wet paint on the same wall, the same painting, the same colors as Noell was seeing—if that hand was truly Gamma's hand—it had to be ages ago and not right now.

But when it all came together—Bea was the one—the one who said it first. "There's the hand again, Mommy."

Bea.

Noell forced herself to breath deeply and slowly.

That usually made her feel at least calmer. And she had, but when they found the dress—Gamma's dress—oh my.

Just now, she had to potty so she ran upstairs to her own bathroom.

Now, sliding down against the door, she braced as she landed on the hardwood floor. Seemed like she had spent many a moment on the floor sitting right where she was, running from fear, embracing the quiet and uncluttered space, and then landing right into her nightmares.

The curse that was hers to bear didn't help at all. Touching things came naturally for people, but when she did … ugh. Most people, ladies especially, touched and sampled the texture of a jacket or sweater—even a wooden table or paneling. Even in a clothing store where products were supposed to be brand new, after people had tried something on, it still held the potential to terrify Noell with voices or visions, or both. Gamma had lost her in a store once, and when she opened the door to the fitting room, she'd found Noell huddled in a corner, under hanging clothes, crying and trembling. The vision she'd seen that day.

When Katty had first gasped and asked Noell if she was seeing the hand, she'd thought Katty must be crazy and had slipped out during the night to buy booze. But then Noell became aware of movement at the wall and slowly a hand became visible, then a brush, and then colored paints. She'd seen it with her own eyes.

The swoop of green and brown for the tree would forever be in her mind. But when Katty had started sobbing, saying "That's my treehouse," Noell couldn't stay any longer. That's when she ran for her room.

She knew what might come next.

She knew her nightmares of flood waters, of seeing her mom

drown were next, right behind any anxiety or fear. One went with the other.

Breathing slowly again, helped. She stroked her long braid. That helped.

Knock, knock.

Oh-oh. Deep breath. Noell opened the door to little Bea. Her face appeared wet, her shoulders slumped and head down. Noell leaned over. "Bea? You okay?"

Noell peeked out the door and down the stairway. No Katty.

"Mommy." That was all Bea said.

Noell drew her head back and to the side as if she was listening.

No. Katty had been doing so well.

Noell picked up Bea and clomped down the steps. "Where is she?"

Bea pointed to the front porch. The porch door was swinging open. She faced the door. "Bad Mommy's back."

Noell stared at her, then at Katty driving away.

THIRTY-SIX

"Hey, Mom?" Mark swallowed and checked his face in the bathroom mirror. "Hey, I got detained, but I'm on my way, now."

She must be in the bathroom because she didn't pick up her phone. That was okay. He could put off explaining why he had taken so long.

Breathe.

Even washing his face hadn't helped. His face in the mirror teared up again. He couldn't stop weeping.

He knew something had happened. He knew he was different.

He knew he'd prayed—thanks to Uncle Ted's letter—but he didn't understand exactly why he felt this … this …

He started weeping again.

This accepted.

This loved.

This clean.

That.

He slumped to the bathroom floor beside the tub and sobbed. Again.

The flooring was cold and hard. As he opened his eyes, grit

and lint became visible in the corners. He wasn't a filthy guy the way he lived, but seeing the floor this close?

Someone or something touched his shoulder as he sat there. He raised his head, bumped it on the sink, and looked around the room. Must have been his shirt that shifted or … there it was again. A touch on his shoulder. What was that?

He stood, still in the emotional, redeeming throes of before.

Quieting his breathing, he flipped on his military training to listen, to sense. He studied videos at the sheriff's department on how to do that. It helped calm his anxiety many times. He stilled his breathing, challenged himself to listen to whatever was around him, whatever was here. He knew something or someone was here.

He searched the room.

Nothing.

But as he looked at the walls, the tub, sink and toilet, something else kicked in from inside him. He could see the walls, the fixtures, but he could also see others. Kind of. He knew they were there.

He slipped to his knees again. "Lord?' Tears dripped onto the tile floor. "Jesus? Are you here? Is that you?"

From somewhere or within him from another dimension, rose a surge of chorus or song, of praise. He could hear it, but not through his own ears or hearing. But it was there.

His chest, his heart was so full it might burst.

A chorus of singing, but laughter.

Joy.

That was it.

And love.

Mark knew he didn't understand, but he knew it was real.

It was real.

His phone buzzed.

Mom. He'd lost all sense of time. He checked his phone, but no time had passed since he came inside his house.

No way.

He knew he should go. Mom was waiting lunch and knowing her, she had a whole banquet set up—for lunch. But he didn't want to leave this … this … whatever it was. He leaned against the tub and swallowed, and hugged his knees. "Lord? How do I do this? I don't know how to live like this." He wiped his eyes again. "Lord, thank you. Thank you for Uncle Ted's … his life, time with him, his letter." He bowed his head onto his knees. "Thank you for this … this, You. Thank you."

Buzz. Buzz.

Deep breath. It was time to go. He pushed up from the tub and walked out the door. As he left his house, the sunshine seemed brighter. The sky was bluer and the colors all around were more intense. He opened the truck door and slid inside.

The note. He'd never get rid of that. He pulled it out, folded it to fit, and slipped it in his chest pocket.

He tapped on his phone that he was on his way. This time he was. He backed out of the driveway. It seemed like he was in a fog, but the edges of the stop sign, the tree leaves, the neighbor's house were clearer and sharper than ever before.

Even in his truck, Uncle Ted's truck, something or someone was with him. "Jesus?" Movement. He held his breath and turned a corner. Wait. Weren't there angels? Mom was always telling him as he left her, something about angels all around him. For protection?

"Angels?"

He lingered at a stop sign. Listened. Breathed. Maybe there wasn't any movement right now. There was not a sound. But in that silence—in the quiet—Mark knew He was there. He knew.

The street swam before him, trees blurred, and the stop sign letters quivered. He wiped his eyes.

His stomach rumbled.

Mom's house. He didn't remember the drive. Because of his

job, he was always conscious of every car, where they parked, people walking to and fro. Every street.

Not this time.

He blinked and he was in front of Mom's house. In her driveway. Laughter burst from him. He almost felt the angels, the beings rejoicing around him.

Mom was gonna know. She was gonna pester him until—

She opened the door as he raised his fist to knock and almost hit her in the face. "Mom!" He laughed. "I almost hit you! Sorry!"

Dang.

She just stood there. "Son." She looked him over. "Are you okay?"

He brushed past her inside the house. "Yep. Sure. Why do you ask?"

She closed the door and followed him into the kitchen. "Well, you don't usually wear your work shirt on your day off … with shorts." She stepped back, folding her arms across her chest. "And you don't usually wear your gun like that." She pointed.

He looked to where she was pointing. His gun was stuffed into his waist in his shorts, like an old-time robber might wear his. No holster. No badge—he wasn't on duty—but he had his work shirt on. One final thing Mom hadn't noticed or brought up … he had his body cam on and the operation light was flashing.

Oh no. He was busted. He flicked it off.

He had rushed into his closet after the bathroom scene and gotten dressed, but obviously, had mixed his work dress code with his personal one.

His chin dropped to his chest. No denying that something was going on. She could see it just in his mode of dress, if not in his eyes.

"Why don't you take a seat while I bring the food to the table." She took his hand and led him to the chair like she had when he was four. Felt like it too. But it was okay. He didn't understand, but he was a different man than the last time he'd come over to visit.

He *was* different.

Mark chuckled as he settled onto the chair, looking down at himself. Reflexes kicked in. His muscles flexed and he almost ran out the door. He made himself sit still. "Mom, that smells amazing." He tried to tuck the gun in his waistband, but it wasn't going to work. "Hey Mom, … uh … I'm gonna run this out to my truck and lock it in there." He held it low and shook his head. "I … I'll be right back."

"That's okay, Mark. I figured you had a YouTube channel."

What? Deep breath. Running out to the car was either a bad decision because he wanted to weep again at the reminder of Uncle Ted's letter, and a good decision to stow the gun and camera.

He paused before shutting the door, then picked up the Bible. No. He patted his pocket as he stood outside the front door. *Breathe.*

Back in the house, the smell of food beckoned. His stomach rumbled again. That Italian food smell was a comfort smell for Mark. Especially Mom's. Better than any Italian restaurant, probably better than any Italian family home smells—because it was Mom's.

He sat down in his chair as Mom placed the casserole in the middle of the table and arranged the serving spoon and knife. "It always needs cutting. The noodles get tough."

He leaned over the table and sniffed the dish. "Your … lasagne?" The parmesan cheese even smelled good. She always sprinkled a thick layer of it on top that made a nice golden crust when baked, plus layers of it inside.

Mom smiled and she served a large chunk onto his plate. The steam rose up heating Mark's face and giving him a direct whiff. "Holy cow, that smells wonderful." He patted his chest without thinking of the note, but he heard it rumple in his pocket at the same time.

"Better blow on it. Even though it sat for a little bit, it's hot." She helped herself to a serving and sat down.

He picked up his fork, but immediately laid it back down. "Wanna pray, Mom?" Stupid question.

"Do you want to offer the blessing?"

No pressure. He couldn't even talk, much less pray right now. He swallowed and cleared his throat. "Dear God." Sounded like one of those Dear Santa letters a little kid might write. "Uh, thank You God for this food and … thank You for my mom." This part he'd always remember—she'd explained it well. "In Jesus' Name."

Oh, he was gonna cry before he could eat. He wiped his eyes and stole a look up at Mom.

She wiped her own eyes and glanced up at him, then quickly picked up her fork and cut a bite. She paused and opened her mouth to speak, but shook her head and raised the bite to her lips. "Amen." She almost let it be and took the bite, but couldn't seem to stop herself. "And Lord, bring Your best woman for Mark to marry." She quickly closed her prayer. "Amen."

Very uncomfortable, awkward, but it somehow didn't seemed to rile him up like it usually did.

"I just want what's best for you." Tears streamed down her cheeks, as she tried to chew. She cleared her throat and sipped a drink of water.

He swallowed and put down his fork. He looked directly into her eyes and nodded. "I know Mom. I know you love me and want what's best for me." He patted his chest for emphasis, but maybe there was a higher reason for him patting right there.

The note.

THIRTY-SEVEN

Katty opened the car door and breathed the fresh air. Even though she'd driven off with a destination in mind—buy booze, no matter where she had to go—the convenience store, out of town to a real liquor store, a neighbor's house if they had any to steal—she found herself driving into the park. She literally turned in, drove through on the little curvy road, and parked at the picnic building.

She stepped out of her car and quietly shut the door. No one seemed to be playing or walking here right now. The trees above her reached for the sky, a long way up. No breeze rustled the leaves or branches. The painting in Gamma's closet just now had more breeze. She glanced south, toward the part of town where her trailer was. The trees in this park were almost like the tree she had painted in her trailer on that crappy paneling.

Quiet.

Silent.

Almost eerie.

Terrifying.

Anytime in Katty's past when emotions or memories became too clear and intense, she ran. Or drove. Or drank. Or all three.

This moment was intense.

Most people found solace in a park. They'd find peace or at least quiet. Quiet from their daily life of what? Work. Family. Thoughts. Overbooked calendars.

Run away.

That's what most would do.

And she was too. Running away from her brutal, childhood memories with Mom. From her life with Phil. From the abortions. There. She pushed herself to even think the word. Abortion.

Running away from the darkness in her life. Running from what was inside Gamma's closet that was freaking her out. Painting on the wall herself was natural, but painting and seeing an actual hand do exactly what she was doing.

Too much.

Oh, for a drink.

Walking back to her car, she noticed a woman enter the park from the convenience store across the highway, and on the other side of the railroad tracks. Shit! That looked like Mom. Long flowing black hair. Impressive toned figure in skinny cut jeans and close-fitting t-shirt under a black and white plaid flannel shirt. Shit, she looked good for her age. She carried two coffee take-out cups.

The words the woman flung at Katty in front of Noell's house the other night were definite evidence of her true heart— still evil. She hadn't changed a bit. As Katty slid into her car, she didn't remember Mom looking that good.

As she softly closed the car door behind her, she knew. It was only her mom's eyes that she remembered. The visuals of her past childhood, her life as a kid with her mom, were always just Mom's black, evil eyes.

So it was a shock when she showed up at Noell's the other night.

Katty peeked toward her Mom. Maybe she hadn't seen her.

The other shock was to realize that Mom's eyes were green, not black.

Green like … Mark's eyes.

"Hello, Katty dear."

God, help.

Tap. Tap.

That voice. "Hello, beautiful daughter of mine."

What? The other night she'd been screaming the same old crap. And now Katty was beautiful? Not on her life. Not here. Not today. Not ever.

The park was no longer peaceful, but … she was no longer going to run.

Katty stepped out of the car. Louisiana Randolph. There. That name even made her cringe. It was like the name of a character in a horror novel. And all the things a person thought of when they opened a horror novel were present in her mom. Evil. Blood. Horrible words. Fear. Terror. Pain.

"How are you this fine afternoon?" Mom stepped closer to Katty and held out one of the coffees. "Need a pick-me-up?" She tilted her head toward the convenience store. "They have great coffee." She held the coffee closer, almost under Katty's nose. "Give us some time to catch up with each other."

Not on your life.

What she needed or really wanted right now wasn't coffee. It was—

"I know we didn't start off very well, the other night—"

"What the …" Katty stopped herself and swallowed. *Breathe.* When Katty was little, this woman had literally controlled her every minute of living, every thought, every hope Katty might have had for her personal life. Even Katty's response to what Mom did or said had ruled her every waking and sleeping minute.

No more!

Katty stomped her foot. "I don't want your damn coffee."

She sucked in a breath. If she used the same words that Mom used, she'd be well on her way to *being* her. Well, she was already half-way there. "I don't want your so called pick-me-up. I don't want time with you." Katty shook her head and took a step toward Mom. "I don't have to sit with you anymore." Another breath. "I don't have to listen to you anymore." Another step forward. "And I don't have to even like you." Face-to-face. Almost nose-to-nose. "You will never rule my life again."

"Uh, ladies?"

Both women flipped their heads toward the voice, their hair flying out around their heads.

"Who the hell are you?" Mom spat out.

"Clarence!" Katty full-on faced him. "Thank God! What are you doing out here?" Katty glanced behind him toward Hillcrest Homes.

He grinned his normal handsome expression. Those blue eyes twittered with his usual mirth and love, but there was something underneath—something was up. "I saw you pull up and I wanted a hug." He stepped closer to Katty, his arms were wide open.

Katty hesitated. Mom was here. Awkward. But for some reason, it felt so right—so according to plan. She held out her own arms and stepped into his.

"Wait." Mom rubbed against them both. "Let me get summa that."

Clarence immediately picked Katty up and stepped clear away from Mom. How did he do that? He was stronger than any younger man, times five. He turned, his arm still around Katty's shoulders, keeping her just to the side, almost behind him, and faced Mom.

Stand-off.

"Who is this, Katty?"

Katty choked. She almost wanted to cry, but caught herself. She chuckled instead and gripped his waist tightly. "This,

Clarence, is my mother." She didn't know why, but she held out her arm and presented her mother to Clarence, like some game show host presenting the next contestant. "Louisiana Randolph."

Mom held out her arms for an expected hug, coffees still in her hands.

Clarence didn't make a move, but nodded at her.

Oh, dear Clarence. God for sure had a special reward for this man.

"Greetings, Louisiana Randolph." No more. He stopped right there. He could have said so much, like it's nice to meet you or it's nice to meet Katty's mom, or something like that. But he didn't. He stopped right there. He didn't even touch the woman. He never left Katty's side. He never stopped hugging her and making her feel ... safe.

Stay strong.

Katty almost faltered and dipped to her knees.

"Huh." Mom did a twist with her head and body back and forth, her jaw jutted out, and her eyes appeared black. "Well, I guess I'll go find someone who wants my time." She laughed a guttural laugh and held the coffees high. "And my coffees." She turned toward the street, but stopped, turned back to Katty and Clarence. "You're still a slut." She grinned, her red lips stretched across her face in a wicked expression. "A scab on my life. Always have been. Always will be."

Clarence's arm tightened around Katty's shoulders and he stepped so close that he and Katty were one body. No words. Just together.

When neither of them spoke, Mom's frown tightened to an evil grimace, her eyes squinted and glared, nostrils flared, and her jaw jutted. "Unbelievable." She turned again to the street and with each step, she spoke one word. "Slut. Slut. Slut." Until she reached Ridge Street at the corner and turned.

Katty jumped. "She's gonna go to Noell's! That's where

she's going. She was there the other night and … I've got to go. She knows where we've been staying. She might get Bea."

Clarence stopped Katty. "No. She's been staying with Grimes, Noell's neighbor." He patted her shoulder. "He lives on the other side of Noell, a couple houses away."

Katty blinked and leaned toward him. "What? How'd you know that?"

He smiled and wiped her cheek, brushed hair out of her face. "We've been watching Grimes and your mom. They spent a little time in jail a while back and we know they've been shacking … uh, living together."

Those eyes. So blue.

Katty stared at him for many minutes, trying to take it in. Mom had been living so close to Noell's and she never knew until now. When her eyes followed to where her mom walked— she was almost past the corner house—almost out of sight. It was all Katty could do to not jump in her car and make sure Clarence was right.

"Katty."

Again.

"Katty."

She slowly turned back to him and bowed her head. "I'm sorry. I didn't trust you." She pointed at the direction Mom had walked. "She's evil, Clarence." It was hard to stand without his arms around her. "I've missed you."

He embraced her again. "I've missed you, Katty. Bea, too." He embraced her tighter.

"You showed up here at just the right time." Katty drew back and searched his face. "How did you know?"

He chuckled. "I didn't. But Mrs. T did." He let those words float around in Katty's mind for a minute.

The quiet of the park returned. A gentle breeze barely stirred the trees behind and above him.

"Mrs. T?" She gulped.

"Yes." His skin crinkled around his beautiful eyes. "She stopped a meeting I was having with Harold and a client. Said I needed to get to the park and protect my Katty." He grinned wide. "That's how she said it. My Katty."

A breeze must have gotten stronger. The trees and leaves were still gently moving, but a fog or mist floated, moved, swirled around them—just like at Noell's. Katty could see it or so she thought. She wasn't drunk. She was sober. She was the most sober she'd been in years. At this moment what was stirring was not evil or fear or gut-wrenching pain.

It was …

Katty looked toward Hillcrest again. "Mrs. T?"

"Oh, well. And I know Mrs. T would add … Jesus."

Katty stared at the building, back at Clarence, then at the trees. Where her brain, her thoughts had been so blocked for most of her life and her eyes had been blinded, something was clearing them away so she could see. A fog was lifting and Katty could finally start to see.

"Oh." She squinted. "Jesus?" More of the fog parted.

Clarence hugged her again. "I've got to get back to my meeting." A sweet kiss on her forehead, and he ran across the street and into the building, leaving his aftershave on her skin.

Katty didn't take her eyes off him until the door closed behind him. She slowly came to herself. But she wasn't herself. Something was different. Back to the door where he had run through. Him? Mrs. T? Jesus? Something was finally making sense in her booze-ridden brain. She didn't understand, but she did.

Clarence and Mrs. T. Her eyes saw Hillcrest, but somehow she saw the old couple from the convenience store. Still married. Still in love after many years and heartache. What had … she'd been blind … what had she said? You'll know when you've found him? You'll know. A faithful man?

Like Clarence?

Deep breath.

Maybe she should get back to Noell's. She'd just driven off without saying where she was going, although if she knew Bea and now even Noell, they had probably guessed.

She blinked.

Driven off to buy booze. She opened the car door. Why had she stopped at the park? She tried to remember. Deep breath again.

Probably didn't matter why or how she'd come here. Just that she had. She leaned against the car door and glanced up the street, her eyes followed where Mom had walked. Mom had come to the park.

Then her eyes were drawn back to Hillcrest.

Clarence had come to the park.

And Mrs. T had, in her sweet old lady way. No. Bea always said Mrs. T prayed. That's how Mrs. T was in the park.

Katty slowly sat back down in her car, leaving the door open, and stared at the trees.

THIRTY-EIGHT

"Mark? Do you want these?" Mom held up some papers, but they slipped from her fingers and floated to the kitchen floor. She laughed. "Didn't mean to throw them at you."

Boxes covered the table and some of the chairs. They'd have to work hard if they were to eat on the table for supper. Mom promised leftover lasagne—the best.

Mark shook his head and smiled. He leaned over and picked up the scattered papers and a card slipped out from among them. He knew he really didn't need any of this stuff. It was just fluff to him, unimportant papers and threads to Dad's drunken life. He recognized court papers. He'd seen plenty of those at work as people passed from jail time through the court system and onto wherever they'd been sentenced.

Like Phil Daynton was now. Mark would be fully satisfied and relieved to see him in prison for all he'd done. Away from Katty and Bea. Phil had spent time in the Polk county jail and was being sentenced soon. Seeing those papers shuffled across Mark's desk would give him deep satisfaction, indeed.

The card.

Dad's drivers license.

Mark slowly leaned down to pick it up and stood upright. Hollinger Carl Scott was the name on it. All official. He glanced up at his mom as she dug through another box, turned away from her and examined the driver's license. Nobody had ever called Dad Hollinger. They'd always called him Carl. What a name. That alone might have made the man drink like he had. Shortening the name to Holly sounded more like a girl's name.

Mark chuckled. A man named Holly. Oh my.

"What are you laughing at?" Mom dumped some papers into the trash bag.

He turned toward her and held up the card. "Dad's name." He shook his head. "What in ... why would anyone name their kid Hollinger?"

"I know. I made sure *I* never shortened it to Holly, because that made him so angry. He should have legally changed it years ago, but he didn't." She paused. "Why would anyone name a sweet baby, Bea?"

Mark blinked. "What?"

"Well, it's the same kind of odd name as Dad's was." Mom tilted her head and tried to smile, but it turned almost into a scowl. "I know. I shouldn't even have brought it up, but ... it is odd, right?"

Mark just stood there. Why would she care? Why would she even bring that up right now when they were focusing on Dad's belongings and papers—on cleaning them out? He loved Bea's name. It was ... Bea's name, so he loved it because ... he loved her.

Deep slow breath.

"Well, I don't know." God help him. No need to insult Mom right now, even though she didn't need to bring that stuff up. Maybe it was the right time, even though it was very uncomfortable. Something fluttered inside and he became almost playful. "Well, what if when Bea was born, Katty saw a bee and named her Bea—only spelled it different? Like the Indians did."

Mom raised her eyebrows. "How could Katty have seen a bee in the delivery room? I mean, really."

Mark stopped and flipped the drivers license back and forth against his fingers. How, indeed? He was pretty sure that Katty had escaped from Phil with Bea intact and was possibly all alone when she delivered Bea.

He slowly brought his eyes to meet Mom's. Not accusing. Not in anger. But in realization of what might have happened.

Katty. All alone. Delivered Bea—all alone. Maybe outside. Maybe in a car.

Mom's face flickered surprise, then understanding. "Did she … uh." She blinked and frowned. "Did she deliver Bea …?" Only she couldn't finish her question. She slowly sat, almost missed the chair, then adjusted and sat. She planted there, staring at the papers in her hand, but obviously not seeing them, although something else became very real to her. Her eyes met Mark's. Not accusing. Not criticizing. Her mouth dropped open just a bit. Her face changed to pity—no—to compassion?

Mark blinked and sat on the only vacant chair left in the kitchen. He didn't know what surprised him more: the fact that Katty might have actually delivered Bea all alone, or the fact that his mom was sitting in front of him having compassion for her. She's never liked her, she'd actually despised the fact that she knew Mark might love Katty.

"Mom?" What was he going to say? What could he say? "Um—"

She waved her hand. Waved the subject away. "It's okay. What do you think about my name? About your name, Mark?"

Right. Avoid the unavoidable. Avoid the difficult subjects. Like always.

She handed him some papers and he threw them in the trash bag.

"You didn't even look at them. What if you want them someday?" She stood and reached for the trash.

"No Mom. I'll never want this stuff." He closed the open trash bag and held his hand on top of it. Patted it. "This stuff is your life, Dad's life, not mine."

"But what if you ever need to find out something--"

"I won't. Dad is gone. I have to build my own life."

"Now I went and made you mad." She opened another box. "Oh, his shirts."

Mark stood and closed the box in front of her and placed it beside the trash. "We don't need his shirts or his clothes."

She reached for the box. "But you might be able to wear them. You're about his size, his shape."

"I'm not him. I don't want his stuff." Mark shoved the box out of her reach. "I'll carry this out to your car and we can take it to Mrs. B's thrift store." He gritted his teeth. "We are not keeping them."

As he carried the box to her car, he released the emotion that was building up inside. Dang. Why did she have to go and bring up Katty and Bea? He slumped. What Katty might have done—had Bea all alone—maybe even in her car or outside—made Mark love her more. Maybe respect her. He'd read her file—he shouldn't have, but. What she'd been through.

He put the box in the backseat and stood, still shaking his head. He'd had some tough times, too, but never anything like Katty had. Plus, Uncle Ted took him in. Mark had someone by his side. Katty had been all alone.

He didn't want to go back inside. Not even for lasagne leftovers.

He would stay and help Mom. He told her he would help. But they needed to change the subject. Or change the mood. Or really face what they were avoiding.

Thoughts of Uncle Ted reminded him of what was in his pocket and he patted it. Get back there, Mark. Get back to God. He didn't even know how to do that, but remembering the note and his prayer helped.

"Be right back, Mom." He shut himself inside the bathroom. He didn't have to use the toilet. He just wanted to hear Him. He breathed a deep breath and closed his eyes. "God help me feel you, hear you, like before." He shook his head. He didn't know how to do this and it wasn't his house or his truck like before. It was the same. But. He sucked in another breath and kept his eyes closed. "God?" He whispered the word. He wasn't ready to talk to Mom about what he'd done. He smiled. The agitation and anger that had begun to rise in him before, left and a definite peace and something else—joy—filled him. Happiness, but different. Joy. It invaded his whole body. Shivers. Goosebumps, kind of. Only … what was this?

Knock, knock. "Mark? You okay?"

Oh Mom. She'd always be Mom. His mom. And she loved him, no matter what he'd ever done or would ever do. She loved him.

Love. That was what filled him just now.

He opened that bathroom door. "Hey Mom? Where did you get my name? It's kind of obvious, isn't it? The Bible, maybe?" Back in the kitchen. "Right? Who am I named after?" He tried to grin. "Oh, and by the way, thanks for not naming me after Dad."

She smiled. "It was a battle to name you. Dad knew it wasn't going to be after him. He hated his name and one of the best things he did for you was not name you Hollinger Carl Scott." She handed him another box. "His underwear. I'm sure you don't want to wear any of that."

Mark took the box from her. "You kept his underwear? Are you kidding?"

"No. I didn't really keep it. I just didn't want to do this, go through his stuff, remember his life and his drinking." She smiled. "That's all. And you're named after Mark. In the Bible. You know, in the New Testament. That Mark."

"Huh. Okay, I get that. It's from the Bible. Why Phyllis?" He grinned. "Who are you named after?"

She stuck her tongue out at him and picked up another box. "Look we cleared off the table again."

He chuckled. "Now we can have leftovers, right?" He took the box from her.

"Not until we take these to Mrs. B's store."

"Meany, Mom. Mean Mom." He stuck his tongue out at her and almost waited for the spanking, or the slap. She'd never been a perfect mom, but she never beat him. He paused on his way outside. She'd lived a tough life with Dad.

What made the difference?

THIRTY-NINE

Katty huddled on the floor of the closet, Gamma's closet, surrounded by journals. She knew she should have asked Noell for permission again, but when she did ask, Noell always laughed and said yes. So, okay.

She was the only one awake and up. Unusual that Bea wasn't even up. She tapped her phone—5:30 in the morning. The birds weren't even awake. Yet. This was the third morning she'd stirred awake. Every time she covered back up, checked Bea next to her, and closed her eyes. Back to sleep. But every time, Gamma's journals drew her.

Most mornings, Katty was haunted by visions of brutal abortions and this morning they had tried to crush her day before it started. But hope wove its way through her dreams. Hope from Gamma's journals now covered the pain, the memories. Those visuals might never leave. But because of Gamma's closet and the journals there, hope wove over and around the pain, strengthening—layer upon layer.

Like the hot pad Noell had made for Gamma. It still hung by the stove. All those pretty colors woven over and under.

Inside the closet, the paintings were amazing. Strange how

the light bulb was never on, but plenty of bright light emanated, radiated from somewhere.

If what Bea said she saw was real, was true, Gamma was helping Katty paint. Or was somehow there painting with her. How?

Gamma was dead.

The journal open in her lap was full of Gamma's writing and little pictures filling every corner, every line, each space. Each page was a treasure—rich in color and in meaning. Gamma wrote her fears, her Bible verses. Katty didn't understand it all. Lines and sentences and stories of what Gamma called revelations from Him.

Him? From God?

How? If that was even true, how did that happen?

She leaned her head back against the bookshelf and stared at the painted wall across from her. That painting. Deep breath. Similar to the one she had painted in her trailer house on that paneling in the living room. Her eyes followed flowers. The main tree. Babies—crazy that this one had the babies, too. But this one also had an amazing sunset. The colors were rich blues, purples, bright oranges. Every color on earth but in a richness that no paintbox or tube of paint could produce.

She tapped on the journal page open in her lap and whispered what was written there. "The Roots." Odd. What did that mean?

Flipping through the next couple pages, she breathed out a breath, then another.

Trees. Trees on every page. Pine trees. Shrubs. Each drawing was labeled as to the kind of tree or plant it was. Oak trees. Oh so beautiful. The branches swooped up and out as if it was getting ready to hug … someone.

Katty swallowed. She swallowed hard again, against a lump in her throat and shook her head. She knew she was related to Gamma. Never studied bloodlines. Didn't know any generation older than Gamma. But she'd only gotten to be at Gamma's house a few times.

Back to the painting—the tree—back to the trees in the journals. She wiped her eyes. Swallowed again.

Why was she getting emotional just reading and looking through Gamma's journals?

Peeked out into the bedroom—Bea was still asleep.

Next page. All drawings of roots—from tiny thread sized roots to what must be oak tree sized roots winding over and around different words.

She rotated the book so she could read each word. "Roots. Vines. Connected. Rooted. Nurtured. Fingers. Threads." The words wound through, over, and between the drawings there, making beautiful and rich pages. Gamma had colored the pages with the typical greens and browns of trees, but shaded with gentle blues and purples and reds.

Some drawings stopped her—dark, scraggly, crusty, gnarly trees. Ugly trees. Why?

Some beautiful to look at, but powerful to ponder. Katty shook her head. Her eyes stared first at the trees in the journal, then at the tree on the wall. She shook her head—not understanding—but she found that the challenge to understand Gamma's writings stirred her.

She turned the page. Ahh. A beautiful drawing of a real tree, but from the roots to the tip of leaves sprouting from every branch. But oddly, there was a broken branch among other healthy ones. The trunk was even damaged on one side.

Beside every part of the tree was a sentence. No. A verse. A Bible verse?

"For he shall be like a tree planted by the waters that spreads out its roots by the river, and it shall not see and fear when heat comes, but its leaf shall be green. It shall not be anxious and full of care in the year of droughts, nor shall it cease yielding fruit." Jeremiah 17:8

Not fear? Not be anxious? That's part of what drove her to those little bottles.

Who was Jeremiah?

Or another one. "I sank down to the very roots of the mountains, I was imprisoned in the earth, whose gates lock shut forever. But you, O Lord my God, snatched me from the jaws of death!" Jonah 2:6.

Did Gamma do a study on roots? Did this verse help her when her daughter drowned?

Another drawing was of a pile of branches, all broken and burned. Trees that had uprooted, their roots tipped toward the sky. The verse beside the drawing was, "Every plant not planted by my heavenly Father will be uprooted." Matthew 15:13.

All this tree stuff. It had started out pretty and beautiful. But several pages into the journal, the drawings had become dark and ugly. The verse was even harsh. "Even now the ax is laid to the root of the trees, so that every tree that does not bear good fruit is cut down and cast into the fire." Luke 3:9.

Ouch.

If this stuff was true, she didn't have a chance. She'd be weeded out just like Bea and Noell did in the flower beds.

Cut down. Cast in the fire?

She thought back to her time in jail. That time on the floor, crying out. She'd murdered—

Burned. That's what she deserved.

Or "May Christ through your faith [actually} dwell (settle down, abide, make His permanent home) in your hearts! May you be rooted deep in love and founded securely on love," Ephesians 3:17.

There was no way that Christ or anyone else would want to live in her heart.

Page after page of beautiful drawings in every color of the rainbow, and words filled with Gamma's wisdom. Each page dated. Every page filled with Gamma's day—what she had for lunch, when she went to the store and what she bought, her thoughts about the bird that might be singing outside her window. And there was the bird, all colored and finely detailed —ready to sing from the page.

Every page was her day.

Every page was her life.

Gamma lived her life in these journals.

Katty'd always felt robbed. Her own mom had robbed her of knowing Gamma personally.

She let her eyes roam over all the journals and books on each shelf. Dozens of them. Hundreds? All about Gamma's life?

Katty shook her head and wiped her eyes. Realization hit her. Maybe she had never enjoyed a real conversation with Gamma. Oh, she had tasted her chocolate chip cookies that she was well known for, but had barely really talked to her. Mom always blocked that. Mom exploded at something Gamma said or tried to do for them, grabbed Katty, and left. Katty had been in this house maybe twice.

But here. Right in front of her, she had Gamma's daily life. Katty had access to conversations from Gamma and from her heart.

Deep sigh.

She hugged the journal to her chest and blinked.

Gamma's wisdom seemed to float down to Katty. As she held that book against her flesh—well, through a flimsy old T-shirt, turned night shirt—that wisdom seemed to vibrate into her being.

Gamma's thoughts and her wisdom permeated Katty's body and she knew she'd never be the same again. She knew that reading those books would help her know Gamma, but in time the words would help heal her heart.

Katty carefully closed the book in her arms and placed it on the bookshelf sideways. She almost laughed. Better find a way to remember which book she'd read and which ones she still should read. She didn't want to miss anything.

Even though she had put the book back, she still could feel the power, the … what?

The love.

Gamma's love.

Had Gamma known back then … months or even years ago … that Katty would find her way into this closet and read the journals?

Her own mother could have had access to Gamma and her heart. Maybe it might have changed Mom if she'd been open to Gamma. Katty didn't even want to go there. Whatever it was that had split the two sisters was gonna be left alone. Katty did not want to explore that evil—her mom's evil.

Ever.

Slowly, Katty knelt on the floor, her hands outstretched against the old worn wood, and a tear dropped next to her fingers, darkening the wood. She closed her eyes. Terrified. She'd never opened her heart to anyone since Phil and Mom.

But now, in this small room that should not be a room, she let it happen. She looked up at the space around her. Magical. This space was impossible if a person checked walls, or a floor plan and measured.

Impossible.

She couldn't explain it to anyone, although Noell knew. Noell had even run outside to check. She didn't need to do that. She'd grown up in this house. She owned this house and knew every inch.

But somehow, the years or the power of Gamma's words, her wisdom, had expanded from what Noell had thought was a normal closet into a whole room that held—Katty counted—nine bookshelves. And a couple walls with paintings.

Whatever was letting it happen, she would not be the one to tell the outside world of the miracle. That was it. It was a miracle and Katty felt it was partly for her. Yes, Noell, too. Bea, too.

She glanced up. So many books.

If it would help Noell's nightmares, her own pain and fears. Even Bea with what she had already—in her young life—experienced.

Wow.

People paid for expensive therapy when, if they had a room like Gamma's Closet, they would be so much better off.

Gamma drew and wrote words of her personal life—her pain, joys, celebrations, accusations. She painted over Katty's hands and with her—Katty had no idea on earth how. But it had happened and Bea and Noell had experienced it, too. They had seen. Katty searched the bookshelves with her eyes. Were there answers here in those books? What could Gamma teach her?

Noell had a gift that she called a curse. But what if it wasn't a curse but a sort of protection. She could feel and hear, sometimes see another person's life. It had protected her from that guy, Mr. Grimes. From other things. And maybe her germaphobe stuff protected her.

Katty straightened. It had to. If she gathered a bunch of junk from someone else and it had bad vibes on it, Noell maybe wouldn't be able to sense what she did now.

What if even her mom's drowning played a part in all this. Awful for Noell to be actually in the water and see and hear ... awful. But, what if—

Bea crawled into the room. "Morning, Mommy. Did you sleep in here?"

Katty chuckled and shook her head. "Nope. I just woke up early and came in here so I wouldn't wake you up." She reached for Bea and snuggled her onto her lap, her head on top of Bea's head. "You're so warm."

This kid.

What were *her* gifts?

Deep breath. Bea still smelled good from her bath the night before. Sweetness. Another deep breath. What had Gamma smelled like? She couldn't remember. She picked up a book and sniffed it.

Ahh. That. The book smelled like … a book, but more than that. It probably smelled like the inks and paints, too. But there was something else.

Gamma's smell was this. And for the time being, that was enough for Katty.

Bea's smell.

Gamma's smell.

FORTY

Noell could see Katty and Bea snuggled inside Gamma's closet. She was sure with everything she was, that they were definitely a part of finding what was in that closet. Gamma's thoughts. Her drawings. If they hadn't moved in with her, she might never have discovered that space.

She tapped her chin. What if … what if the only reason it had been discovered was for them, but … for them all? What if it hadn't even been there, not even existed, until … until they were all in Gamma's room, in her house.

Perfect timing, if that could even happen.

Noell shook her head. That drawing on the wall and actually seeing Gamma's hand, or someone's hand, paint. If only. If only she could hold that hand again. If she could kiss it, feel it comb through her hair like when she was little, again.

Noell slipped away from the door, into the kitchen.

She wanted to join them but didn't want to interfere with their mother, daughter time. They had been through a lot in their lives that only recently Noell had learned something about. Getting to know them was wonderful, but hard.

But reality. She almost knew what was in some of those

diaries, in Gamma's journals—or could guess. And that was the real reason she backed away from the closet.

Noell was terrified.

When Katty brought up something from *her* past, at first Noell understood, but then after a moment, she struggled. At least Katty had a mom. At least Bea had a grandma.

At that point, Noell always retracted her accusations. Even she would never forget Katty's mom's eyes from just recently. Black, they were. There was something evil lurking in those eyes —in her—and it reminded Noell of Mr. Grimes. The afternoon that younger Noell had found herself lured into his house. He had asked for help—playing on the down-trodden expression on his face and the walker he was tapping with his fingers—almost to draw attention to it. The evil there revealed itself—so obvious to her pure heart—that she had never forgotten it. Shivers even now ran up her arms, years later, at the memory.

At the Public Power office, she could literally breathe in and know Mr. Grimes had been there. Using autopay was her salvation. She loved going there to visit the ladies, since she had worked there previously for a very short time. The ladies there were so nice and caring—especially since Gamma died.

But even their kindness was no match for Mr. Grimes' evil that she would probably absorb just entering the office.

She stared out the kitchen window toward his house. He was pure evil. A blink opened in her mind—like a tiny video played there—of Mr. Grimes with Bea.

Oh no! What was that?

She dropped onto a kitchen chair and covered her face with her hands. No way was that man ever getting his hands on pure-hearted Bea. No way.

She hugged herself, rubbed her arms, rocked back and forth. Goosebumps. No windows were open. She had made sure last night. The nights were getting cooler and she didn't want to pay extra for utility bills.

His house was too close for her own comfort. Either she should move, or he should leave. Somehow.

What would Gamma do? There was a whole library, a whole eternity of teachings in that closet. Without thinking about it she stood and faced toward Gamma's room. She knew they needed to get at them and study up. Noell heaved a shaky sigh. Parts of those journals were going to hurt. She knew beyond anything she could ever imagine, that Gamma had written about the drowning in those journals.

Ugh.

Gamma had probably written about Noell's own struggles, too. Gamma knew about Noell's nightmares. She knew about every night Noell woke up either screaming or crying. She seemed to have a sixth sense about when Noell needed her. Her loving and kind face always appeared.

In the recent years, especially—Noell's nightmares had become very real, exceptionally terrifying. She woke up crying, "Mommy! Mommy! Don't go."

Every year it grew worse. Each dream began to seep water in real life. Water even splashed under Noell's bed. In the last year, water even poured into the front porch when she tried to change her outside boots into brand new slippers to protect her feet. She had no doubt also, that her germaphobe stuff, her fears, had begun then. If she couldn't control river water pounding at the car doors, keeping her and Mommy inside, hearing Mommy scream Noell's name, gulping in too much water until strong hands lifted her away from the terror, then at least she could control her room, her surroundings.

As she stared into space, had those strong hands been Grampa's? Or were they someone … or something else? Back then, she'd been sure, because Grampa had been there. He'd crushed her in her arms, sobbing at the same time.

She'd been saved.

Mom had drowned.

Oh, why had she gone so deep this time? *Pull back. Pull back in, Noell.*

Breathe.

It wasn't like she was afraid that the floors might be dirty. She wasn't afraid of bugs or dirt. She was afraid of drowning. She was afraid that because the water had become real—her shoes or slippers even got wet and the heavy totes floated against the wall—that some day the water might get deeper and deeper and she wouldn't be able to swim out.

She was, bottom line, afraid to face that night.

There wasn't much research on dreams turning real. Not that she'd found, anyway. She scoured the actual library and had gotten very good at asking every search engine on the internet pertinent and creative questions.

Never any answers.

She and Gamma were total opposites when it came to housekeeping. But maybe it wasn't really about housekeeping but more about what each person had experienced and how each individual dealt with things—how each person healed—or didn't heal. Gamma had lost a daughter. Noell had lost her mom. Same, but different. Everyone must grieve differently.

Because of her curse—Gamma had called it a gift—what was it, really? A molecule attack? What was the science behind it? There had to be something, some study, somewhere. Doctors. Answers. She wanted answers to not live in fear.

Sometimes Noell felt trapped or at least closed in. She usually did that to herself, but mostly it made living her life tolerable. Back in high school, she pretended to be sick many days, to stay home. Entering a certain classroom, the one she was most interested in, was intolerable. Science was her favorite subject and when the bell rang and it was time for that certain class, her skin crawled. Her stomach lurched. She always wore some sort of protective jacket with thick sleeves.

Classmates teased her about having cold hands. She didn't

have cold hands. Noell pulled the thick sleeves down over her hands so no skin came in touch with the doorknob or drawer handles. Not one molecule. But even then, she had become good at sensing the atmosphere in the room, or outside. It wasn't the air quality ... like in oxygen or hydrogen.

It was something else.

One day Noell had literally walked the town. Up one street and down the other, sending out feelers, if she could call it that. Sensing. Concentrating on what she felt or could sense. Certain buildings seemed okay, almost pleasant. She would have guessed that the library would be the worst since all kinds of books were in there: books on the supernatural, fiction about anything, even some children's books terrified her. But no. It was fine. Great even. Noell knew the director there, and the others who filled in on her day off. They were probably the reason it felt good.

She expected the bar and grille to be bad. It was. As a personal challenge, she even walked up to the door—she knew she was underage—and almost touched the handle. Almost. Couldn't do it. No way. Especially when she saw little tendrils floating out along the edge of the door itself.

No way.

Some churches, like where Gamma's funeral service had been, gave her the creeps even from the street. But another church made her feel happy—so happy that she had walked up to the door and touched it, touched the handle and opened the door. She entered the building. Breathed the air. Her breathing had become faster, but not really because of any evil. She was just nervous.

She especially didn't feel trapped at Mrs. B's store though. Why? It felt better than any of the churches. Better than her own home—better than Gamma's house. She loved Mrs. B. What was the difference?

Noell jumped.

Katty tiptoed into the kitchen. "I saw you peek into the closet." She reached for Noell's arm, but stopped before she touched her. "What are you seeing?" She pointed behind her toward Gamma's bedroom—the closet. "You turned around and left. Are you okay?"

Noell shivered. There had to be a window left open. "I'm okay. Just deep … thinking … about stuff."

"You've got goosebumps all up and down your arms." Katty did touch her, gently on her shoulder. No one had dared look so directly into her eyes as Katty did now. Oh, to run. Run to her old camper outside. Her room upstairs.

But she didn't run.

Feet planted.

Katty reached for her hand. "Come back in the closet."

"Well, I thought you and Bea would need some time together."

Katty smirked. "We're always together—her and I." She tugged on Noell's hand. "I know. I get it. Kinda." She squirmed and twisted side-to-side, like a little girl shyly asking for candy. She came by that move naturally. Bea did it well. "So, I don't know exactly what you're going through. But. Please. The painting is changing."

Noell jumped again. "What? How?"

"Come." She pulled harder on Noell's hand. "Come and see."

In the closet, Bea was snuggled onto a blanket, asleep again. Sweet, beautiful face. So pure. Beautiful clear skin. Almost angelic.

Katty backed into the closet, still pulling on Noell's hand. She pointed at the wall. "That is a painting of my treehouse, but something happened just now." She peeked at Bea. Still asleep. "The hand appeared again with a paintbrush and look."

Where Katty pointed there appeared a car in the background.

"Okay." Noell was never good with cars. They all looked alike. Fletcher—even Grampa—would comment on a person's car and Noell could never recall anything about it. Four tires, hopefully. An engine and windshield. That was all. Maybe the color. "Okay, it's a car." As she stepped closer, the car began to move. Slowly at first, as it drove. Noell gasped and stumbled backwards, almost stepped on Bea. She couldn't take her eyes off the painting. The sky turned dark and wet. She stepped close to the wall and touched it.

Wet. She touched it. Her finger was wet with dark paint.

"It's raining, right?" She glanced back at Katty. The look on Katty's face must be exactly as her own. "That can't be." She plunked onto the floor. "It's like watching TV. A video."

She rushed to the bedroom and checked the windows. Now in the closet, she shook her head. "It's not raining." Her chest tightened. Her skin felt clammy. Goosebumps again. Slowly she slid to the floor.

Katty joined her, next to Bea. "Just a thought. The painting is like my painting back at our trailer house. Almost exactly. Mine at home has more babies—"

Just as she said the words, babies appeared. Babies floated into the tree, sat on the grass.

Noell turned to Katty. Her eyes popped wide. Mouth open, just like her own.

Katty pointed. "Look. The storm is coming."

It was. The sky was dark. They both jumped toward each other, when a streak of lightning hit the tree. They grabbed each others hands. Thunder. Just like watching a storm chaser video.

Bea stirred and opened her eyes. "Mommy?" She spied the painting. "Oh, it's raining." Her eyelids fluttered closed.

"I don't get it." Noell's analytical mind tried to figure out the possibility of the painting moving right in front of them. "This can't be happening. Raining. Bea saw it too." Hard to whisper. What would Gamma do? Or, what was Gamma doing?

She would be praying.

Maybe.

Noell grabbed Katty's hand in hers. "God help." That was all she could say. When the car appeared—when the hand seemed to paint, no it did paint—it was freaky enough. But with the rain. She checked the floor at the base of the painting. Tapped the floor. The water. It was real. It was wet. But the lightning. The thunder?

She'd … been there. She'd been to this place before. The painting looked like a real place that she almost remembered.

As she watched the scene unfold, tears began to fill her eyes. Her chest tightened. "No. Mom." She reached toward the painting, but never released Katty's hand. Tighter. She knew she must be hurting Katty, but she couldn't stop.

Bea woke again. "Mommy?" She rubbed her eyes and sat up.

Rain poured down in the painting. The car seemed to float, skid back and forth, and go out of control. The creek became a river overflowing its banks and soon enveloped the car.

The car disappeared under the water.

Noell screamed.

FORTY-ONE

Mark shoved the boxes over on the back seat to make room for the one he had carried from the house. The last one. Well, the last one for now, if he knew his mom. She was in clean-out mode and that meant days and days of opening boxes, examining every piece, every item in it, then deciding where it should go—back in the box to donate to Mrs. B's consignment store, to the trash bag open on the floor, or on a shelf or counter to keep.

It all took an amazing and exhausting amount of time.

Every day that he helped Mom, he always went home and threw something of his own stuff away. Even if it was a piece of junk mail—he threw something away. If he didn't find junk mail, he made himself open kitchen cupboards and find some odd dish or melted plastic bowl. If he didn't find something in the kitchen, he intentionally walked to his closet. He always found a faded T-shirt to toss.

The note from Uncle Ted would always be in his pocket or wallet. Always. He might even frame it.

"Ready to go?" Mom opened the passenger door and she stood there waiting. As if they could get another box inside her car.

"Let's get this done." Mark opened the door and slid onto the seat. "We should have loaded everything in my pickup. It would have held more." He started the engine and shifted into reverse.

"But things might have blown out if we'd loaded it in the back … in the—"

"In the box?" Mark shook his head as he backed out and started down the street toward downtown. "In the pick-up bed? Naw. I wouldn't have driven that fast and besides it's only a couple blocks from your house to downtown—to Mrs. B's store. Which reminds me, I forgot to bring some old junk of mine that I wanted to donate."

"We can go to your house and get it." Mom pointed the direction of his house behind them. "Right now. It won't take much time."

"Naw. I can pick it up later and take it." He pulled into a parking space downtown in front of Mrs. B's store. The store window was always intriguing, luring customers inside. Today she had displayed pumpkins, fall leaves, old canning jars. Tons more stuff. All in the window. Odd display.

"Look, Mark." Mom pointed as she got out of the car. "She's got all kinds of old stuff—antiques, I should say—fall … decor." She chuckled. "I like her display better than those big stores." She scanned the store window. "I love this. I should get my fall decorations up."

Mark opened the back door and pulled out a couple boxes and walked to the entrance. "Hey Mom. Give me a hand? Open the door?"

Mom made a move toward the entrance door, but another woman inside beat her to it. She grinned and pulled the door wide and held out her hand to enter. Like that woman on TV— all of those fancy models who introduced the prize. This woman looked familiar. She was maybe Mom's age or a bit younger, but wore heavy eyeliner. He could see it from outside. Hot pink lips. Tight jeans with a button-up shirt. She'd forgotten to button the top couple of buttons, because Mark could see her—

"Why, thank you for holding the door for us." Mom to the rescue. How had she run from the open car, grabbed something, and rushed to the door? Fast Mom. "Lovely day today, isn't it?"

The woman cocked one eyebrow up and smirked. "Yes." She oozed kindness—sort of. "Cleaning out, I see? Can I help you with your things?"

Mom glanced at Mark. "Well, uh, we should talk to Mrs. B, first."

"Oh, Gelda? She lets me check people in, so put your things right on this counter and I'll get busy."

Mark hesitated a few steps from the counter. She seemed so familiar. Where? Seemed nice enough.

The woman grabbed his top box and slid it onto the counter and turned back for the other one. Mark beat her to it and pushed it against the others. Where was Mrs. B?

There. He'd never seen a scowl on that woman's face—ever. As Mrs. B headed over to where he stood, she seemed to be mumbling something to herself. She brightened when she saw Mark and her scowl turned to a smile. Her eyes seemed to be pleading for help, though, as they landed on the strange woman.

"Hello, Mrs. B." Mark stepped up to their boxes. "What can I do to help?"

Mrs. B's eyes spoke again … or was Mark seeing things? He thought he heard, "Rescue me from this woman." Naw. But there was certainly something off and Mrs. B wasn't happy about it.

Mark tapped the woman's shoulder. "Hey. We need to check our stuff in with Mrs. B. She's here now, so if you'll excuse us?"

The woman stopped digging through their boxes and backed away. "Oh. Sure. Just trying to help." Something about her. She seemed ordinary enough, a regular person.

"Don't I know you from somewhere?" Mark tried to remember.

The woman adjusted her blouse to reveal more of her chest and bra.

He blinked, like scales fell off his eyes.

Or some kind of disguise had been removed from her. Or both.

He'd seen this woman half naked in the park with Mr. Grimes and they'd both ended up in jail the other day. That's where he'd seen her. And he'd seen way too much of her that day. Almost like she was trying to reveal now.

She grinned, knowing he recognized her. "Now you remember." She stepped closer and shrugged her shoulders.

Mark stood his ground.

She stepped face-to-face and licked her pink lips. Something rose in him—that old desire, the same as when he'd lived in Omaha. His breathing quickened, and he felt like he was standing next to a fire pit.

Wait. Something else rose up in Mark and he put his hands on her shoulders as she pursed her lips, ready for a kiss.

He held her at arms length and pushed her behind him. "Not here. Not now." He swallowed and spoke louder. "And not ever."

She snickered and swiveled her hips. "Oh, you'll come around. I know guys like you."

"Well, he's not like those guys." Mom stepped in, crossed her arms across her chest, her nostrils flared. "Ever."

"Mom." He chuckled. "I'm okay."

The woman slithered away, but not before throwing him a kiss and Mom a tongue. Slimy.

Ding. R'ling.

The entrance door flew open and two women and a little girl walked in.

The woman greeted them, loudly. "Katty! Bea! Noell." She rushed to embrace Bea, but the little girl quickly hid behind her mother.

Katty withdrew from her, ready to leave, her hand grabbed the door handle, again. "Mom. What are you doing here?"

Mom?

The woman glanced at Mark. "I was just shopping around. Trying to help this cute young man with his boxes."

Katty's eyes met Mark's. Her eyes spoke. Not accusing. Her expression seemed to apologize because then she glanced at her mother, then back at Mark.

Her mom scanned between Katty and Mark. "Oh, you two have met, I see." She swirled around between them all, including Phyllis, eyeing them all. "One big happy family."

Why did this feel so slimy? Could there be anymore toxicity in this store all at once? Even Mrs. B felt it—her lips were still moving like she was talking to herself. Was she praying?

He stepped past Katty's mom and leaned down to Bea. The minute she saw his face, she brightened and held her arms up, but immediately, her eyes flitted to Katty's mom behind him. He lifted Bea up in his arms and stood in front of Katty. Their eyes met and she clearly relaxed a little.

She moved so he was between her and her mom and mouthed, "Thank you."

He nodded. "Hey Bea, how are you doing?"

The woman, Katty's mom didn't miss a thing.

Interesting mix here in Mrs. B's store. Mom hadn't missed a thing, either. She seemed rooted to the floor. Her usual jovial greetings to Mrs. B was a silent nod and her lips began moving, too. But her eyes jumped from Mark's, Katty's, Bea's, Katty's mom and back to Mrs. B. Back to Mark. She visibly sucked in a deep breath and stepped close to Mark.

Patting him on the shoulder, then Bea on the back. "Hi, sweetie." She played the part of rescuer well.

Bea hid her face in Mark's neck and peeked out at her. She offered a sweet smile, then hid again.

That evidently stirred up competition in Katty's mom

because she stepped close to Mark and tickled Bea. She held out her hands. "Come to Grandma, Sweetie."

Nothing doing. Bea strangled Mark's neck and was not letting go.

Katty and Noell moved into the store and Katty pushed past her mom. "Here, Bea. We wanted a drink, didn't we." She flinched as she said the word drink, but held firm. Her eyes were on Mark's as she pulled Bea from him. Even a slight smile on her lips. "What do you want?" She mouthed thank you on her lips, again. "A smoothie? Strawberry?"

Noell took her cue and moved to the order counter.

Mrs. B smiled and stepped behind the counter. "What can I get you, Noell?"

Katty stepped beside Noell and swayed with Bea from side-to-side, waiting her turn. Bea still clung to her neck, her eyes on Mark behind them.

"Mom? I'll go get the rest and be right back."

Phyllis nodded.

Whew. Good to get outside for fresh air. Mark reached in for the last box and shoved the door shut with his foot. He turned and the door was open, only it wasn't Katty's mom who opened it again, but his own mom. "Thanks, Mom." He searched the store. Katty's mom appeared to be shopping down one aisle.

He set the box down on the counter next to the rest. "Do we need to take these to the back?"

Mrs. B heard him and shook her head, no. "It's okay. We'll price them there and scan them into the system." She scooped ice into the blender. "Less steps that way." She nodded at Mom. "Thanks Phyllis. Good to get rid of stuff, right?"

Mom nodded and smiled.

Mark knew he was going to get an earful on the way back to Mom's house, until he left to go home. She had promised him leftovers to take home, so he guessed it might be worth it. But

Mom's eyes never left Katty, her mom, or Bea. Even Noell drew her interest.

"Not staying for a drink?" Mrs. B was doing her best to defuse the charged atmosphere.

Mark checked Mom's face. "You want something, Mom?"

She shook her head. "No thanks. We just ate, so I don't think I want anything." She nodded at Mark. "But you get something if you want."

"I'm fine. Let's go back to your house and clean up the mess." He knew good and well, they'd already done that, but he also sensed Mom was ready to leave.

Katty picked up her drink and looked for a place to sit. Noell stood right behind her.

He waved. "See you girls later." Oh that felt good. What if someday that would happen. That he might see them—her later tonight for a—

Katty's mom stepped up and made eyes at Mark. She bounced her eyebrows up and down and winked a couple times. She was just trying to stir up trouble. It wasn't going to happen —either with him or with Katty because she had intentionally sat at a small table with only three chairs. Just room enough for her, Bea, and Noell.

"Ready, Son?" Mom walked to the door, standing just behind Katty's mom. The two almost side-by-side. He glanced at Katty's mom, then at his own. One was dressed kind of like the young girls—maybe like Katty and Noell, but she left nothing to the imagination with buttons open at the top of her shirt. Her jeans were tight, but that seemed to be the style now. His own mom wore jeans, too and they fit loose, but stylish. Both wore button-down shirts, both were pretty, but very different in what each breathed out.

Mom opened the door and stepped outside.

"Thank you Phyllis and Mark." Mrs. B was always so gracious and kind.

He waved. "We'll be back with more another day." One last peek at Katty. She appeared to be deep in conversation with Noell. Bea was playing in the Kid's Corner.

"Wait!" Bea jumped up and ran to him. "I want a hug, Depdy Mark."

Not going to pass that up. He leaned down, but Katty's mom intercepted and tried to pick her up. Bea fought, kicking, until she got away. "No no." She stomped her foot. "Not you." Then pointed at Mark. "Him."

Oh-oh. That did not go well with her grandma. An angry expression flitted across her face but she recovered quickly with a smirk. "Just like her mother."

Bea found him and gave her best hug, while she kept an eye on her grandmother.

"Bye, Bea."

She released him and drew back, looked into his eyes. She patted him on the shoulder. "You be careful out there, Mr. Depdy Mark."

Mark swallowed hard. "I will."

FORTY-TWO

Phyllis struggled to keep quiet. Her usual response to someone like Katty's mom would be to clam up and run away.

It was difficult not to stare at the woman. She might have been pretty at one time.

Phyllis stole a peek at Katty, even Bea. They were beautiful, if you judged by the world's view or standards. Was she even sober right now in the coffee shop? Probably not. Coffee might help. Being with her ... cousin Noell would help. Noell seemed to be a solid young woman.

Phyllis glanced at Mark. Why couldn't he be attracted to Noell, instead of—?

She tried to stop shaking her head. She sensed she might only be doing it slightly, but when she saw what the woman was doing and how she was dressed, it just happened. She shook her head.

"What?"

Oh-oh.

Caught.

"What are you staring at?" The woman held out her hand. "I'm Katty's mom." She looked behind her at the table where they sat. "And Bea's grandma." She snickered. "Yeah. Probably not your typical grandma, am I."

Phyllis hesitated and started to hold out her hand, but Mark intervened.

"Mom, you sure you don't want something to drink?" He winked at her. "My treat." He took her hand and led her to the counter, pointing at the menu board. "They have a great selection."

Whew. Saved by her son. Mark was a hero, because she wasn't sure where that woman's hands had been or what she'd been doing.

"Do you want something, Son?" Would it be obvious if she ran out of the store right now?

She could almost feel the woman's eyes on her back. There was something about her that gave Phyllis the jitters. She didn't know what to call it, but she knew it wasn't good. And probably the same stuff was on Katty and her little girl, Bea.

She couldn't let Mark end up with a woman like that. What had she worked so hard for all these years—raising Mark, praying for him—to have him end up with a family like that?

Never.

"Mom? You okay?" Mark chuckled. "You seem far, far away."

"Uh, I'll have what you're having, I guess." She spoke before she really looked at what he was having. It was huge and topped with whipped cream or something. "Wait. I just want a small one." She stepped to the counter and tried to breathe.

Her little plan of time with Mark, feeding him lasagne, cleaning out his dad's stuff, and maybe have some Bible study with him wasn't working. Even pray with him. Her deepest desire was for him—

She felt a hand on her back and moved closer to the order counter. Only this didn't feel like his touch. He was always so respectful and gentle with her and this gave her the jitters or goosebumps. She shivered and turned around.

No one.

Mark ordered their drinks, stood right beside her, his hands on the counter—not on her back.

She turned the other way.

No one.

Someone or something had just touched her on the back, she was sure of it. But as she turned both right and left and all the way around, there was no one there. She felt silly, like she was dancing in the store, in public, like a little girl—like Bea might.

The woman was watching her and as their eyes met, something so raw came over Phyllis, so evil that she grabbed Mark's arm.

"Is this okay?" He held a drink out to her.

"Oh, yes. It's fine." She took it in one hand and held onto his arm with her other. Not letting go of him.

Something so terrifying and evil had come near her.

The woman laughed.

It felt like just the woman and Phyllis were alone in a movie and the rest of the world had been pushed behind some sort of veil or mist. She could just barely see the store and the other people—Mark—through some kind of fog, but she saw clearly the woman and herself. Just the two of them, like an old western stand-off. The two of them facing each other, The woman stepped closer, closer, until she was right next to her.

"Scared?" She breathed into Phyllis's face. "Am I scaring you? You poor little religious, righteous woman." She circled around Phyllis. "You've never seen the likes of me, have you. Never run into someone so powerful as I am."

Phyllis blinked and gasped. A terrible stench rose up. She couldn't even smell the drink she held in her hand and it must be strong. Even though the drink was hot, her hand was cold. She shivered as the woman continued to circle her. Pictures rose up in her mind—pictures of this woman with a little girl about the size of Bea, but not Bea. Pictures of the little girl screaming, "It's hot!" And the woman laughing like she was now. Awful things she did to that little girl.

Where was Mark? Where was God?

Help!

"Mom?" Mark put his arm around her shoulders. "You okay? You just trembled." He chuckled. "Glad we didn't get a cold drink. You're always so cold and that would put you over the edge." His voice sounded so far away—like when Phyllis had surgery and was waking up to someone talking to her. He sounded like he was in the next room but the door was closed. In a closed room next to where she stood.

At the same time Mark chuckled, the woman laughed in a raucous voice.

The only other person she could see besides Katty's mom, was Mrs. B and she stood still, her lips moving silently.

Shivers ran up Phyllis's spine. How could she get out of this … this … she wasn't used to using words like dimension, but that's what came to her mind. How could she get back to Mark and what she thought was her reality? How could she—

Something touched her back again, only this time she felt a strengthening. Power. She could breathe again. The weight she had felt, the heaviness and the evil lifted and she could breathe freely. She sucked in a deep breath and blew it out. And again. The mist or whatever it was seemed to clear and the store was visible. All of the shelves and stuff for sale once again appeared sharp and clear. People moved around. The coffee maker or whatever it was, was loud as it hissed. Colors were vivid just like before.

Somehow, as the mist lifted, Phyllis wanted to run to Katty. Her arms ached to embrace Katty and Bea because of what she had seen of that woman. She could hardly breathe as she remembered and she blinked tears away. How could she explain her emotion to Mark, here, now? Never had anything like this happened before. Never had she seen into the invisible world. Frightening, yet enlightening.

She tried not to look at Katty, at the woman. What had Katty lived through?

Phyllis straightened. What might be God's plan for Katty's life.

Without thinking, Phyllis sipped from her drink, not expecting the rush of coffee through the sweet cream. She gasped.

Mark turned to her. "You okay? Is it too hot?"

She shook her head. "No, Mark. It's just right." She swallowed. "I'm just not used to such … a rich drink." She smiled. "It's delicious."

Mark turned to Mrs. B with a thumbs up. "I told you she would like it."

Mrs. B smiled and nodded. "Good. Glad you like it Phyllis." Her eyes smiled too, but there was something deeper. A knowing, or … wait. She'd been there in that other—

"Ready?" Mark turned toward the door.

Phyllis did too, but that woman stood in their way.

"I just realized something." The woman's head was held high, her chin jutted forward. "It's time for Bea to turn five." She said it loud enough for all in the store to hear—even above the whirr of the coffee machine. She whirled to face Katty and all at that table. "Isn't it?" She clapped her hands. "Let's have a party for her!"

Exciting news, but the look in her eyes didn't resemble a grandma excited about a granddaughter's birthday party. Her eyes looked like she was trying to stir up trouble, or worse.

The expression on Katty's face seemed shocked. Horrified.

Phyllis had never contemplated the fact that this woman had terrified her own daughter. Katty was still scared of her own mother.

Katty's expression imprinted on Phyllis's mind, on her heart.

What had that child been through at the hands of her own mother?

"Come on, Mom." Mark hooked his hand through her arm and pulled her toward the door.

Phyllis pointed. "Um. We should—"

"No. I have no idea who this is and why she thinks she is Bea's grandma." Mark kept pulling on Phyllis's arm. He got her to the entrance door and grasped the handle.

"But can't you see the resemblance?" At just the moment Phyllis stopped him and pointed from the woman to Katty, the woman turned to face him with a smirk on her face. She'd heard her. Katty sat just behind the woman, against the wall.

Mark bumped into the door as he realized the truth. "I-I have to go, Mom." He yanked the door open and stepped outside. "You coming?"

"Hey." The woman clapped her hands together. "I said, isn't it about time for Bea to have a birthday party?" She directed her glare first at Mark and Phyllis, then to Katty. And Bea. "We're all here. Why not now?"

Bea perked up from her drink and coloring. "A birthday party? What's that?" She bounced off her chair and clapped her hands along with the woman.

Oh my. This was going to get ugly. Phyllis stepped outside. She couldn't help herself. She glanced back inside as the door closed behind her. The look on Katty's face was heartbreaking. Katty slowly rose from her chair, pointed at her mom, and opened her mouth. Phyllis almost covered her ears, even though she was outside and couldn't hear what Katty was saying.

Even though Phyllis hadn't said what Katty's mom had said and stirred up *that* bit of trouble, she had stirred up trouble of her own.

Phyllis swallowed and bit her lips. She followed Mark to the car and silently slid onto the seat, as he held the door open for her. Not going to say any more. Not going to criticize Katty or Bea. Not going to say bad things about Katty's mom. What a … not going to say bad things about Katty or her mom. Not going to make it worse.

Looking out the window was easier than trying to hold her breath.

She could almost feel Mark fuming beside her as he drove her home.

"I didn't—" She clapped her hand over her mouth.

Out of the corner of her eye, she could see Mark shaking his head.

"Please don't, Mom."

She drew a deep breath in, then slowly blew it out. In again. Then out again. She'd blown it with the biggest, most important issue in her son's life—his life mate. How could she ever fix this? She'd messed up lots in her life, in her marriage, in raising Mark. But this time was different. It affected his future, her future with him, possible grandkids.

It was her prayer to have grandkids, but for Mark to be happy in his marriage.

Now he may never trust her again.

What if he never spoke to her again?

FORTY-THREE

Katty followed Noell and Bea inside to the kitchen. Bea slurped from her smoothie cup, set it on the table, and picked up a red crayon.

Katty's thoughts tumbled over each other. The visuals of her past with her mom—the abuse, the slaps, broken crayons, broken bones. They stirred with pictures of a couple days ago, but of just now at Mrs. B's store. Those eyes pierced her very soul—everything she had hidden down deep was no longer hidden but visual. Other visuals morphed and mixed over the insanity of her past. Visuals of that woman—her eyes opened up another realm of evil lurking behind that fake green of her eyes.

Something had stirred, moved, writhed behind the green that made Katty cringe even now as she stood inside Noell's house.

Mom had stood there, rooted to the spot, like she expected Katty to run and embrace her.

Something clicked or snapped in Katty and she ran for Gamma's room.

"Mommy?" Bea ran after her. "Who was that lady?" She pointed. "At cute Gelda's store?"

Katty found her purse. Her keys. She ran past Bea and Noell.

Bea ran after her. "Bad Mommy's back."

As she ran out the front door, she could hear Noell begging her. "Katty, stay. You don't have to do that. Stay here. It'll be okay. Don't start again."

Katty stopped at the dollar store. She had no idea why. As she stumbled through the store, she saw birthday party decorations. Streamers, cards, balloons, and banners screaming, "Happy Birthday!"

Katty almost stopped breathing.

Birthday?

Gasp.

Her feet stuck to the floor. She became immobile, like a statue made of stone. She'd never had a birthday party for Bea. Blinking back tears, she could hardly remember when her actual birthday was. When Bea was born, Katty was in a full-on drunken stupor. Probably the worst pain killer anyone could ever use for birthing a baby.

And now she was—well, almost—on her way to buy more booze. That was what she had run out of the house to do—get drunk. Numb out. Or die.

Part of Katty begged to get back in the car, drive to the convenience store, and buy shooters. She hadn't had anything to drink in days. And right now her body, but her emotions screamed for booze, especially after seeing and hearing her mom.

Birthday colors and sparkles blasted her on every shelf, every hook.

She still couldn't move.

Bea always talked about the angels. Did an angel have her glued to this spot? Stopped here to see ... to realize ... to remember?

Standing in the middle of a public store, not being able to move, and with tears streaming down her cheeks. She could hardly wipe her eyes.

Painful.

But. What if she could stay here, rooted to this spot, in front of all this happiness, and make herself experience the pain.

Oh. Dear. God.

Embrace the pain.

Without anything to numb it.

Without the booze.

She knew Noell had seen her leave.

Bea knew. Katty had heard her as the door to the porch slammed. "Bad Mommy's back." Tears ran freely down her cheeks now. She didn't dare wipe them away.

Let them come. Let them flood the place. Drowned by her own tears.

Not running away this time. Not numbing out with booze or anything else, People used all kinds of things to run away to: drugs, sex, shopping, anger, TV shows. Hiding. Running. Not facing the truth. Not facing the lies.

Mom's voice echoed in her mind. "You're just a slut. I should have killed you when I had the chance."

Were those words the truth or the lies?

Something broke in Katty and she grabbed a banner, a couple rolls of streamers in several colors, cake toppers. Cake toppers? Birthday cake? How could she do that?

She better check with Noell before she went that wild. She'd never baked a cake before. She'd never created a birthday party before.

Katty stared at the birthday cards in front of her.

She'd never had a birthday party.

Mom had never celebrated Katty's birthday. Well, why would she? Mom regretted the day Katty had been born.

Katty made herself go there, but this time with Bea. Katty had been through some very hard times with Bea—all because of her own stupidly—but she had never, ever regretted birthing

Bea. Ever. She had loved that baby girl from the very first minute she'd pushed her out and wrapped her in old towels.

Never. She gulped. Her chin quivered. Her whole face crumpled.

An employee seemed to be hovering. Did she even have the money to buy this stuff?

She nodded. The money she was going to use for booze was perfect. She was not buying booze today or any day. Ever again.

"Need some help?" The man had kind eyes.

She gulped again and blinked. Nodded.

She definitely needed help.

He held out his hands and smiled. "Birthday party? That's always fun."

"Yeah. Fun." This was the dollar kind of store. She had enough money. She wasn't going to buy shooters today. She smiled. She was buying birthday party stuff. She'd never done that.

She continued to smile as she followed the man to the checkout.

"Did you buy candles for the cake?" He grinned. He was older—maybe a grandpa—and had obviously done the whole birthday party thing.

"Uh. No. I forgot." She hadn't forgotten. She had no idea on this earth how to make a birthday party. She followed him back to the party aisle, wiping her face with her sleeves.

"What color do you want?" He laughed. "What about every color? Do it up right."

"Sure. Okay." She came to. "How much are they?"

"Oh, they are cheap." He grabbed one of every color and started toward the front of the store.

Katty reached into her pocket. A twenty. She held her breath as he scanned each item in. Twenty-Two dollars and forty-seven cents. "Uh, I only have—"

"Hush." He pushed his hand at her, reached into his pocket,

and pulled out his money. "My birthday present to you and your little one." He rang it up and handed Katty the change. "It's on me, today."

Katty stared at the coins in her hand, then back up at the man. Tears started to flow again. "I can't … I—"

"Pretend I'm your dad or better yet, your grandpa." He nodded very slowly, his eyes appeared sincere. He handed her the receipt and carried the full shopping bag to the exit door, his arms outstretched.

Oh no.

Katty was aware of each step toward him. She wasn't used to kindness in a hug. She was used to—

She walked into his hug.

He didn't let go right away.

Pure love and kindness.

When he released her, he wiped her cheeks with his hand. Warm hands. "Have a great day and a wonderful party."

Katty couldn't talk, only nod. The man's eyes were dark brown, not black. But they made her feel like she was looking into Clarence's blue, blue eyes.

Kindness from Clarence.

Kindness from this man.

She nodded again and found her way outside to her car. Wiped her nose on her sleeve. As she sat in the driver's seat, she found herself wanting to slow down time. She wanted to remember how this felt. What she saw.

Deep sigh.

But when was Bea's birthday?

FORTY-FOUR

Memories of Katty being led into a jail cell, handcuffed, meshed with visuals of when Mark himself had led that woman—her mom—half-naked, into another jail cell. His mom didn't know the half of it. And she never would—not from his mouth. As he had walked to the car with Mom, pictures flashed of both women handcuffed and in that jail cell, both pretty drunk. How could a guy get that out of his head?

He pulled onto the street and started toward Mom's house.

He knew there were several trauma-based groups available for police officers. When they had been called to a particularly horrible accident, the whole department attended to recover. Super helpful, even though uncomfortable to be that vulnerable. Mark didn't like being that transparent, like most men, but he knew that if he didn't at least take part in some of it, those visuals would live in his mind forever. He'd met some long-term deputies. They had become hard-hearted men.

As Mark pulled in the driveway at Mom's house, he put up with her good-bye's and chattering.

"Good-bye Mark. Thanks for helping me get rid of those boxes— boxes of Dad's stuff."

She had swallowed. Here it came. She couldn't stop herself from always—

"And thanks for the coffee … drink. It was good, once it cooled down." She chuckled. "Nice to see Katty and her daughter, Bea." Mom would not stop. "She is so cute. Bea that is. Katty is … nice."

Holy cow, Mom. It had been a long time since he had wanted to yell shut-up at her. He'd done it a couple times as an immature teenager. But he almost did again, now. He clamped his lips shut, like back when he tried to stop her from giving him icky medicine as a little boy. Not going to yell at her—even though right now he wanted to defend Katty. With a mom like hers, why *wouldn't* she be the way she was? Why wouldn't she run away with whoever came along—Daynton? Why wouldn't she turn to booze—Mark had read too much of the archives. Why wouldn't she want to numb out from the pain of her past?

The more Mom chattered on about it, the more he realized that even since jail time, Katty seemed to have changed. Nobody would ever be perfect—he wasn't—but something was different in her for sure.

And for sure, something or Someone was different in him.
Breathe, Mark.

Katty hadn't yelled, tripped on her way in, hadn't patted her pockets. He knew she wanted booze when she did that. She hadn't hidden her eyes. She had looked directly into his.

Her eyes were deep pools of beautiful brown.

For some reason, his thoughts turned to Katty's painting on the walls of her trailer—those clouds and babies, the tree. He had to believe that the paintings were the true Katty. They comprised the truth of who she really was, instead of the abusive, addictive and … post abortive woman she showed to the world. The paintings were Katty's true heart.

Even this last arrest and her time in jail. He knew something had happened to her in that cell and to him on the floor outside

the door. Something or Someone had invaded her hard heart …
and his. Someone had changed her somehow into the young
woman he had seen just now at Mrs. B's store. She spoke softer.
She hugged and stroked Bea's hair because she seemed to want
to, not just for show. She was even respectful of her mom,
almost. Her mom didn't seem to deserve any of that.

What was making the difference? Yes, those moments in jail,
but what else?

Mom's chatter broke into his thoughts. "But, you have to do
whatever you feel led to do, Mark. I'm not telling you what to
do." She sighed. "You're a man now and have a life of your own.
I just pray you are happy with whatever and whoever you
choose." She looked up at him. "You're my only son and I love
you."

He swallowed and let his chin drop to his chest, then looked
up at her. "I love you too, Mom." He got out and walked around
the car, taking his time to breathe deeply. She was especially
frustrating today. He opened the car door for her and she hopped
out. She was amazingly spry for her age. He guessed she was't
that old. Mrs. Nosy—Agatha—was really old. Mom wasn't as
old as Agatha.

"You need to come in to get your leftovers, Son. Lasagne."
She unlocked her front door and held it open for him.

If there was any way to lure him back in, it was through
lasagne. He loved that dish, but especially his mom's. He
followed her into the kitchen and watched her dig some out of
the dish and fill smaller containers—lots of small containers.
"Mom, you better save some for yourself. I'm not the only one
who loves it."

She nodded and pointed to a medium container. "There's
mine. And it's enough. I'm trying—"

"I know. You're trying to lose weight." He rolled his eyes
and shook his head. "You look fine. You always say that, but you
look better than all of your bible study friends."

"That's nice of you to say." She shrugged and dished another piece into a container. "I'll never look like Katty's mom, though. She's all … how do you say it? Buff? Trim. She can wear those skinny jeans better than most young girls." She licked her fingers. "Better than her own daughter." The baking pan was empty, but she scraped the sides. Always the frugal one. She was busy with the leftovers and chatted without thinking.

She packed his containers into a plastic shopping bag, held them out to him, and kept on chatting—almost without thinking about what she was saying. She just kept on. "Skinny jeans and unbuttoned shirts are not for a woman of God."

Mark just stared at her. She couldn't be thinking about what she was saying. She was just flapping her jaws, like some people said. Meaningless chatter. But somewhere deep down inside, Mom was letting what was inside her heart puke out of her mouth.

Maybe she still had a lot of pain from Dad, but she didn't need to talk that way about Katty and Bea. Even Katty's mom.

"Mom, I gotta go get some things done at home." The box with some of Dad's stuff she thought he needed was in his back seat. He might drive back over to Mrs. B's and drop that off there, too. Mom would never know.

"I said something wrong." She put her leftovers into the refrigerator and reached out to hug him. She stopped, then pursed her lips. She opened her mouth to say something, then closed it. Again. "I did it again." She peeked up at him. "I'm sorry, Mark. I don't mean to hurt you." She fiddled with the top buttons of her shirt. "I just want the best for you. I've tried to be a good example of a woman, a wife. Well, with your dad being who he was, and all the drinking that he did, I'm sure I failed a lot. But I tried to represent who you might want to marry someday."

"Mom." He held out his arms to hug her. "You have done a great job of being a good woman, a good wife—in spite of the obstacles that Dad set before you." He leaned his cheek against her ear. "I can't help it that … I didn't ever plan to … uh." He swallowed. Hard to speak it out loud. God help. "I guess God had a different plan than either one of us did."

Had he just admitted something? Yes, he kind of admitted—or started to admit—to loving Katty. But He had just spoken something about God, that he'd never even thought of saying before.

Before that note.

Before that prayer.

Mom nodded her head against his cheek. She was trying. He knew she was.

She seemed to have fallen asleep, standing up. After another minute, she raised her head and looked him right in the eye. "I'll stand by you and whoever you choose to marry." She pushed away and stood facing him. "That's my vow. I will stand by you and her and whoever she brings into the marriage." She tapped her chest. "I give you my word."

What? Never in a million—

She reached out and grabbed his hand. "I give you my word, Mark."

Whew. Mark knew she meant it. He was totally taken by surprise at how sincere she was. She meant every word. He didn't even wipe his wet cheeks. "I believe you, Mom. And I thank you from everything I am. I know this has been—" He shut his mouth. "Thank you. Because Katty might be the one."

There. He'd said it. Admitted it before the world—well, before Mom … and God. That truth burned into his very being, every cell.

It was just as solid as the prayer he had prayed earlier.

FORTY-FIVE

Phyllis waved from the front door as Mark pulled away in his truck. She stood there for several minutes after he was no longer visible. Whatever or whoever might have been driving in front of her house, or walking their dog might have gotten a wave from her, but she didn't see them at all.

The only thing she saw or felt was Mark still in front of her, his eyes filled with tears, his face wet, and the tremble in his voice as he said those words.

Katty was the one.

Katty was the life mate he would marry.

Katty was to be the mother of his children—her grand-children.

She was the one that Phyllis had prayed for all these years.

Oh my.

The realization of what that meant hit her like a punch in the stomach. She had faithfully prayed for Mark's life mate ever since she herself had started following Jesus. Phyllis had a prayer list and at the top of that list was to pray for protection for the woman he would marry. Her vision blurred as a car drove past. She blindly waved. Phyllis wiped her eyes. She had prayed that somehow God would get ahold of Mark's future life mate as a little girl's heart and draw her to faith in God. She had prayed for a good childhood and that God would keep her heart pure.

Well, it had been *her* list. *Her* will for Mark's future wife.

She sucked in a deep, ragged breath and closed the inside door. Turning to her living room, she slowly sat at her favorite place on the sofa and closed her eyes. "Lord, I'm sorry for trying to … for controlling … for—" She stopped herself and shook her head. She knew she always tried to make things happen, to control things and people's lives. She patted her chest. "Lord, I'm sorry for always … I know I'm not in control and I'm sorry for thinking I even was… ever."

Yes. That. "Lord, I give you my son, Mark." She chuckled. "I don't have to give You his name. You know who he is, don't You." She could almost feel God nod and hear him chuckle. "And I give you his future, his life mate and whoever she might be, although I think I know if she accepts." She reached for a tissue. "I ask you to take care of them and whatever family they might end up with--that little girl, Bea, is so precious."

Her heart opened to the possibility. Love from Him flowed and filled every part of her. Little flickers of joy began to tickle her insides.

Was this how it felt? Was this the joy of the Lord?

Phyllis had always thought of herself as a mature Christian woman. But today, that little girl inside her was waking up, too. She was remembering who she was and even from the time she was a little girl, what she might be someday. That little girl was learning to receive and embrace the love of a Father so generous and life-giving. That little girl had blossomed in His love and was ready to pour out love.

Pour out acceptance of others.

Release her will to His plans.

She knelt down beside the sofa and bowed her head. "Your

will, Lord and not mine." Deep breath. "Your plans for Mark, and not mine. I release him and Katty to You, Lord."

Sitting back on the sofa, she continued. "Lord, at first I wanted Mark to cut all ties to that woman and her daughter." She cleared her throat. "Katty and Bea. But when Bea jumped on Mark at the store, and he held his arms out to her, I knew, Lord. I know now that Katty and Bea are important to Mark—essential to him."

She spent a couple more minutes sitting on the sofa just breathing in and out. She'd been wrong. Terribly wrong. So wrong that it might have cost her a very important relationship with her son. Never worth it. Being right was never worth the heartache of losing someone so precious.

Ring!

She felt her pockets. No phone.

It wasn't on the counter where she'd dished up the lasagne.

Ring!

Where was that phone? It wasn't what they called the old phone—the land line.

It was her mobile.

She followed the sound as it rang.

Finally she pulled the utensil drawer open and there it was. Three rings. Mark's name was on the read out. He might have hung up already. She grabbed it and tapped it on. "Hello?"

"Hi, Mom."

"Hi, Mark." Was he psychic? He might have heard her words before but he couldn't have heard her prayer. "How are you?" Stupid. Stupid.

He chuckled. His voice seemed different. "I called to tell you that I'm sorry for being impatient with you before."

Impatient? He should have been angry or down-right mad. He had the right to be that with all she had said.

"It's okay, Mark. I'm glad you called." Deep breath. "I'm

sorry for what I said about Katty and Bea. About her mom. I had no right to say those things, Son. I'm so sorry."

There was a long silence on the other end. "Mom."

"And I forgive you, too." She interrupted him.

There was a deep sigh from Mark. "Thanks, Mom. I forgive you. I better … oh, thanks for the lasagne." He could be grinning. "It was good today, but it'll be even better the next time. Lasagne leftovers are the best."

She laughed out loud. "I know. My pleasure. Enjoy. Next time I'll make you peach pie."

He groaned. "I'll carry all the boxes you want for a piece of your peach pie!" He seemed to be shuffling dishes around. "Putting the lasagne in the fridge. Yeah. Peach pie." He must have closed the door. "Well, gotta go get a couple things done before work tonight. Talk to you later." A pause. "I love you, Mom."

She blinked tears away. "Thanks, Son. I love you, too. God keep you safe."

"Amen."

Phyllis put her phone on the counter and sighed. The thought of where she'd put her phone before—in the drawer—made her laugh. She spied the charger on another counter and attached it there. Easier to find it when it rang again. She giggled again. So funny. "Thank you, Lord." A deep sigh filled her lungs, and she blew it out. In again. Out again. She felt lighter than she had for a long time. Apologies were so healthy—in every way. Emotionally. Spiritually. Physically.

She paused at the counter remembering her earlier prayer. "Lord, if it's your will for Mark and Katty to marry, I ask you to make it clear. But if it's not Your will, please give them some sign—not me—them. Both of them. So they don't make a huge mistake."

Her thoughts tumbled in of her own marriage. It had seemed so right in the beginning. And maybe it was. But she'd had no idea that he was an alcoholic from the start. Her own dad had tried to talk to her, but she wouldn't listen. He had smelled alcohol on Holliger and warned Phyllis, but she had thought Dad was meddling and told him it didn't make any difference. She thought she could change him.

She had tried through the years to do that very thing. She invited him to special events at church. She played the guilt card when little Mark had a part in the Christmas program. She had played the part of match-maker to try to get Carl to love the Lord, but had come to realize that it wasn't her job. She couldn't do that. It had to be from God and not her pushing him toward God.

The alcohol took it's toll on Carl, on her and their marriage, and in time they separated and finally divorced.

At first she felt she had failed—as a wife, as a follower of Jesus, as a mom, too.

Mark was the shining light as a result of the marriage, though. He was priceless and would always remain that.

She tapped the counter. The boxes they had taken to Mrs. B's store had lifted the heavy burden of that broken time in her life. She could breathe easier now that most of it was gone. She shrugged. What was even left? She'd given more memorable things to Mark. Carl was his dad, so it was the right thing to do. Carl had taken his personal things like his clothing and all, but for some reason had left other stuff behind. And when he died, he had left everything to her. Which she guessed was okay.

His personal effects. Where else would a mortician or judge deliver them? He had no other family, except her and Mark. They had to do something with it all. It wasn't theirs to throw away.

She took her birthstone ring off, held her hand under the lotion spigot, and gave it a push. Interesting. It always felt funny without her ring on. Felt naked almost. Like something was definitely missing. As she rubbed in the lotion, she blinked.

Something else had been missing off of her hand for years.

Her own diamond ring that Carl had given her when they became engaged. The size of it had impressed her dad and mom for sure. It had definitely dazzled her.

Where was that ring?

She rushed toward her bedroom, but ran back for the birthstone ring she had just taken off and put it back on. It hadn't been that long since she had ransacked her drawers to find it before.

Where was it?

She pulled open her little jewelry chest and searched through it all. She didn't wear half of the rings, earrings, and necklaces stored in there. She should go through this whole little jewelry box and take it to Mrs. B's store later. She could carry this whole jewelry box by herself.

The ring was not there.

She tried to remember. She knew at one point she had just wanted to launch it into the creek or flush it down the toilet. But, as she thought about it, she realized way back then, that it might help out someday for it had a sizable diamond in it, plus some tiny ones around the main one. She knew she had kept it, but where had she put it?

It hadn't been that long. She knew it had been in this jewelry box that time, but where was it now?

Oh God, please help. She didn't think she'd thrown it away. Hadn't she thought of giving it to Mark then? Only … then she had envisioned him marrying someone totally different than Katty. Didn't matter. Phyllis had released that to God and now where was that ring?

She studied the ring on her finger—her mother's ring. It was a tiny chip and meant more to her than her own engagement ring, even though her own was ten times bigger. As she slowed her breathing, trying to remember where she had put her own ring, other thoughts surged through her mind. Should she give Mark this ring?

Let him choose?

Another thought popped into her mind. A picture. She knew. She had read an article back then about hiding things in places where robbers wouldn't think to look. Unusual places. Hiding things in plain sight, not in a Bible or safe or under a mattress.

She couldn't remember where she'd hidden it. Good hiding.

If a person hid something so well, that they couldn't find it, it must be the right place. But what if that person wanted to find it again and couldn't?

Her heart pounded in her chest. She now had a goal or a reason to find it and it wouldn't appear.

Memories flooded her brain of those last years with Carl. He'd go on a binge and she'd threaten to lock him out or to have him arrested. Especially one time when he'd come inside from the garage. Phyllis had called him for supper, knowing he'd been drinking. When he opened the door to the house and saw the beautiful supper she'd laid out, he had smiled.

He sat down in his chair and began to load his plate without any acknowledgment that she might have worked hard to create all this. Potatoes. Meat loaf—two slices. Baked beans and corn. His plate was loaded. He picked up his fork and dug in. But, then looked at her face. Something had clicked, something had triggered a memory or a thought and he flew at her in a rage. He accused her of poisoning the food, of trying to kill him.

She had shook her head and immediately began shoveling her food into her mouth. Even the food off of his plate to prove he was wrong. He accused her again and again. "I've heard of wives doing that to their unsuspecting husbands—preparing a beautiful meal and it's all poison. Don't you ever try to manipulate me again. I had enough of that with my—"

The ring!

She remembered. A visual of where it was exploded in her mind.

On the counter in her bathroom was a vase full of artificial flowers. She ripped them from the vase and there was the ring. She had used it as a sort of holder, like a wire tie, for the stems of the flowers. When they were in the vase, the petals and leaves covered the ring so no one could see it.

"Mark?" She ran to the front door, knowing he must be gone, but she was willing to run after him no matter the distance. She stopped at the front door. No Mark.

She held the ring in the sunlight.

Beautiful.

FORTY-SIX

Katty moaned and rolled over in the bed.

Dreams. Bad dreams. Nightmares haunted her. Visuals of babies floated by her. Of babies accusing her, taunting her. Strings tied and linked them all together and to her. Blood covered them all. They all stared at her, wide-eyed.

Then the voices began. Babies crying, but more. "Mommy, Mommy."

"Why'd you leave me?"

"Why didn't you want us, Mommy?"

"What did we do to deserve this?"

All crying out. All children's voices and baby's voices. Some cried. Some accused. Some yelled. Some sounded like Bea. Many sounded like her own voice.

Still sleep, Katty cried and moaned.

Then other voices started. Voices of men and other people. Some loud. Some in a low, sinister whisper. Some hissed at her. "You are a slut."

"You deserve to die."

"You aren't even worth the air you breathe."

That woke her and she rolled over, her back to Bea so she

wouldn't wake her. She pinched her lips together and tried to hold back the sobs. She flipped her wet pillow to the other side and closed her eyes again, but the visuals were clear and wouldn't leave her mind.

Slowly, she crept out of bed and grabbed her sweater from the chair. It had begun to get chilly lately. Fall was here. The bags from the dollar store rustled under the bed. She'd have to find a better hiding place or Bea would find them.

Bea seemed to be sleeping deeply.

She was so pretty always, but especially in her sleep. Her long eyelashes rested against her pale cheeks. She always got sweaty when she slept, so her hair tumbled and curled around her face.

Katty shook her head. She hadn't realized her hair was getting so long—it was halfway down her back now. She blinked. Bea was growing up. She was changing right before her eyes into a little girl, not a baby.

Baby. Babies.

Such a horrible contrast of her dreams just now and this beautiful little girl sleeping before her. The pain of those nightmares. This beautiful child in the bed. The babies she'd killed or Phil had killed. And this little girl—living, breathing, growing more beautiful every day.

Katty knelt beside the bed, afraid to touch Bea for fear she'd wake her, but wanting to cuddle her right now. She slumped down on the floor and let the tears flow down, into her hands, onto the rug. She sobbed silently for all the babies.

Who would ever want her? She was a murderer.

She patted the sweater pocket. That was such a habit, but even more right now. She needed a drink badly. She knew there was no booze in Noell's house. She'd been sober for a few weeks now.

Help, God. Help.

Almost panic-stricken, Katty raised her head. Bea was still sleeping.

Katty crawled to the closet on the carpet. The door was always open now, since they had discovered it's treasures. It still mystified and amazed Katty—Noell, too—how this could be. It wasn't possible. They'd all three tapped the walls inside, in the closet, to discover where it connected with the rest of the house. Then they had checked outside and learned where the inside walls were in the structure with the outside walls. Noell had even drawn a diagram of the inside and outside.

Nothing made sense.

The closet was too big for the house.

When they were outside, it was just a normal house.

When they were inside, Gamma's closet was five times the size it should be, but that didn't show on the outside.

Katty sat in a corner in the closet and shook her head.

It didn't make sense, but they didn't want to tell anyone—especially a contractor or builder. What if this house was haunted—in a good way? What if Gamma had some sort of power, even still after she was dead, that made the closet big when it didn't make any sense?

Katty rolled her head back and forth against the wall and studied the bookshelves as she had many times now. She counted them—nine in all—filled with books and notebooks. Noell called them journals. There was the wall space where she had painted, that they now called the magic painting.

That was another thing that still didn't make sense to any of them. Katty saw the painting being painted--incomplete. Wet paint. Noell saw dry paint on a completed painting.

Both saw something so beautiful. The scene was similar to the one Katty had painted in her trailer house, but it was ever so much richer here. The details were clearer. The colors were brighter, richer. That tree almost brought Katty to tears.

Her Rescue Tree House from her childhood, where she

escaped to if the weather wasn't too cold. How mom had never discovered it. Another miracle. Katty spent long hours there, drawing, coloring, even singing songs from her heart.

She wiped her wet cheeks and glanced into the bedroom where Bea still slept. Bea was like that. Bea sang songs from her heart. She drew and colored pictures.

God please keep Bea safe.

No matter what happened to her own life, God please keep Bea safe and pure.

Whew. She'd just prayed.

What kind of a God would hear the prayers of a murderer?

Katty tapped the bookcase next to where she sat and reached in to pull a journal out. Interesting. Just as she'd pulled the book to her, a deep breath pushed out of her chest. Another one.

She hadn't known Gamma well while she was alive, but somehow, she was knowing her now.

She opened the book and words poured out. She wasn't even reading them. They just poured out from the books. Thoughts flowed out. Words of wisdom. Verses from the Bible. Words that created beautiful paintings like the one still unfinished on that wall. Pictures drawn with ink and colored in. So beautiful.

She glanced up at all the shelves, each shelf lined with more journals: some black, some colored, all different. Katty shook her head at the wealth of words and wisdom in this room. This magical room.

Where should she start? Which journal was the first one that Gamma had written in? Which was the one?

It was overwhelming, until she glanced down at the one she held in her hand.

Huh. She opened it to the first page. The journal was lined, like a regular notebook, which made Gamma's words and drawings even more rich and interesting. She flipped through the whole book, letting the pages open and close. The overview was even beautiful. It almost took her breath away.

Back to page one.

"Bernie died years ago and it doesn't get any easier." Both pages were covered in hearts in various sizes and colors of pink, red, and white. Green vines wound through them all, tying them together. Tiny words threaded and edged each heart—words like love, peace. Katty had to turn the journal upside down and sideways to read them all.

And who was Bernie? Some male cousin, maybe, or had Gamma had a man friend after Grampa died? Bernie. Who—

Wait. Bernie was Bernadine, Noell's mom. Had to be.

The journal flopped to her lap. Oh no. Noell hardly talked about her.

Gamma was writing about losing her own daughter. She'd drowned.

"She and Katty had spent time together. Bernie had taught Katty how to crochet."

Katty gasped. She was in Gamma's journals? She kept on reading.

"It's hard not to cry, even now. People who haven't lost someone close to them don't realize the pain."

Katty shook her head. How on earth did Gamma keep on living? How had she not wanted to die, herself?

Another entry, after another row of hearts. "'You are my Strength, my Everlasting Hope." Who was Gamma talking to, there? "Without You, I am nothing. Without You I can't go on. Without You there is no hope. Without You Who I stand upon?"

She'd written a poem? Who was the You Gamma kept talking to? Katty stared at the painting in front of her. Who was the other person painting the wall? Katty had seen the arm and the brush.

Goosebumps started at her right lower leg and marched on up to her right arm. She shivered. Something was happening. A slight breeze flipped the pages of the journal she was reading.

Had Bea opened a window last night? She peeked into the bedroom. The curtains weren't even moving.

But the journal pages flipped up and down. Words bounced up as a page flipped up. "Bound. Pain. Freedom. Love. Missing her. Never the same. Noell."

Wait. Noell. What about her?

Colors meshed with the words. Reds. Pinks. Reddish-browns. All seemed to flow together obscuring any words she might read.

Blank pages became visible as the pages flipped and fluttered. Katty jumped. Blank pages. She turned more pages. Some were blank. She looked around the closet. She knew she shouldn't. But the blank pages called to her, lured her … to paint. To draw.

Where were her paints?

She'd have to make do with Bea's paint sets.

Her stomach fluttered and she knew it wasn't hunger.

These were Noell's Gamma's journals, not her own. If she knew what was right and good for her, she'd put the journal back right now.

The painting on the wall blurred and the hand appeared to beckon her.

Wh-what?

The hand pulled at her, beckoned with fingers waving her in, appearing to call to her. Katty was the only one up, the only one in the closet right now.

Katty crawled to the open door and peeked at Bea. Huh. Still sleeping? Bea was always the first one up, bugging Katty to start the day.

Katty held her breath, crawled to the living room door, and shoved off her knees. Even Noell was still sleeping, or at least still upstairs. Katty tip-toed into the kitchen and carefully picked up Bea's paint set.

She chose a paintbrush and tip-toed to Gamma's closet,

waving the paint brush in the air, pondering what to paint. Glancing down at the open journal, the leaves and hearts seemed to speak to her. Hearts and plants. She almost danced around the closet, but stopped. Bea might hear. Katty hadn't felt like dancing in … a very long time.

She might need water. The paint set was dry. When had Bea painted lately?

She couldn't stop dancing, the paintbrush skimmed the air. Katty could see it in her mind, swirls of yellows, greens, pink hearts with red highlights. She swirled and danced.

"Mommy?" Bea stood in the doorway, rubbing her eyes. Sleepy little girl. Then her eyes grew wide, as she woke up. "Mommy! You have paint on your face." She stepped inside the closet and pointed. "You painted your face? Can I do that?" She giggled.

Noell stepped inside right behind her. Her eyes were just as big, her hand cupped her open mouth. Laughter bubbled out—oh that melodious laughter.

Katty grinned. "What are you two laughing about? Paint on my face?" She touched her cheek and started, then held her hand out in front of her. Pink paint on her fingers?

She ran for the bathroom mirror just around the corner and screamed. "There's paint on my face!" She gasped. "In my hair."

Bea followed her. "Mommy. It's pretty." She pointed again and again. Giggles brought tears to her eyes. She couldn't stop laughing. "Mommy." Bea jumped. "Where's your phone?"

Noell let out a full-on belly laugh and reached into her pajama pocket and pulled out hers.

Before Katty could hide, Noell had tapped several photos and showed them to Bea.

They were both laughing.

Noell caught her breath. "Why did you paint your own face? That's like something a little kid would do."

Bea nodded. "Littler than me, little kid."

Katty leaned closer to the mirror and touched her face again. "I didn't ... I ... didn't paint it." She checked her fingers. "It's wet." She caught Noell's eyes in the mirror. "Like on the wall the other day. Can't be." She pushed past them into the closet again. "I was just doing this."

The beauty and joy returned as she lifted the paintbrush into the air and rotated. "It feels so good in here. Like I'm floating and dancing."

Noell and Bea followed her.

Noell shrieked. "You *are* floating." She shook her head, her fists balled at her mouth.

Bea snuggled onto the floor right at Katty's swinging feet and held her hands under them. "Tickle, tickle, Mommy." She rolled over to her other side and back again, still laughing. "Mommy's floating and dancing above me."

Noell shrieked again. "Katty. You're—"

"I am not." Katty kicked her feet. "I am not. I'm ... not." She shuffled her feet again and gasped. "I'm ... dancing in the air."

Noell sank down beside Bea and stared at Katty's feet, then up to her face. "This can't be ... happening." She reached under Katty's feet. "Nothing. Your feet are above the floor." Back to her face. "Your face is green now. Are you okay?"

"I'm a leaf now." Katty gurgled. "Leaves are green. I'm a plant." She waved the paintbrush in front of Bea's face.

"That tickles, Mommy." Bea's face turned green.

Katty jumped and lifted the paint brush from Bea's face. "I didn't touch her face. I didn't paint that."She shook her head and stared at Noell. "I didn't do anything!" She stopped and carefully lifted the brush to the air and painted a line in the air.

A green line flowed from her brush and stayed in the air. She touched the red and did the same thing. Red flowed in a line and crossed some of the green.

Katty turned and checked Noell's face. Surprise—no shock —registered there.

"Mommy!" Bea's face was shining, her eyes sparkled. "You don't need paper anymore."

Katty sputtered and laughed out loud. Oh, that felt good. She stopped. "I don't remember the last time I did that."

"You never did that before, so how could you remember?"

Katty laughed and shook her head. "No. I haven't laughed out loud like that for … forever."

Bea nodded. Her eyebrows lifted. A knowing, wise look on her face.

Katty dipped the brush into paint again and circles appeared in the air, over and over. Rings of yellow. Rings of light. Circles with bright green and red. All inter-weaving each other. All rings of color overlayed.

"Paint my name, Mommy."

"Okay. B." Katty pretended to forget how to spell Bea's name. "What is it? What comes next?"

Bea laughed. "Mommy. You're funny." She stood, her hands on her hips. "It's B, E, A. Bea!" She jumped up and down and clapped her hands.

"Okay. B. E. A." Katty stepped back and read it. "Bea. What a great name." Her lines were squiggled but if she really stopped and thought about it, this shouldn't be happening.

Noell daubed at the paint in the air. She lifted her finger away and it had green paint on it. She held it for Katty to see. "It's real." She walked around the word and lines Katty had painted, behind the lines. They showed on her face, making shadows of Bea and the lines. "I can see them from here." She pointed.

Katty shook her head. Laughter bubbled again.

"Good Mommy is here." Bea smiled.

Katty nodded. "The little girl from the treehouse is here."

FORTY-SEVEN

Jasper folded his arms across his chest, his sword in the sheath and his feet firmly planted in the old woman's closet.

He knew that the parameters of the closet compared to the actual, physical house messed with the humans. He caught the eyes of the other angels surrounding the closet and grinned, shaking his head.

This was always fun for the angels. Challenging the humans. Not from the angels' point of view or desires, but fully in accordance with the Father's plan.

That was a trip. Allowed to be different. No, commanded to be different—to create a space that Father in heaven knew would challenge the human's thinking. Father always knew how far to take them in order to bring about his final plan.

Jasper nodded at Michael.

Oops. It *was* Michael. None other.

Jasper had been off in his own world of thoughts and missed Michael's entrance. All the other angels were kneeling in obeisance, their arms bent over each chest of armor.

Jasper found his knees as Michael stepped past him. Was

there a hint of a curve around Michael's mouth—almost a smile or a smirk?

Probably.

Jasper had been caught daydreaming, almost. He had always been a deep thinker. Pondering the things of God and His mighty plan. Watching and listening to others—to angels, his Father, all the creatures of the kingdom. Even to demons at times.

And right now, he was humbled into bowing before his commander.

Since Michael was in Gamma's closet, that definitely meant that the battle for Katty and Bea, even Noell, had reached a higher level.

Michael reached out to Jasper and gripped his arm, pulling him up. "You are in charge here, Jasper." He smiled. "No need to kneel. We are on the same team."

Jasper nodded and let Michael pull him up. Not on the same level, though. This Michael was the Supreme Commander, of all angels. Maybe the same team, but definitely not the same level.

Michael walked through the paint in the air. "These humans are beginning to transcend, to become." He turned toward Jasper. "Am I seeing this?" He turned again and watched as Katty lifted a paint brush and released paint onto the air's atmosphere.

Mesmerizing. Jasper realized that his dear Katty was learning to tap into the kingdom, into Father, without knowing it. She had no clue. She was just following her instinct, her happiness, her bliss, and it was all leading her to the Father's heart.

"Michael." Jasper followed him as he inspected the host of angels and what Katty was creating.

Michael turned, a smile on his lips, twinkles in his eyes. "You're thinking what I'm thinking?"

"Um." Jasper was caught. "Maybe?" Hearing the conversation between mother and child just now, had stirred him. This creativity, this release in his human, was inspiring.

A beginning. A beginning of supernatural collaboration in the kingdom of God.

Katty had already painted letters in the air and they were still there, visible to every angel, but also to her and Bea. Noell, too. Ha. The scientist in Noell would challenge it, but realize that she was seeing reality. All of them were seeing it and touching it, experiencing it for real.

Jasper grinned and knelt again.

There was no limit to what they could do in the Christ. The Eternal One. The Spirit.

Noell, herself with her gifting was already on the way to discovering facts about her gift, but also her world. The science —Father's laboratory on this wonderful sphere called earth— was already being discovered in a big way. And there was so much more.

But Noell would soon open up to personal science—her own gifts, just like Katty was now. To help others. What could she learn? Would she help Clarence and Sheriff on some cases because she learned things about her world and her gift and how to exploit and perfect them?

Bea, too.

Jasper chuckled as both he and Michael leaned over Bea. That child, birthed in pain and trauma, would become a menace to the enemy. She would rise—

Jasper stopped. There seemed to be a charge in the air, vibrations, frequencies. How else could the paint remain in the air?

He and Michael and the other angels walked around the paintings in the air but didn't stir or destroy them. Beautiful color flowed from Katty's brush. Beautiful emotion flowed from her heart.

Experiencing Katty finally free. Extraordinary peace and joy flooded the room. Jasper knelt once again—not in obeisance to Michael, but in gratitude to the Father and His plan.

Jasper had his own hopes for Katty and Bea, but ultimately it was all up to the Father and the young woman. And seeing it open up in his human was overwhelmingly satisfying. Gratifying. Powerful. If just these three humans would experience freedom in Christ and use those gifts widely for Him, well—

"You *are* thinking what I'm thinking." Michael grinned and knelt beside Jasper. Clapped him on the shoulder. He withdrew his sword from its sheath and held it up.

Jasper immediately did the same and held his high. "Unto Him!"

"Yes! Unto Him!" Michael stood and marched past each angel lining the closet, his sword still high.

Each angel drew his sword and shouted, proclaiming, "Unto Him!"

FORTY-EIGHT

Something was up.

Something had changed.

Katty glanced around the closet, her brush poised in her hand.

The air around her seemed electric. Her skin tingled. As she breathed in deeply, a distinct fragrance entered her nostrils.

Something was happening to her insides at the same time. Inside her. Every cell, every organ. Her heart pounded. Jitters and goosebumps burned up and down both arms and both legs. Shivers all across her chest and back.

She'd been very drunk in her life and no sensation compared to this. Even when withdrawals were the worst, just before she'd downed another bottle, the tremors and shivers were nothing compared to what was happening to her now.

Every cell was lit up and not by anything she had put into her body.

Oh if this could last.

She could almost feel her body changing as she stood swabbing paint into the air. Somehow she separated from the actual physical motion of swiping the paint into lines onto the air. And she could almost step back, totally unengaged, and watch the paint flow.

She knew painting into the air and having it stick was impossible.

But she could see it.

She dipped her brush into another color—blue, this time—and painted over the red lines, outlined the letters for Bea's name. Without thinking what she was doing, she stepped to the other side of Bea's name and painted on the back—on the A, then the E, and the B. Peeking around the word, it remained red on the first side and blue on the back.

Was Noell seeing this?

Yup.

Noell's eyes were wide, her mouth open. She watched every move Katty made.

Bea even watched. "Mommy. You made my name pretty in back, too." She rolled on the floor so she could see. She lifted up on one elbow, her eyes intent. "Can you teach me how to do that?"

A visual of Bea sticking her brush or crayons into the air and making a mess almost crumpled Katty to the floor. A bubble of laughter burst out from way down deep. Again, the sensation of her heart expanding and almost bursting was real. Her heart was free to laugh, to sense weird things, to embrace whatever this was, whatever might be happening in Gamma's closet.

She was free. Freer than she had ever been. Freer than when she was in her treehouse, as a kid.

Noell laughed her beautiful laugh. She must have had the same visual as Katty. Yes. Bea would make a mess. But wait. Who was doing this or making this possible? Maybe Bea could do it too.

Katty breathed in again. There was that wonderful fragrance. "Can you smell that?" She breathed in again.

"What?" Noell sucked in a deep breath. "Smell what?"

Bea sat up. "What Mommy?"

"It … it's a clean smell."

Noell nodded. "Like—"

Bea nodded too. "It's like the flowers in Noell's garden." She breathed in. "No. It's like …" She was so pretty. Her eyes twinkled. Then she looked down at the floor. "Well, 'member when I opened the window in the car. We were driving." She giggled. "You were driving. Annnnnd it was breakfast time." She glanced around the room. "It smells like that—the window down and the flower garden." She clapped her hands. "Both! Together."

Katty jumped and paint splattered all over the space.

Bea pointed. "Pretty."

Noell nodded. "Pretty." She pulled Bea onto her lap.

Katty wasn't sure what to do. Should she wipe the paint up off the floor, or … out of the air?

FORTY-NINE

Katty held her breath and unlocked the door to the trailer house. It had been weeks since she and Bea had been back. She told Bea she was going to the grocery store for peanut butter and cereal. Her two most favorite things in the world.

Katty had lied—or at least at that minute she'd lied. She would go to the store on her way back from checking the trailer house. She made sure she had enough money before she left so she wouldn't lie.

She had lied so many times to that baby girl.

Not ever again. She was not lying to her ever—no matter how hard it might be. And she knew just by her own experience that there would be hard times to be honest.

She shook her head and scratched at a blotch of paint still on her hand.

She breathed out a breath and pushed the door open. Gag. How long had they been gone? A couple weeks? She hadn't even gone inside, yet. As she pushed the door open, a stink pushed back. "Oh sh—" She stopped herself. She hadn't cussed much in the weeks she'd been away either. "This is so bad. Man, it stinks."

Birth certificate. Repeat those words, find it, and get out. Wait. Did Bea even have one? Katty had been so high on drugs when Bea was born. She didn't even remember the date. She could only guess.

Maybe Clarence had one? Or could get one?

The stench overwhelmed her.

The memory—or partial memory of when she'd left—came back. She'd been pounding on Mrs. Nosy's trailer door and not her own. She'd been drunk. Out of her mind. She cringed at the memory, as the door swung back and forth. Mark had arrested her at Mrs. Nosey's and taken her to jail. She hadn't come back to her own trailer until now.

The door swung in again, making visible the trash on the floor, spilling out of the trash can.

Katty blinked.

She held the door open and made herself see. Made herself see every nasty, dirty part of what her and Bea's life had been.

One step inside.

She held her arm over her nose and mouth and took another step. Quickly, she pushed a chair against the door to hold it open. She didn't care what animals might sneak inside. It was almost as if she let the door slam shut and she was still inside, she would be trapped here forever. Trapped in this horrible life all over again and she wouldn't ever make it out.

Another step inside.

Dishes still filled the sink and the counter.

Hardly a healthy environment to raise a kid—to raise her Bea.

Tears stung her eyes. She knew it wasn't just the stench and fumes burning from this crappy trailer house.

Bea's latest—or rather her latest from weeks ago—drawings covered the table, scattered with crayons and pencils. All colors.

Katty circled the table, She picked up a drawing. Then another. Bea had drawn pictures of the usual unicorns and dragons, Daryl & Dumpty, flowers and bunnies. But mixed in with all that were babies.

Babies in clouds. Babies on the unicorns. Babies—

She turned abruptly toward the wall.

Babies.

Her painting.

Babies on clouds, in the blue sky, in the tree.

Her tree. Something about seeing that tree painted on the wall again almost broke her, almost did her in.

That treehouse had been her only salvation back then. Her only place of peace.

Seeing it again on this wall stilled her heart. Quieted her. But seeing it, brought out all the pain from back then. And the babies floating around it reminded her of all—convicted her of all she'd done—Phil had done. What she had agreed to and she herself had done.

She almost sat on the sofa before she thought about how dirty it might be.

When had she cared about sitting on this sofa? When she had lived here, she sat anywhere, ate everywhere, slept anywhere. Even on the floor. When had she become so picky, so finicky about all this?

A visual of Noell's hoarder house popped into her mind. There were totes and boxes all over the house. Books stacked in the kitchen against the walls. Noell was adamant that she had already taken many boxes of books to Mrs. B's store to sell.

Katty had never really thought about how many there must have been before. Stacks and stacks.

But the house was clean.

It didn't stink.

As she sat on her old sofa and looked at the tree she'd painted, she remembered the tree she'd—no, she and Gamma had painted in Gamma's closet. Gamma's hand. She shook her

head. She'd seen it. She'd painted it. She'd seen the hand. Terrifying. Definitely sobering.

Because of living at Noell's with Bea, Katty had already
changed, way over and above not drinking anymore. Something
in Gamma's closet—her drawings and paintings, her words in
those journals—something was changing Katty to the very core
of her being.

She must have grown out of the person she'd been while
living in this dump.

Somehow.

She had no idea how much time had passed with her sitting
in her old crappy trailer house on the dirty sofa, staring at the
painting on the wall. Her head dropped down to her crossed
arms. So much had changed in just a couple weeks. There were
still times when she desperately needed a drink.

Something flipped inside as she had that thought. There had
to be bottles hidden here in this house. She glanced up. In that
kitchen cupboard, behind the canned veggies. Maybe in the bathroom and even her bedroom.

Breathe.

She hadn't come this far to—

Leaves waved from the tree.

Babies twirled, waved, floated closer. Floated into her—
through her—touching her.

FIFTY

Mark checked both ways before turning the corner.

Back on night duty, which was okay. Kinda. It was hard to get enough sleep in the daytime. But it freed time during the day to help Mom, and do his own chores. On his nights off, and it was dark outside, he just wanted to sleep and not clean his house. Maybe watch TV, but he was gone so much, that he found himself out of touch with whatever was the popular TV series at the moment.

Around the square again.

He hadn't scoured the outskirts of the county much lately. There had been too many accidents right close to Osceola, so there hadn't been time.

He drove toward the highway and stopped at the stop sign. The convenience store was busy. End of day purchases. Pick up the milk for breakfast because the kid would be hungry before school. Buy the beer because the night would be long without it.

He shook his head and waved as he drove past and on east toward Shelby. This highway had taken a beating—the surface was fine because the road department had resurfaced it a couple years ago. Even with all the accidents, it was safe. The crew that worked with the fire fighters always did a great job.

Mark had watched them as the crew paced back and forth. Each man took a different section of ground, head bent, eyes down, they scoured it bit by bit. Some carried a to-go cup of coffee as they walked. Back and forth. Every inch inspected for debris.

Mark chuckled at a weird thought. If they ever needed to search for a body or a person—a child—they should ask *that* crew because they inspected every blade of grass, every dirt clod.

Yeah. That was weird.

Slowing through Shelby, he scanned the cars parked at the convenience store there. Just for fun, he turned in, drove around to the back of the building and again to the front. Nobody there. Nothing going on, that he could detect.

Parking along the outer edge of the lot, he waved at a trucker who was gassing up his semi.

If he was going to drive through the county tonight, a cup of coffee might be good.

As he headed into the store, a visual of a strange memory popped into his mind. Katty had been here that time and almost caused an accident. The shooter display was full. He always checked those, knowing that she bought them regularly.

Back by the coffee machines, he nodded at a woman there, stirring her coffee. The store had added more coffee machines. Cold brew? Many more flavors and brews to choose from.

The woman chuckled as he held back. "They have added a lot of choices, right? I circled this aisle three times before I decided on my usual—French Roast Medium."

"It's crazy." He needed to get on the road. "Yep. Medium Roast for me too." He pulled a cup from the dispenser and filled it. A little sweetener might taste good tonight.

The woman tossed her straw into the trash and walked past

him. "Have a good night, Deputy." She stopped and backed up to stand beside him. "How can I pray? I have to drive to Omaha tonight. Might as well use the time for a good cause." She sipped her coffee. "Anything specific?"

No one had ever asked him that before. He was caught off guard. "Uh, I don't know." He should know. Mom was always … wait. "Yes. Angels around about me and the Sheriff's Department. All of us need protection and … wisdom."

She nodded and stepped away as another woman appeared around the corner.

"And … healing." Oh-oh. There it was. Speaking out loud for them all. And yes, they needed prayer for healing after all of the tragedies they came upon: accidents, bar fights, abusive marriages. Humans against other humans.

She looked back at him. Her eyes pierced into his soul for a nanosecond. But she saw. She knew. She nodded and left.

Whew. He'd never been that honest with a stranger.

He tore the sugar packets open, dumped the sugar into his cup, and stirred. "Oops. Sorry."

A woman purposely sidled next to him, her hip against his, and smiled. "Hey Copper." She pulled out a cup and filled it.

Mark stepped away and smiled. He'd met her before, somewhere. He could only guess. Jail? County court? "Greetings and salutations, Ma'am." He nodded as he walked away. "Have a good day … er, night."

The cashier waved him on. "No charge, Deputy." The cashier smiled. "God keep you."

He bowed slightly. "Thank you." He started toward the door. "And thank you. God bless you, too."

Outside, as he walked the distance to his cruiser, he chuckled. Quite a contrast in people tonight. He unlocked his door. One woman was a prayer warrior. God help. God teach. And one was a … well, quite a contrast to the prayer warrior. He checked his mirrors and logged in.

He turned back toward Osceola and found himself driving past Noell's. Katty's car wasn't there.

The next stop he made was the trailer court. There it was—Katty's car parked in her drive-way. He sipped the coffee again and shook his head. He shouldn't.

Mark opened the car door and got out. The trailer door had been propped open with a chair. He raised his hand and knocked.

No answer. God, please don't let her be going back to those bottles.

Knock. Knock.

He pushed the door open more. "Katty?" He hadn't whispered, but he hadn't called her name loudly, either. As he stepped around the chair inside, he stopped.

Katty stood there in the living room. The place was a shambles. A chair at the kitchen table was overturned and the table was cluttered with crayons, bits of cereal, mail.

Katty seemed oblivious to it all. She was beautiful. Almost shining. There was no light streaming in from any window—the shades had been pulled down. But there was definitely light that glowed around her, from within?

She appeared to be painting, but not where he expected her to be. He loved what she had painted on that wall and he checked. Still there. The tree stopped him. Magnificent. Real. The branches spiraled up and around with leaves fluttering from each branch, each twig. And tucked within the biggest branches was a tree house. Sweet. He'd had a tree house—sort of. Babies floated in and around the tree on fluffy white clouds or that's what Mark thought of when he saw them. Flowers. Grass. Blue sky.

The whole wall seemed alive. Like it was flowing. The leaves seemed to float—same with the babies.

The radio from his squad car sputtered. Oh yeah. He'd left the trailer house door open. Chantell's voice reported a complaint—something about neighbor's dog barking and scattering trash. He moved the chair and closed the trailer house door.

Katty was painting.

But what she was doing was impossible. And she seemed totally unaware of his presence. The scene before him was unbelievable and magical at the same time. Her dark hair was up in a loose knot with tendrils cascading down around her face and neck. Her pale skin glistened.

Katty was engrossed in what she was doing. She held a paint brush poised in the air and as she swiped the brush across in front of her, a swipe of paint appeared in the air. Red. Blue.

No canvas. Not on the wall.

On or in or on the air.

On the air?

Had he been drinking? Of course not. He was on …

Mark swallowed. This was the most stunning thing he had ever seen. Katty herself was beautiful and totally oblivious to his presence. But there was a sort of hush in the moment, a quiet reverence in what she was doing.

He reached behind and knocked on the front door once again, softly at first. Then when she didn't appear to hear him, he tapped a little louder.

She jumped and at the same time, dropped the brush, and the paint scattered to the floor—all over the carpet under her feet.

"Oh!" She screamed. "Oh no!"

He rushed to her and caught her before she fell onto the paint. "Katty. Are you alright? This is … amazing." He stuttered. He didn't know what to say. "What was that?" No booze on her breath.

She came to, out of the fog, and realized who he was and where she was. Her brown eyes were startled and wide. Dark lashes framed them. Her eyebrows arched over her eyes.

And she lingered there … in his arms.

Their faces couldn't have been more than a couple inches apart. Eye to eye.

Oh, he shouldn't.

She didn't move away, her face turned toward his.

He bent his head and brushed his lips against hers.

"I-I'm sorry." Mark gently, slowly released Katty and knelt on the floor. "I shouldn't have done that. I'm on duty. I … shouldn't have."

He hadn't realized he was weeping, until Katty knelt beside him and wiped the tears away.

And kissed him back.

Did you like Redeemed? Grab the next book, Resurrected, Book 6 in The Great Escapee Series, Book 3 in Katty's Story! www.bonnielacy.com

Katty has to choose between an evil, abusive man who hates her art and pressures her because he is Bea's father … or a loving, but equally flawed man, who loves her art, and wants her to be free to choose.

AUTHOR NOTES AND ACKNOWLEDGEMENTS

I know. Go back and check out the dedication.

"To God and all the Beings of Heaven?" What does that mean, exactly?

I get the "To God" part. Right? I mean, it's God.

But, I am just beginning to discover what or who they all are! Somedays it feels like I'm in a movie or a game set. But if we read the Bible, it's all there. They're all there.

I want to much to write the angels and demons correctly. What would they do, really? What are legitimate names for them? How do I know what they're thinking? What they might do? I just have to trust in the Lord speaking to me, through me.

I have learned so much. Yes, about the angels and demons, but about the world, about who we are and how we got here on this earth.

But, there is so much more to learn. I love this adventure!

That's what writing does for me—it helps me figure things out. I don't know everything, but the more I seek Him, the more I learn.

Katty has been through very tough things. Some are her choices —her decisions—but some she had no choice but to hold on tight. Abuse by her mom. Horrendous. Probably in a future book, I'll dig into how her mom got that way, when her own sister,

Gamma, was sweet and kind, even though she had hard stuff happen, too.

It's hard to write those things: Katty driving to buy booze—time after time, little Bea wandering and being abandoned at times—abused at times, Katty reliving her childhood and the abortions.

That stuff is hard.

I needed to write that scene when Katty was in jail. We sometimes do bad things. Having her angel, Jasper, see the Father enfold her with his love made me cry. (Yes, authors weep over the pain that they cause their characters to go through.) We need to know His love, His compassion. We need to let Him embrace us, no matter the pain, or guilt.

He is always, always there.

We just need to ask. And let Him in.

So, in writing Katty's struggles, I am writing my own.

You knew that, right?

———

First, as always, a disclaimer. The actual nursing home, the grocery store, the sheriff's department, the antique store—all the real, physical places in Osceola, Nebraska, and their staff are wonderful. If I wrote about how wonderful they really are, nobody would read my books.

No conflict—no readers!

So I make things up.

And that's the fun of being an author!

———

A huge thank you to Dearly Beloved. He works hard driving truck, is gone a lot, and provides so I can pursue my writing career.

Thank you to my kids, who are always asking how the book is going and encouraging me to keep at it.

Thank you to my grandkids—all ten of them—for keeping me laughing, hugging, and thinking. Your questions, your kisses, and your texts are always wonderful and loved.

Thank you to Jane Dixon-Smith who always understands where I want to go with a cover. I never stress over them. A book cover designer has such an important gift to draw readers to pick up a book.

Thank you to Steve Rzasa, my editor. I am so grateful for him. I always get nervous when I send the manuscript to him. Will he think it's terrible? But when he sends it back, what I need to change is so clear.

Thank you, Jan. I don't know how you do it—reading my manuscript three and four times, send it back to me, I revise and read it multiple times and send it back to you. Then you read it again—three or more times! Thank you, dear Sister. You are more than a blood sister. You are a friend, a confidant, my sister in Christ.

Thank you Prayer Warriors. I know, beyond any doubt, when you are praying. I might have, at that moment, bowed my head into my hands, totally freaked out by what I'd just written. But, you prayed. God heard. And my heart stilled, quieted. And I knew it was your prayers. Thank you.

A special thank you to my parents. Writing these books makes me even more appreciative for my sister and my parents, who loved us, taught us about Jesus, provided for us (I had no clue that we didn't have much!), supported us in everything we wanted to do.

And really, that thanks is directed to the Lord Jesus Christ, too. For I don't know that we get to choose where we grow up on this earth. Where I got to grow up was wonderful.

Thank you, Readers. There are many of you who stay in contact (always feel free to contact me via text or email!). I can write another day/month/year when you do that. It's not about flattery. It's about genuine heart-felt encouragement that keeps me at the keyboard.

I pray that my books point you to Jesus Christ, Yeshua, the Son of God, the Anointed One. Back to the verse at the front of the book: *"It is because of the Lord's loving kindnesses that we are not consumed, Because His [tender] compassions never fail. They are new every morning; Great and beyond measure is Your faithfulness." Lamentations 3: 22, 23. Amplified Version.*

His kindness and faithfulness. He never fails. He never lies.

Ask Him. Believe in Him. Breathe Him in. Take another breath.

He is here.

Believe.

THANK YOU, READER!

Thank you for reading my books! If you have a minute, would you consider leaving a review anywhere you purchase books? It is a huge help to any author! Ask for them at your Public Library. Even though you get to read them for free, I get a little kick-back, too.

It's not all about the money. But it helps when I pay an editor or book cover designer.

This is Katty's Story. There are more to come—another book for Katty and Bea.

They've become like family to me and I hope also to you.

There is a trilogy for Clarence and Harold, too, and The Timmelsen & Dexter Agency—a detective agency they run from Hillcrest Nursing Home. Michael is in it. Katty and Bea. Noell appears, too.

Yeah, Phil is jumping up and down. "What about me?"

Ugly, evil man.

But what if …

Noell is drawn to that pool in Rescued, Book 2. What are her other gifts? She goes to strange places in her own trilogy!

If you want to keep up with my characters (literally!) go to: www.bonnielacy.com. Scroll down and you'll see "Join My Newsletter." There you can fill in your info and hit the subscribe button. There's always a giveaway. I won't blow up your inbox, for sure … just keep you up on releases, maybe a doodle, and excerpts from my daily journals. You'll be added to my email newsletter list, but you can unsubscribe anytime.

Keep in touch.

Be Blessed!

ALSO BY BONNIE LACY

Fiction:

Released

Rescued

Restored

Revealed

Redeemed

Resurrected

Nonfiction:

Rage Rising: My Walk Through the Dark Tunnel of Anger

Cash Envelopes: You've Never Had So Much Money

Cash Envelopes: You've Never Had So Much Money Companion Workbook